Head Count

Head Count

JUDITH CUTLER

Allison & Busby Limited
12 Fitzroy Mews
London W1T 6DW
allisonandbusby.com

First published in Great Britain by Allison & Busby in 2017.

A CIP catalogue record for this book is available from
the British Library.

First Edition

ISBN 978-0-7490-2085-9

Typeset in 11/16 pt Sabon by
Allison & Busby Ltd.

The paper used for this Allison & Busby publication
has been produced from trees that have been legally sourced
from well-managed and credibly certified forests.

Printed and bound by
CPI Group (UK) Ltd, Croydon, CR0 4YY

For Chance to Shine
With thanks for all they do to give young people the
lifelong love of cricket my father gave me

CHAPTER ONE

*I'd seen kids like that a thousand times on TV. Thin –
emaciated really. Heads crawling with lice. Dirty. Not just
grubby because they'd been playing outdoors. Filthy. Some
of them ill. Some dressed in the remains of a parent's idea of
best clothes. Some with little bundles. Some with nothing.
Some even with something tattooed on their wrists. But
here? In the Garden of England?*

So there I was, head over heels, if you'll forgive my
occupational pun, in a very thorny hedge, with plenty of
time to reflect on my summer holiday so far.

Everyone knows that schoolteachers are an overpaid,
idle lot, enjoying all sorts of fringe benefits, including
enormously long holidays during which they do nothing
but doss around. Meanwhile, parents have to scurry round
in search of expensive and elusive childcare unless they are

lucky enough to take a holiday that is hugely overpriced simply because it's not in term time.

On the other side of the school fence, you might hear different facts. One of which, sadly, is that when the longed-for breaks finally arrive, the first thing the average teacher does is succumb to an evil virus that takes at least a week to shake off – by which time you should probably be starting your preparation for the next academic year.

The bug is no respecter of persons either. It doesn't knock on the head teacher's door and slink away when it's told she's too busy.

Not in my case, anyway.

I lost my voice on the last day of term. Perhaps people thought it was because I was so choked up at the transfer of some of my lovely pupils to the wicked world of secondary education. It might well have been. They were moving from a tiny school with only a hundred or so pupils to the giant world of a full-sized secondary – whether it was co-ed or single sex, a grammar or an academy, they would cease to be big fish in a tiny pond and become the smallest of minnows. If I had wept, I'd have tried to swallow my tears, for the sake of the kids and, let's face it, my dignity. But swallowing anything was a pretty painful option, and remained so long after the last child had waved goodbye.

All through the rest of the day. And the day after. Which was interesting, because I'd been roped in to act as Wrayford Cricket Club's substitute umpire, the regular one having succumbed to an attack of gout, which trumped my laryngitis.

Wrayford were playing St Luke's Bay, down in the south of the county. The ground was in a lovely setting with the sea one way and wooded hills another. The village itself was small, but its harbour bulged with vessels of all shapes and sizes. There were a few working boats, but most were chic yachts that looked as if they didn't really want to get their keels wet, any more than their owners would want their hair windswept.

The Bay team had produced county players in the past, and were already contributing girls to the Kent under-19 women's team. So the match promised to be a good contest, and we had all signed up for a fish supper at a proper old-fashioned chippie, which had so far resisted attempts to gentrify it. There was also a good pub next door, according to Ed van Boolen, the captain.

Tall, broad-shouldered and blonde, with the bluest eyes in the world, Ed ought to have been a Viking. He'd actually come from the Netherlands. He'd arrived in the UK in his teens with his sister, both intending to study fruit growing. She'd married and given up on the idea – I had a feeling they were no longer in touch – and he'd turned instead to landscape gardening and cricket, in whichever order. The Netherlands were a growing presence on the international cricket scene; Ed was the driving force of Wrayford CC. We'd had a lot to do with each other ever since I'd persuaded the governors to let the cricket club use the school playing field. I insisted it would benefit everyone: club, village and school. The club wouldn't have to close down, the village would have the social fun of a few fund-raising events, and the kids would get year-round coaching instead of the short burst that the wonderful Chance to Shine cricket charity provided. Yes, the club members involved would get the relevant background checks. Win, win, win, as far as I could see. The children didn't just have role models, but next year would get the chance to play in the under-twelve team Ed and the club were now planning. I had my eye on a girl I was sure would become a founder member.

And rumour had it that Ed had his eye on me, which was good for my ego, at least.

He'd hired three minibuses for the players and supporters to take us down to St Luke's Bay. We'd be dropped off one by one outside our own front doors in case any of us were too relaxed, as it were, to manage the stroll from a central point.

As it happened, we never made it to the chippie or to the pub because the captain of the Bay team, Marcus Baker, had organised a barbecue for us all, all the more generous in light of their eight-wicket defeat. Marcus's house was halfway up the steep hill to the north-east of the harbour; apart from a patio bigger than the whole of my garden, a lawn the size of a tennis court dropped towards a low wall overlooking the bay. Tonight the sunset was spectacular. The food smelt as good as only the open air can make it, and the drink was free-flowing. But by now I could hardly do more than sip iced water. My head throbbed in time with the loud music; my eyes found even the fairy lights dazzling; I could no longer attempt to join in any conversation. Then one of the Bay's players, extremely drunk already, started jabbing me in the chest, complaining about a leg-before-wicket decision I'd made. He'd argued at the time, with a lot of obscene words to emphasise his point. And another short, equally unacceptable gesture had ended his tirade as his fellow batsman, mouthing his apologies to me, propelled him off the square towards the boundary.

I shook my head: 'Come on, Dennis, what's played on the pitch stays on the pitch,' I whispered.

'I could have bloody killed you!'

The Bay umpire and another Bay player appeared, telling him it was time he left. He did, but not quietly. A couple of people came to offer their apologies. All I could do was smile pacifically, all the time longing for nothing more than paracetamol and my bed, with no one but Nosey the Bear for company, thank you very much.

But I had to wait for the minibus home: if I tried to call a cab someone would insist on driving me, which would break up an otherwise friendly party. So I looked for somewhere nice and quiet. Soon I found myself down by the back wall. Chunks of a poem I thought I'd forgotten years ago came unbidden to my mind as I leant heavily on the stonework and looked out towards the harbour:

The sea is calm tonight.
The tide is full, the moon lies fair
Upon the straits; on the French coast the light
Gleams and is gone; the cliffs of England stand,
Glimmering and vast, out in the tranquil bay.
. . . sweet is the night-air!

It was certainly sweet for a couple entwined in the shadows to my right. I would have averted my gaze from any lovers' private moment but was even swifter with this pair: not for anything would anyone learn from me that the giant of an opening bowler was snogging the wicketkeeper, whom I had rebuked only five hours ago for the foulest mouthed macho sledging I'd ever heard.

11

I turned my attention to the sea,

. . . the long line of spray
Where the sea meets the moon-blanched land . . .

The sea, or rather the inlet, was full of life in the descending dusk. All the boats were lit up, either from the cabin spaces or with what I dimly remembered were called riding lights. So I was surprised when one vessel slipped in in complete darkness, mooring out of my line of sight. As I peered round I was joined by our host, who asked abruptly why I was out on my own, and what was I staring at.

He stood rather closer than I expected to follow the line of my finger as I pointed. 'Just someone driving without lights,' I rasped.

He ignored my comment – might not even have heard it. Hardly moving away, he waved the bottles he held in his right hand. His own glass was in his left: it was very elegant, more at home on a candlelit dinner party than in the chaos of a big al fresco bash. Bravely he put it on the wall. It wobbled once but stayed put. 'Another drink?' I shook my head. 'No thanks.'

He topped up his glass with red wine. 'You've lost your voice completely? Really? We should have argued more with your decisions, shouldn't we! Though, to be honest, I thought you were very fair. Even when you awarded five penalty runs against us when the ball hit the helmet our wicketkeeper should have stowed somewhere safe. Very good all round.' He didn't even add 'For a woman'. He raised his glass in a silent toast. I responded with mine, mouthing painful thanks.

I couldn't work out why he bothered to stay with me, but he did, sipping his wine. Each time he wiped the glass rim with a tissue before drinking again. He might have been sharing a communion chalice except that there was no one there except me. The silence deepened. I was supposed to do something, wasn't I? Interact. Utter polite nothings. He was a pleasant enough young man, after all, but fairly nondescript in appearance – there was nothing to mark him out as a keen sportsman who'd once hoped to play at county level. I had an idea he was something in the family firm of lawyers, which would explain the size of his house and garden. Sadly his wife looked as if she'd been dipped in a bucketful of resentful unhappiness, and every time I'd heard her speak it was to complain about something – from the sugar-high children who refused to go to bed, to the smelly dog stealing burgers out of guests' buns and the fact that one of the minibus drivers had gone AWOL. Marcus, on the other hand, seemed serene enough, even if he must have been spitting tacks at being run out by his partner Toby something-or-other when he'd been on the verge of his first fifty of the season.

'I'm sorry about your half-century,' I growled.

He put his ear close to my mouth. I repeated what I'd said.

'Shit happens. But I'll put the little bugger in to field at very short square leg next match. See how he likes that.'

Yes. The most dangerous place on the field. I hoped Toby would wear adequate protection but couldn't say it. All I could manage was a wry smile of agreement. The burning pain in my throat was spreading through my sinuses and lungs.

The silence returned.

Another boat was moving about unlit – this one was leaving the harbour.

'*Where ignorant armies clash by night,*' I gasped meaninglessly – and fainted into, someone told me later, his arms.

By Monday morning I'd tried everything the Sainsbury's pharmacist had to offer, though she warned me she was sure that I only had a virus, which no antibiotics would touch. Otherwise I would have been pleading, presumably via text messages, for an appointment with the local GP. As it was, I resigned myself to salt-water gargles, silent communion with Nosey, the teddy bear that had come into my life a few months ago, and an indolence quite foreign to me.

I should have enjoyed myself in my latest temporary home, normally a holiday cottage, which was equipped to the highest standards. I could bask in either the tiny walled garden or the chic living area, working my way through a year's worth of unread books. Sadly and bizarrely, reading made my throat worse – even the silent reading I always encouraged when playtimes were too wet for the pupils to go outside. I felt too weak to start packing up for the move to my new home in the village, knowing that in any case it was in such a poor state that until essential work like repairs to the roof and drains, the installation of a new kitchen and a new bathroom and total redecoration had made it habitable, there was little point anyway. And now rumour had it that some do-gooder was applying to get it listed. Just what I needed when I'd run to earth the only house in the area I could afford – thanks to my long-awaited divorce settlement and to a major change in my employment conditions thought to merit a respectable pay rise.

Fortunately my new landlord, Brian Dawes, the chair of the school governors, promised to let me stay as long as necessary. Furthermore, he was charging me at the low-season rate, which he could easily have tripled in the summer. Possibly he sensed that being generous to me would enhance his reputation in the village. But he didn't demur when I suggested that at the very least I should pay the weekly cleaner's bills.

Even though I was living on the outskirts of the village, news of my illness soon spread: a couple of wild-flower posies appeared on my doorstep, soon followed by soups of various sorts, some more successful than others. The things that brought the biggest smile to my face were the get-well cards crafted, perhaps lovingly and certainly proudly, by some of my pupils. There was also a mauve teddy bear, which Nosey eyed with disdain, and, from the cricket club, a canvas carrier bag containing a litre of whisky, a jar of local honey and a net of organic unwaxed lemons. A bunch of late sweet peas from Ed himself arrived late one evening too.

After a week of inertia and too much television, I found myself feeling better – though still silent. My new psychotherapist thought it might be something to do with being too angry at or even too upset by recent events to be able to speak. My own theory was a bit homespun, of course, but one shared by the GP to whom I'd had at last to report: that my throat, battered by all the end-of-term activity, had succumbed more heavily than most to what was a decidedly nasty bug doing the rounds in the south of England. So rest, gentle exercise – and no antibiotics. There was no reason to lurk self-pityingly indoors, he said, now my fever had subsided. Canterbury cricket week was coming up any day now. I smiled my approval: Dr Mike Evans and his practice had been generous in sponsoring the school Kwik Cricket team. Meanwhile, he asked, why didn't I take advantage of my silent state? Why not buy a bike and explore the countryside?

Mouth agape, I pointed to my chest. Me, cycle?

He nodded, playing his trump card: 'Two legs good; two wheels better.'

I couldn't argue, could I? Firstly, I was still in Trappist mode. Secondly, I had to applaud his literary allusion.

One place within cycling distance would be my new school. No, I wasn't leaving the one in Wrayford, but gaining another, in Wray Episcopi. It was tinier than mine with fewer than eighty pupils on roll, and, as its head teacher had retired, was threatened with closure – unless some kind fellow head could be bribed to take it on in addition to their duties at their own school. Kind – or ambitious. Unwilling to identify my motives, I quickly established that this would involve appointing deputy heads and freeing the head from teaching duties. Sadly teaching was what I enjoyed most about the job – but getting on the property ladder was important, so I was prepared to trade it. And, perhaps simply on geographical grounds, I got the post.

There had been a lot of negotiations: we might have been discussing the merger of two multinationals. I'd wanted the unions involved from day one: the rights of the teachers, my colleagues, on whom I would have to depend totally, were as important as saving local authority money, despite the swingeing cuts. The only male teacher at Wray Episcopi opted for voluntary redundancy, on the grounds that teaching wasn't what it used to be and he wanted to live long enough to enjoy his retirement. No one could argue with that, but I drew the line at recruiting a young, untried replacement. Being trained was one thing; knowing the job inside out was another. The latest statistics showed that new recruits to the profession generally stuck it out for only three years. So I wanted someone battle-hardened, even though that would make a bigger dent in my staffing budget. I was also quite keen to recruit a man, to give the boys a role model since all the other staff at Wray Episcopi were women. On the other hand, I would really have liked my deputy there to be a woman, to balance Tom, my deputy at Wrayford. But I wouldn't get any deputy till Christmas at the earliest, given notice periods, unless I could snap up one who'd been made redundant and wouldn't mind a bit of rural downsizing.

At last the job descriptions were drawn up, and advertisements placed. All I had to do now was watch and wait – and pray I could make myself heard, in every sense, at the interviews.

After the overwrought garrulity of the school, in one way I enjoyed the enforced quiet. In another I loathed it. I discovered I was more sociable than I'd realised: I wouldn't have had much of a career as a contemplative nun. I missed my elbows-on-bar gossips with Diane, the landlady of the Jolly Cricketers, who had sent me some magical ice cream, assuring me when I texted my thanks that she was simply using me as a guinea pig to test her new machine. She might even have been serious.

With only the birds and loud agricultural machinery for company, then, I followed Mike Evans' advice. I bought a bike. I bought a helmet. I bought a hi-vis waistcoat. I bought gloves. What I found I couldn't do was go the whole Lycra-wearing hog. I saw the point, I really did, but I wasn't into that sort of statement. Overstatement, in my case. Any athletic skills I had had always involved keeping my feet on the ground, or at least running and jumping around on it. So, with everyday trainers on my feet and clad in old jeans and tops, I got on the saddle, waving a dubious Nosey goodbye. At first I confined myself to nice, secluded, dedicated cycle paths, even if that meant hoisting the bike on to the car – yes, I'd bought a bike rack too – and driving there. Gradually I progressed to country lanes, but I soon learnt that these might not be as idyllic as you'd think – learnt the hard way, too.

Suddenly I was flying. Suddenly I was on top of a hedgerow, which seemed to consist entirely of brambles, wild roses, and nettles. Ah, there was some barbed wire in there too. Probably rusty.

'Help!' But no sound came out, of course. And, for the time being, I couldn't reach my phone, tucked in my bumbag.

Before I knew it, I was being rescued. Painfully. Pulled through a hedge backwards, as the cliché goes, but this was literally happening.

'We've dialled 999,' a man's voice said. Oldish. Kentish.

'I'm fine,' I protested, though it's possible that over the grunting of their own exertions they couldn't hear my

18

guttural whisper. By now I was making my own efforts to free myself, but could find nothing to give any leverage.

It was hard not to squeak with pain when my rescuers resumed theirs.

'Come on, Doreen: don't just stand there!' he gasped.

'You're just making it worse,' the woman said. She too was oldish and Kentish. 'And you know your heart's not what it was, Harry.'

What if trying to help me killed him? 'I'm safe enough here,' I gasped. 'Do you live nearby?'

'Just across the lane – well, a few yards.'

'Maybe you've got such a thing as a stepladder, Harry?'

He had. His footsteps retreated.

'I'd best help him carry it, silly old bugger,' the woman said doubtfully. 'If it's OK to leave you?'

Certainly I wasn't going anywhere. I promised her I'd be all right.

And soon I was. Maybe I really had been hoping for the wail of an ambulance siren. Certainly I hadn't expected the throaty pulse of a motorbike. Not just any leather-clad rider, either: the miracle of a mobile paramedic, who introduced himself as Ian.

I suppose he had a list of guidelines to follow, because he fired a series of questions at me. No doubt my rescuers' helpful suggestions drowned some of my replies: it took time to persuade him that my lack of voice wasn't as a result of today's activities.

Eventually, though I didn't wish to challenge his professionalism, I risked a suggestion: 'Ian, you're practically wearing a suit of armour. You could even put your helmet on again. Couldn't you just push your way through and hold me up while I wriggle free? Look, all my toes and fingers work, and I promise you I've not lost any feeling anywhere. Anywhere at all,' I whispered emphatically.

'I ought to get backup, Jane.' For some reason he dropped his voice too. 'Ambulances carry equipment I can't. Then we could slide a back-board under you and fix a neck brace.'

'I'm sure you ought. But I'm sure a quick tug and Harry's stepladder under me will free me.' Please let it be quick: otherwise it would be like having a slow tooth extraction or a leisurely leg wax.

He did his best. In a matter of seconds I was standing in my tattered jeans and shredded top on the dried-out grass verge. One foot hurt more than the other: I'd managed to lose a trainer at some point. My helmet was still in place, however, and things could clearly have been a lot worse. Even the blood – though there was quite a lot. I might have been embraced by razor blades.

Doreen and Harry were both, as I'd suspected, in their seventies. For some reason they dressed as if they were in a fashion time warp, he in grey flannels and she wearing a wrap-around pinny. Both were more appalled by the sight of all my blood than was reassuring.

'The trouble is,' Ian said, 'I can't take you to A&E. We need an ambulance for that.'

'But I don't need A&E. GP surgery or Minor Injuries, maybe. The scratches are all pretty superficial. Aren't they?'

He was checking them carefully, and was clearly inclined to agree. But there was no doubt he registered my pathetic shaking.

'I've only just had a tetanus booster,' I added, as if that would put an end to the discussion. 'It's surely just a matter of putting dressings on the worst.'

At this point, Doreen – it turned out she was Harry's sister, not his wife – insisted that we all adjourn to their bungalow so that the paramedic could treat me there and then in what she called decent privacy. I was very grateful, even though she kept popping in and out of the lounge – a strange choice of room, perhaps – with towels and bowls of hot water, as if I was an injured hero in an old black and white Western. Ian pretended to be appreciative, although he had a seemingly endless supply of disposable wipes; my husky thanks for the pot of tea for both of us were absolutely sincere, however. The cup rattled less and less in the saucer.

'I suppose you didn't get the reg of the guy that ran you off the road?' he asked, probably to distract me while he diligently extracted a thorn.

'He came up from behind. I think. I can't recall seeing anyone coming my way. Bloody hell, Ian!'

'Soon be done. There's no one who's out to get you, I suppose?'

Now wasn't the time to regale him with my life story.

At last he announced he was satisfied. I was to take a taxi home and call my GP or the NHS helpline if I had any problems. We waved him off.

Doreen, who clearly disapproved of wasting money on a taxi, declared that Harry and she would drive me back to my cottage, even though my bike would have to await its turn in their front garden – a charming picture-book place with old-fashioned flowers surrounding an immaculate lawn. It was so lovely that I asked, flourishing my phone, if I could take a photo with them in it, but she simply pointed to a loft window she'd left ajar and dashed in to close it. Then she had to double-check she'd locked the front door. And nip round the back to see that all was secure there. Shades of my paranoid mother.

Harry let himself into an elderly two-door Fiesta, which looked as if it had last been cleaned the year he bought it: it was completely out of place against the neatness of the house. It had left a patch of oil on the driveway at the side of the cottage. Doreen was checking that all was clear for him to reverse into the lane, reassuring him with decidedly ambiguous arm movements.

'What I can't work out,' he said through the open driver's window, as he pulled up with two wheels on the verge, 'is why that man drove at you. He did, you know, didn't he? That man?' he prompted as Doreen held the front passenger door open and tipped forward the seat. Somehow I was to get into the back seat. At last I managed. I dared not speculate on how I'd get out.

'What man?' She took her place beside him.

'The man that drove at Jane, here. In the big car.'

'Oh, the blue one.'

'No, it was black. With tinted windows.'

'Blue with tinted windows. One of those that look like a van. Ugly great things.'

'More like a young lorry. What do they call them on *Neighbours*? Utes? Only with the back section covered up. Yes, you ought to tell the police, Jane. Who would want to do that to an innocent woman?'

'I've no idea.' Nor had I. Not precisely. The trouble was

that though Simon was still in prison, he had plenty of cronies on the outside. On the other hand, I'd have thought they'd have done a more efficient job of despatching me. Who else could it have been? – assuming, of course, that it wasn't a simple accident. I'd had problems when I'd arrived in the village but now I seemed to be on reasonably good terms with everyone.

'We'd be witnesses,' she continued.

'Thank you,' I said, without irony. 'I don't suppose you managed to remember any of the registration number?'

'They've got such complicated ones these days, haven't they?'

I took that as a negative. 'Or the make?' I added, more in hope than expectation.

As if they were an old married couple, bound together for fifty years, they bickered all the way to Wrayford: make; model; colour? Somehow I didn't think there was much for the police to work on, even if I'd been able to make any intelligent guesses.

The only time they were silent was when, ready to say goodbye, I asked them for their address and phone number. They flinched as if I'd asked them to give classified information.

'So I can phone you before I come and collect my bicycle,' I whispered gently.

'Oh, there's no need for that. All you need to do is open the gate.'

I shook my head, trying to be patient and to sound even more grateful than I was. 'You know, I think I must have banged my head after all. I haven't,' I declared truthfully, 'a clue where it all happened.'

Their contact details safe in my phone, I waved them goodbye, unable, however, to rid myself of the idea that they wanted nothing further to do with me. I wouldn't have been surprised if the cycle had appeared unannounced in my own front garden. But it hadn't when I ordered a large bunch of thank-you flowers online next morning, including the message that I'd arrive in my car the following day.

I did. To find the bike still in place. It was absolutely pristine: they must have cleaned it when they cleaned their car, which I presumed they must do occasionally – an annual treat, perhaps. Meanwhile, far from spruce, wilting on the sun-baked doorstep, sat a large bouquet.

It must have been a combination of the virus and the accident that meant I could only stare, nonplussed, for what seemed like several minutes. They were out. That was all. Or perhaps it wasn't. I took a prowl round the bungalow. A peep through a window showed me that everything was almost unnaturally tidy: it reminded me of how my mother used to leave the family home before our summer exodus to the seaside; my family hadn't discovered cheap package tours abroad. Even the dishcloth was hung carefully to dry over the mixer tap. Some fairly deep tyre tracks led me to a long shed, the roof of which was so concave I couldn't imagine it holding up much longer. What it held would remain a mystery, because it dawned on me that what I was doing was snooping. Even so I registered another puzzle: why two people should need such an inordinately long washing line. But perhaps they had once offered B&B accommodation and needed to dry loads of bedlinen.

But none of this was anything to do with me. I gathered up the flowers so I could return them to the Canterbury florist. Next time they might not leave anything unsigned for lying casually for all to see. All? Well, the odd sheep.

In the cycle shop, as the mean and lean owner sucked his teeth over the damage to the bike and worked out an estimate for repairing it, I looked at helmet cameras. The next person running me off the road had better smile.

CHAPTER TWO

Having bravely run the risk of being bled on, Nosey was very relieved when my scratches began to heal. Then my voice improved, apparently in sync. I was almost as disappointed as he was. Even though I'd have had to exchange two wheels for four until my bike was better too, I'd planned silent visits to some of the most famous tourist destinations in Kent: Dover Castle, Dungeness, Sissinghurst. But now I could read without throat complications, could I turn to my enticing pile of books? With Nosey on my lap? No, I told him: I'd better apply myself to the files of my new outpost, none of which would interest him. I'd arrived in Wrayford itself with precious little opportunity to prepare, and a whole heap of problems no one could have envisaged. So naturally I resolved to prepare this time for every single foreseeable eventuality.

I read the file of every child and every adult associated

with the school. I knew the first name of the plumber who responded to what seemed an unnaturally high number of call-outs; I also knew the cleaner had a problem with punctuality, though not the reason. But the most interesting thing I discovered seemed to me a policy worth adopting at Wrayford itself: every family whose child had been offered a place at Wray Episcopi school had a home visit from one of the staff – sometimes even with Maggie Hale, the head, if it was felt there might be problems with either location in a very rural area or with a family known for a less than co-operative attitude to authority. The plan was not to snoop around, but to introduce to the child and its parents a member of staff whose name and face would be familiar on the child's first day at school. It was also a chance for the parent to raise issues about behaviour, illness or allergies. A handwritten appendix to the file showed that this was not a universally popular policy: one extremely rich local worthy had been so incensed by the idea of what he wrongly construed as a check on his granddaughter's home life that he'd paid for a private school place instead. Another noted that as a result of the teachers' visit the RSPCA had been summoned to check on the family dogs. Clearly all was not going to be straightforward, and I suspected that some of the Wrayford governors would be against the idea from the moment I first mooted it, unless I did so with extreme tact – otherwise known as low cunning.

I would certainly need the chair of governors on my side.

Brian Dawes and I had enjoyed an uneasy association from the moment I was appointed: at times he'd shown downright hostility, with his massive head and threatening shoulders unnerving me, but on other occasions he'd proved a wise and committed professional. There was no doubt he'd been as shocked and horrified as I by a series of tragic events resulting in the loss of several promising pupils – the death, indeed, of one of them. Chastened, perhaps feeling a modicum of guilt, he'd recently been more constructive than destructive in any criticism of me or my colleagues. As well as being my generous landlord he had also invited me to a number of social events, which probably caused no little gossip in the village, though I could have assured anyone interested that our friendship, if so it could be described, was strictly platonic.

As was my relationship with someone for whom I'd once had far from platonic feelings: Pat Webber. For a long time he'd been my utterly reliable – *relionable*, indeed – police contact for when my violent ex-husband forced his way back into my life yet again, finding me wherever I'd moved to. At last, however, Simon was tucked away in Durham jail, and, after I'd changed my name and as much of my appearance as I could manage without actually going under the knife, Pat's bosses, mindful of their budget, no doubt, thought I could look after myself. Pat had plenty of other work to do, and perhaps other personal responsibilities I still didn't know about. It was those he had to deal with, one way or another, to his own moral satisfaction; in any case, officers like him were never supposed to develop personal feelings towards their vulnerable clients – and certainly not act on them if they did. There was talk that an officer's initiating a sexual relationship – Pat with me, for instance – would become a criminal offence, with a jail sentence for the offender.

Meanwhile I needed to work out whether I was genuinely

attracted to Pat or simply profoundly grateful for all he'd done. So like fairy-tale lovers we'd separated for a year and a day. Seriously, we'd not spent any time together for about six months now. OK, we'd had the very occasional contact by text or email. How he felt about mine, I can't tell. Once I'd held my breath till the next one from him. Now I was accustomed to not hearing from him, and I'd pretty well ceased to imagine reporting a particularly weird or pleasant incident to him. Actually, even without Pat on the horizon, Brian didn't stand much chance. I needed solid friends more than risky love affairs – and if I did date him, what if the relationship ended? No, it was best for us to be strictly professional in our doings.

I was preoccupied too with the alterations to my new home. Or lack thereof. I was working through a succession of builders who might, you'd have thought, have leapt at the chance of several weeks' solid work. The one on whose assurances I'd gone ahead with the purchase went bankrupt within two days of the cottage becoming my property; another refused point-blank to have anything to do with the project. Was it because it was remotely likely to attract historical officialdom? They never replied. Several insisted that they were committed to projects that would mean no work on mine till next Easter.

Add to that the complications of even builders taking normal summer holidays, my progress was slow to non-existent. Now I could speak firmly down the phone, perhaps my progress would be better. Perhaps.

In fact, the whole village seemed to be in a state of suspended animation, the natives being replaced by visitors in search of quaintness cheek by jowl with the advantages of urban living. They couldn't believe there were no shops, no post office – nothing but the pub. Even the church was relying on visiting clergy, as Brian remarked when we met – by chance – in the Jolly Cricketers' bar.

'And now we've got damned Operation Stack again, too!' he added venomously, as if the M20 being used as a car park for hundreds of vehicles waiting to cross into France was somehow the fault of the Church of England.

'What's the reason this time?' I asked. It wasn't just one major road being blocked, as media reports might have implied: access to others was severely limited, and some minor roads were gridlocked as drivers sought to beat the appalling jams only to find bigger, better ones lying in wait. Last time the delay had been caused by insufficient security staff to check travellers' documentation and search cars, if necessary. I missed all the chaos because of my virus, of course.

Brian shrugged those huge shoulders. 'Which one this time? Migrants trying to get into the Tunnel and closing it? A broken down lorry? Striking French fishermen blockading the port of Calais?'

Diane shook her head. 'Rioting refugees. A boy was killed in the Tunnel. Some sixteen-year-old trying to ride a lorry. The dreadful irony is that he was entitled to come over here anyway – he has family in the country already. But officialdom just took too long . . .'

Our sympathy for the boy, hardly more than a child, didn't chime in with Brian's mood, so she added dryly, 'And I hear our government doesn't think there's sufficient demand for a lorry-park to be cost-effective.'

'They should try living down here,' Brian snorted. He turned to me, effectively cutting Diane out of the conversation. 'What's this I hear about you having an accident, Jane?'

I wasn't sure how I felt about his narrow-eyed scrutiny. 'Some idiot knocked me off my bike,' I said. 'I landed in a good solid hedge, so there was no real damage done – except to my dignity,' I added ruefully. 'They'll be able to repair the bike and my skin's healing.'

At last he seemed to register my linen trousers and prettiest long-sleeved top – there seemed no point in displaying my scabs to the world. 'You've not been cycling long – did you wobble at the wrong moment?' His laugh was meant to be indulgent.

'I certainly wobbled when the SUV hit me. On my side of the road.'

'Hit and run!' Diane put in, passing me a Pimm's she would put on my tab.

'Exactly,' I said.

'Any idea who did it?' Brian asked seriously.

Diane, giving me a wink, moved off to take food orders at the far end of the bar.

'I've wracked my brains. I can think of any number of people I've annoyed,' I said with a self-deprecating grin, 'but I'd rather people moaned to my face than upended me on a public road. Anyway, a passing motorcyclist rescued me, so here I am.' I was being economical with the truth, of course. I was rattled by Brian's assumption that it was my fault, of course, but for some reason I didn't want to bring Doreen and Harry into the anecdote, just in case I blabbed about their elusiveness. And I still tried to block from my mind the idea that the whole thing might not have been a genuine accident.

At this point a cheery voice greeted us all: Ed van Boolen's.

Brian bristled like a hostile dog as Ed approached us, greeting me with a kiss and a rather sweaty hug. When I'd seen him earlier, he'd been leading his teammates in a vigorous fielding practice. But now he was back in gardening mode: when was work going to start on the new place so he could turn my tangled garden into paradise?

Pointedly ignoring the double entendre I spread my hands: 'No one seems to want to tackle the job. If it was new-build I think they'd be interested. But it's simply renovation: I'm not changing the footprint of the existing cottage. Diane contacted one of her friends, but they were booked up well into the new year. Come on, Ed, you must know people round here: if people need pretty cottage gardens, it stands to reason that at least some of them have bought cottages to go with them. Give it some thought, lad. And you, Brian, of course.'

Though he almost blushed, Brian was at his most repressive. 'The firm that did mine is tied up over in St Margaret's Bay. Long term.'

'More of your empire, Brian?' Ed asked dryly. Presumably Brian didn't use his services. When he got no reply, he continued, 'As it happens, I do have an idea. Leave it with me, Jane – I'll see what I can do.' He downed his shandy in one draught and, patting me on the arm, strode off, as if already on his mission to rescue me.

Part of me could have wished that Ed had eaten at the Cricketers too: it would have spared me an impending tête-à-tête with Brian, who would assume, as he always did if he found me here, that he was welcome to join me and then insist on paying the bill, becoming tetchy if I declined. But tonight I was spared any embarrassment. Just as he was reaching for the menus, his phone rang. Excusing himself, he turned aside to answer it. He frowned, and then, with no explanation or even courtly apology, he headed off into the still warm evening.

CHAPTER THREE

Although I should have been working, the next day was so lovely that I couldn't resist collecting my newly repaired bike and tootling off – with my camera switched on – to the place where I was knocked off in the first place. To be strictly honest, I was really more interested in Doreen and Harry's cottage. Actually, in them.

After a trip mercifully without incident I propped the bike up against their fence, but decided it was pointless to venture further. Or was it? Despite the heat, all the windows were firmly closed. When I peered through the kitchen window, I could see that the dishcloth was still draped over the mixer tap. But it seemed to me that the deep tracks I'd noticed before had been ground a bit wider by a vehicle somewhat larger than a Fiesta – which hadn't, as I recalled, been kept there anyway, but on the side drive. The oil patch was no longer fresh. All of which added up to precisely nothing that was any of my business. Why did I feel uneasy? For one thing, they were such a garrulous pair, Doreen particularly, that I was surprised they'd not mentioned a forthcoming holiday – especially when I'd asked for their contact details. For another – well, that was probably enough. And once again I was snooping, and indeed trespassing. Switching on my helmet camera, I set off home. Slowly. Not just because my joints had stiffened. I was keeping an eye out for another cottage that might loosely be described as neighbouring. Nothing. So blow me if I didn't turn round and cycle equally slowly in the other direction. Nothing. What a strange isolated life they must lead, even with a car. After my recent brush with silence, it certainly wasn't one I'd choose.

I headed back, guiltily, to Wray Episcopi to assuage my conscience with some work.

As I propped my bike up by the school gate, an Audi pulled up, the driver waving. With a grin I trotted over: it was Jo Davies, whose policeman husband Lloyd had been immensely supportive during an outbreak of vandalism centred round the school. Now Jo was not just a friend but also an invaluable part-time maths teacher busily improving Wrayford Primary's results.

'So this is the latest outpost of your empire! Can I come and have a look?' She zapped the car's central-locking system with some intangible panache as she walked with me – for so short a woman she had a very long stride. She stopped abruptly as she stepped into the entrance hall, so small it was barely a vestibule. 'God, why do schools always smell the same? Even when there are no kids around? Every single one I've ever taught in smelt like

36

this. And you can't blame it these days on overcooked cabbage or burnt rice pudding.'

'Nor even on sweaty clothes and trainers: I asked my predecessor to insist that absolutely everything was removed at the end of term with the promise of the skip or a charity shop for anything left behind. I needed only a small skip and one trip to Oxfam. But there are some things that leave a different sort of stink.' I pointed to the PTA noticeboard, currently stripped of any paperwork, but with scribbled graffiti still showing despite my best efforts with bleach and abrasive pads. Nasty old-fashioned racism with nasty old-fashioned words, even if the targets were refugees from a hideous twenty-first century war zone. Syria had proved too tough for the culprit's spelling. Yet I sensed the writing was adult.

'What are you going to do?' Jo asked, shocked.

'I've written to the PTA chair – he's called Gerry Paine – telling him to get a new noticeboard. He's not favoured me with a reply yet, though I've tried two or three times. It's PTA property so I can't bin it out of hand unless they fail to act before the start of term. Hey, where are you going?'

'Getting a screwdriver from my car: we can at least take the damn thing down. There you are. Woman-power,' she declared a couple of minutes later, as we lowered the heavy board to the floor.

'Just so I don't get accused of criminal damage – you never know with committees like that, do you? – I'll fasten the screws and Rawlplugs to the back. Provided there's an envelope and sticky tape somewhere in the school office,' I added cautiously.

There might have been, but everything was meticulously

37

locked away. As for my new desk, in my cubbyhole of a room, freshly decorated and carpeted at my own expense, it was completely empty. 'Sorry: I've not got around to stocking up on all things headteacherly yet.' All the usual stuff. Plus tissues. Wet wipes. Even pads for kids getting their first period. 'Drat. But I'll stow the detritus in my desk, for safety's sake.'

We continued our tour. Most of it looked terribly down at heel with none of the usual artwork and exhortatory material schools use to paper over cracks – sometimes quite literally. But Jo was quick to pick up the connection between the odd white splodge on my hair and the newly painted reception classroom.

'I wanted the littlies to feel welcome and valued at the very least,' I confessed. 'It's quite therapeutic,' I added, perhaps defensively. 'Plus the decorating firm pulled out at the last minute: the gaffer broke his leg. Boss,' I added by way of explanation: not everyone got my Midlands lingo.

'And I suppose you'll say it was a very good way of checking every inch of the fabric,' Jo said tartly. 'Fine. But who'd have come to your rescue if you'd fallen off a stepladder? At least you've got the grace to look ashamed of yourself!' She looked around, assessing the work still to be done.

Despite my good intentions, I found myself scratching a scab.

'Hang on,' Jo said, pulling up my sleeve. 'I wondered why you weren't wearing a T-shirt. What have you been up to?'

I explained. Partially.

'If you're that accident-prone, ladders are *verboten*.

38

OK? Now, which room do we tackle next? I'll be here tomorrow. Carys and Geraint are bored to tears and even I have to admit they've completed all their holiday work . . .'

There was quite a party atmosphere the following day. Geraint and Carys tore themselves away from teenage technology to wield a useful paintbrush and roller and actually seemed to enjoy themselves. Lloyd, their father, who described himself as an old-fashioned cop, joined us after work one afternoon to help too. Why could Simon and I never have functioned as a family like this?

They were making mock of his efforts when there was an authoritative peal on the old-fashioned pull-operated doorbell, the sort you associate with National Trust houses.

'Cassandra Preston,' the tall woman announced as I opened the door. She'd be in her late sixties or seventies, but it was hard to tell precisely from a face that had obviously spent a lot of time in the open air. Was she ex-military? She had the posture and demeanour, but her clothing might have been donated by a bag-lady. 'And you are?'

'Jane Cowan. The new head teacher.' I would have offered my hand but to do so would have involved wiping it on my particularly tatty jeans – a gesture I dismissed, somewhere deep in my psyche, as being somehow subservient. Instead I spread both hands to show the paint. It wasn't intended to be an invitation to step inside, but was taken as such.

'I'm afraid it's very messy in here, Ms Preston.' My apology inched out of its own accord. Or was it really a polite warning? I straightened my back. Did she hear the clunk?

'Ms! I heard you insisted on that weird form of address.

Well, I'm Lady Preston, as it happens. Are you sure all this is appropriate work for a headmistress?'

I suspected there might be slight stress on the second two syllables; however, I would pick my battles and the title on my office door would certainly be gender-free.

'It's not term time yet,' I countered. 'And I didn't want decorators interrupting schoolwork. Besides, a clean bright classroom might encourage everyone to observe the uniform code. Anyway, Lady Preston, how can I help you? My office is just through here.'

'I know exactly where it is. I was a governor here for years. Why have you taken down the PTA noticeboard?'

'Offensive graffiti it was impossible to remove. The PTA will have to replace it.'

'And the paintings?'

'Paintings? The children's artwork?'

'I said paintings and I meant paintings. Oil. Landscapes and such.'

Oh, dear. They must have been donated by the Preston family during a previous head's incumbency.

She stood arms akimbo in her irritation: 'The ones that always hung in here. I've heard from the Wrayford people you're always making unnecessary changes. Not that I'm here to criticise in any way, you understand. I just wanted to see for myself what's going on.'

And see the family pictures, of course.

I would not rise to her bait. 'I've never seen any paintings apart from children's efforts during my many visits to the school. Perhaps the previous head teacher found another location for them. We're still in regular touch to ensure a straightforward changeover so I can enquire.' *Ask!* Why

40

hadn't I said *ask*? What a craven toady! I pushed open my office door to let her step in first. 'How can I help you, pictures apart?' I checked my watch. 'First, if you'll excuse me, I must see my fellow decorators off the premises.'

They announced that they'd tidy everything away while I finished with Lady Preston: apparently we were all going bowling together in Ashford.

I didn't think that such a frivolous way of passing an evening would suit her ladyship's idea of pedagogic dignity. In any case, I didn't need to tell her why I needed to keep our meeting short.

She was looking around my office, but had not taken a seat. 'You know how to spend money.' Her voice boomed round my little domain.

'My own, as it happens,' I said crisply. 'Now, how may I help you?'

'I told you: I wanted to see what you were up to since you're here all hours.'

'But you would like your pictures back if I can locate them?'

'Mine? Good God no. My grandfather's. Lord Langleigh.'

The vowel sounded far too long to be a simple *Langley*, which was in my experience far too humble a town to give rise to a lord.

'The one who donated the land for the school,' she continued. 'What's all this about a school running track?'

She certainly had her aristocratic ear to the ground. 'Not here.' There was scarcely room in the playground to swing a kitten: Lady Preston's ancestor had skimped on some things, if not on others. 'Over in Wrayford. The aim

41

is to get the children – and staff! – running a mile before the start of school.'

'Well, good luck with that, the way people are today. Why not here?'

'Circuits of the playground.'

She nodded. 'Not a lot of fun compared with a field. Come over to the Great House one day and we'll see if we can find a bit of field for you. Good day to you then, Miss Cowan.'

She was not the sort of person to twitter good wishes and thanks to. 'When would be convenient, Lady Preston?'

'You can come round tomorrow. We're just round the corner. I'll expect you at eleven-thirty.'

I was going to get a good score if it killed me, so I rolled up my sleeves purposefully and weighed the ball. Lloyd stopped in his tracks. 'Well?'

There was no point in prevaricating. 'I told Jo: I had an argument with a hedge. It won.'

He shrugged, and seemed to accept it. But over a curry later – a fairly good one too – he returned to the subject of my injuries. He listened while I gave a cheerful precis of the affair, but didn't join in the general laughter at my expense.

'You didn't think to report it to us? To me in particular?'

'Come on, Lloyd, what could I have said? I didn't see the vehicle that tipped me over because it came up from behind. The witnesses gave garbled and mutually contradictory accounts and haven't responded to any of my calls—'

'You tried to call them?'

'Several times. To thank them. And to make sure they'd received some thank you flowers I'd ordered.' I still sounded bright and positive but airing the details once more was nurturing the doubts I'd tried to kill off. 'And actually I couldn't have spoken on the phone to anyone – I had that throat bug that silenced half Kent.'

'Lame excuse, Jane. You can phone them but not me? And in any case you could have emailed or texted me. Hmm.' He gave me a hard stare. 'No problems since?'

'None. Or I would have told you.'

'Good. But not good enough. I want more details. I promised Pat I'd keep an eye on you.'

'Thank you kindly, good sir,' I said dryly. 'Actually, it's no good trying to talk to Doreen and Harry. Whenever I've been round, there's been no one at home. The place is locked up. No sign of their car. But I get the sense that someone else has been on the property. Someone with quite a big vehicle. Probably just someone else looking for them,' I conceded.

'Probably. But keep me in the loop. Meanwhile, I'll run a few checks – see if any of your ex's known associates live round here. And I want you to think much harder than you appear to have been doing: is there anyone whom you upset down here enough for them to want to rub you out? It's hard to make someone on a bike have just a little accident, Jane, as you ought to know. I'll expect to hear back from you with a few ideas, OK? Tomorrow evening latest. After all that's happened to you, you can't afford to be so damned cavalier.' He nodded home his point. I found I was hanging my head. 'Now, Geraint, I'll fight you for the last of this jalfrezi.'

Lady Preston's notion of how many metres constituted just round the corner was pretty liberal, and I was already having misgivings as I made my way towards the Great House, which I never actually got to see: her ladyship was waiting on the gravelled drive by the estate gatehouse, a cramped cottage with a turret, no less, atop the tiniest of rooms with arrow-slit windows. It no doubt fulfilled some Victorian landlord's idea of romantic tweeness, but I couldn't imagine anyone taller than Victoria herself being able to live there – and on her own at that.

Her ladyship was on horseback looking, like her mount, magnificent, despite her faded baggy top and filthy trousers. Her boots gleamed, however, as did everything about the horse. I approached gingerly.

There was no greeting, and definitely no suggestion of shaking hands.

'Over there.' She pointed with her crop. 'I'll show you.' She had no difficulty at all making herself heard; indeed, it was probably years in the hunting field that had honed her voice, just as it was life in the classroom that had developed my own skills of projection. The terrain was much rougher for a human than for a horse, and it would have been a struggle to keep up had it not been for all those morning runs I'd done with my Wrayford colleagues and the kids. But I wouldn't risk going full pelt and ending with one foot in a rabbit hole.

'Come on, keep up. For God's sake!' However exasperated she was with me, she'd have to slow down or wait for me when she'd reached the field or paddock she had in mind. She waited. I made her wait longer.

'Now what are you doing?' she called. 'Well?'

I was taking photos on my phone. 'It's so much better than the playground,' I said truthfully, 'but most of the children are very young: I think their little legs might have difficulties with grass this long, but I may be wrong. So I thought I'd canvass my colleagues' opinions.' I was fairly sure they'd see the same problem: on a wet day the kids could be soaked up to the waist.

'Consult your staff? It's your job to make decisions. In any case, I don't see a problem.'

She wouldn't, not from up there.

'I'm a townie, so forgive me if I'm asking a stupid question: is it possible to mow this field?'

'It's supposed to be wild. To encourage wildlife. So no. Absolutely not. Couldn't they run in wellies or something? Oh, I suppose you want them to have proper trainers and all that.' She clearly considered the idea of proper footwear ludicrous, despite her own boots and indeed her hard hat or helmet or whatever it was called. 'Or do you want them hurtling round my front lawn or something?'

'Hardly, Lady Preston,' I laughed.

I wasn't the only one laughing. Through the still air came the unmistakeable sound of children enjoying themselves not very far away. I was about to smile at her ladyship to share the pleasure. But, as if someone had turned a switch, everything went quiet again. Suddenly and unnaturally quiet. 'Do you have family staying?' I asked, smiling anyway. If she did it would give her something to talk about, and ease the strange tension. I always found grandparents even happier to talk than parents themselves.

'No. Why on earth should you ask that? Silly question. OK, long grass, short legs. So no deal.'

'Actually,' I said, embarrassed at having made such a gaffe, 'I think this meadow could be a most valuable resource, more for the wildlife than for running. I wonder how many species of flowers grow here?'

'No idea. Never counted them. Don't want any ragwort in here, that's all, do we?'

'Indeed not!' I agreed enthusiastically; I'd have to find out why later. 'Really, then, the pupils checking the flora and fauna every so often would be mutually beneficial. Do you have an estate manager with whom I could discuss things?'

'Matt Storm. Looks like a kid but he's got his head screwed on. You'll find him—' but she and the horse were already in motion and what she said was lost in the wind. But she turned round, and I caught the words, '. . . pictures and be bloody quick about it.'

Thank you, your ladyship. As for Matt Storm, I didn't find him. Couldn't. Then, as the heat pressed down like a physical force, couldn't be bothered.

I strolled back to school and, opening all the windows wide, mounted another search. And still couldn't find the pictures. Or any response to my emails from my predecessor, Maggie Hale, who, I recalled, was on a Greek island learning Creative Writing.

I also recalled I was supposed to be doing my homework for Lloyd: I'd better get jotting now.

CHAPTER FOUR

'The problem is that my brain's been AWOL ever since the throat virus started,' I said, passing Lloyd a photocopied section of an OS map: I'd marked the precise location. Clipped to it were Doreen and Harry's details, and a sheaf of photos I'd downloaded from the Internet of vehicles I thought might fit their garbled descriptions. 'But you're right – I should have taken more notice.'

'That's something we agree on, at least,' Lloyd said grimly, his tone at complete variance with the evening, which we were spending on his terrace waiting for the barbecue to be hot enough for the food the kids were currently preparing. 'Now, as far as I know there are none of Simon's nasty little friends down here, but there may be nasty friends of nasty friends after the goings-on in the spring. Let's start with the obvious question: have you had any threats?'

'Apart from those I got umpiring a needle village cricket match? Oh, they were jokes. Blokes letting off stream. Cricketers are nice people. They don't just have rules; they're Laws.'

He didn't respond to my laugh. 'Cricketers? Or one cricketer? Ah, you're not very good at lying, are you? Name?'

'I wish I could remember. Everything about the day's gone really foggy. I could ask some of others what they recall . . . I was so ill at the party afterwards I actually passed out. The virus, not an excess of booze. All I could manage was water.'

'Which could have been spiked?'

'I poured it myself from a jug meant for diluting the kids' juice, and carried it with me everywhere like a good-luck charm. After I passed out they shoved me in the team minivan and ferried me home. According to the pharmacist I saw, my symptoms were absolutely typical of the virus: the passing out, the amnesia . . . Which is why I only remembered about it a moment ago. But please don't go chasing round the countryside asking who responded to being given out lbw by killing the umpire.'

'Of course I won't.'

'Apart from that I might have made a bit of an enemy of Lady Preston, mightn't I? I still haven't found her pictures.'

'That'd be the governors' problem, not yours, surely? Unless she drives one of these babies,' he said ironically, spreading the photos, and jabbing a bright-blue Ford monster. 'Are you sure you didn't see anything, anything at all, of the vehicle? They're hardly unobtrusive, Jane.'

'If someone creeps up on you in the street and whacks you, you don't necessarily see them,' I countered. 'I know you're a good cop, but you're far more interested in what turned out to be quite a trivial incident than I'd expect. Has someone else had the same experience? Ah! Gotcha!'

He straightened the pages into a neat heap. 'There has been another incident, yes, in the same sort of remote location – no witnesses at all, this time, and no CCTV or anything, of course. Another female cyclist, who sustained slightly more serious injuries – though not life-threatening, fortunately. Of course the incidents may not be connected.'

'I love it when you talk policese,' I said dryly. 'Am I allowed to know who? Sorry, silly question.'

Geraint was offering me a glass of Pimm's. The conversation was at an end.

Ed van Boolen pulled a face when a couple of days later I asked him, in the Jolly Cricketers' bar, about Matt Storm.

'Does he live up to his name? It's a bit Mills & Boon, come to think of it,' I added as we clinked glasses.

He didn't pick up on my comment. 'He's not from round here.'

Any more than I was – or him, of course – which made it pretty peculiar that he'd adopted the most judgemental phrase he could. I waited without comment.

He took a long sup. 'He's got qualifications – went to the Royal Ag college in Gloucestershire – only now it's a uni, of course. Got some sort of degree, I suppose. But I can't say I know anything more about him,' he added emphatically.

'Not even where I'd find him? Or, more to the point, the estate office? I've tried googling it, but the more I look the less I can see it.'

'It's built into the twelve-foot-high wall at the end of the big yew hedge. OK?'

'Great. Thanks. Ed – I was really ill when I umpired that Bay match. So ill I'm only now beginning to recall the odd detail. Did I make a complete hash of it? I seem to remember I upset one guy with what he thought was a really bad decision. One of our side? Lbw?'

'Only me – and I admit I was plumb. There was a guy on their side who moaned; I'd need to look at the score sheet to see who. But people always moan, and you can't undo decisions even on the field, let alone at this stage.'

'Even so . . . If it was a shocker I could apologise next time I see him.'

'Absolutely not recommended. Hey, Dwayne! Over here, mate!'

Dwayne, a short, square man who aspired to bat above number ten, headed over. Ed explained.

'That'd be the Menace. Dennis, of course. Dennis Paine. He's actually quite a decent guy, but he always argues, even when he's sober. When he's had a couple, he's keen on his fists. And he was way out of order, arguing the toss when your finger went up. Full and straight. Middle stump. Only he put his leg in the way. Even more out of order mentioning at the party. He's had a written warning. You can't have players sounding off like that, can you? Trouble is, they really need him – he's one of the best they've got.' His phone sang. 'That's Trish: supper's ready.' And he was off.

'There: I told you not to apologise, didn't I? Now, how about I challenge you to a game of snooker?'

As I disliked losing almost as much as he did, we didn't

talk much while we were playing, and afterwards I turned talk to the Test series that England had just won. When we'd chewed that over, he changed the subject abruptly.

'Are you still seeing that policeman?'

'Have you stopped beating your wife yet? If you mean *seeing* as have we been in touch recently, the answer is yes, occasionally, but if you mean *seeing* as in dating, that's never been the situation. He was my police liaison officer before my ex got sent down. Now he's in the nick, I don't need that sort of protection.'

'Thing is, I've got a pair of tickets for a One-Day International. The Oval. September. I know you'll be back at school, but I wondered if you'd fancy coming.' His habitually ruddy cheeks burnt as I hesitated for the blink of an eye. 'As a mate, if you like.'

'As a mate'd be great.'

'So you have got . . . someone?'

I had a sudden vision of him and Brian fighting it out over my non-existent affections. 'Oh, yes. About two hundred someones. You've no idea how teaching swamps your life, Ed – I'm not saying I'm signing on as a lifetime spinster, but until I've got the new school sorted out and until I'm keeping my head above water at the present one, I'm going to be on eighteen-hour days. Eight-day weeks!'

'Yeah. It was like that when I was building up my business. Still is at busy times of the year when you've got people wanting instant gardens. Like old Dawes did, the only time I worked for him. A right tartar, he is. How do you cope with him? Running in and out of your office all day – "Do this. Do that. And do it all yesterday".'

'He's very conscientious and very proud of the school,' I

said, his knowing grin showing we both knew I was being diplomatic. I half-expected him to insist on walking me back to the cottage, but one of his mates turned up and pressed a pint into his hand. The newcomer was quick to turn his back on me, and there was clearly no question of Ed introducing me – in fact, he was quite definitely excluding me from any conversation.

I could take a hint. But I was intrigued. I recognised by sight most of the men who used the pub these days, but had certainly never come across this one before. And it didn't seem to be just me he was keen to avoid. The two hunched their way first to the corner by the darts board and then, not happy that someone wanted to use it, outside – presumably to the smokers' den. At least there was no sign of them at any of the tables in the popular patio area, where some of my pupils still played while their parents drank. It was not, I had to remind myself firmly, a school night, so I passed them all with a smile and a wave.

CHAPTER FIVE

The first home visits for new pupils at Wray Episcopi School went well enough. In a larger school, Karenza would have taught the reception class but in this one she had to combine the new intake with the children who'd already completed a year. She was a tall young woman – she could look me in the eye – in her early thirties and striking rather than pretty. She treated me more as a colleague than as a boss, and with the new parents was charming and friendly but astute. If all that sounds stilted and official, blame the pile of references for the new deputy I was currently wading through, all couched in the sort of prefabricated phrases that would have driven George Orwell to drink.

Nor was Karenza afraid to tackle problems like the one in this, the third house we visited – a beautiful barn conversion, with a kitchen so modern that it made even the state-of-the-art one in Brian's rental cottage look inadequate. The whole house looked like something from the advertisement pages of *Kentish Life*, even to the blonde wooden floors and pale furnishings. How on earth did a normal mischievous little boy fit in here? Was there a nice untidy nursery somewhere? Certainly when his *Hello!*-styled mother told him sharply to take himself off he headed up the stairs.

'I see Robbie's still in nappies,' Karenza said, as if that were the most acceptable thing in the world. 'But he's a big boy now and all his new friends can use the loo themselves.'

The mother stared. 'But that's what schools are for. To teach children. They never bothered with nappies at nursery,' she added in the face of Karenza's forbearing silence.

'I think he'd be happier if he'd managed to learn before he started. All the other children are toilet-trained and I'd hate him to feel different – especially if he was teased. Which we would not allow, not if we heard it . . .'

'You're paid good money. It's your job.'

'I think in child development terms most children are clean and dry by the age of three, Ms Carnaby,' I said. 'Don't imagine that any school I'm head of will countenance bullying, not for a second, once we get wind of it – but children, even Robbie's age, can be very cruel.'

She shrugged her shoulders extravagantly. 'It'll cost the fucking earth but I'd better get a nanny in to sort it, if you insist.'

'I'm sure Robbie will be very grateful,' Karenza said, entirely without apparent irony.

The next calls passed without incident. Just. We found that one child had asthma, but there were no problems with peanuts, and another could read so well that we would have to make sure she was never bored. A final interview went swimmingly: we could enjoy the sun for the rest of the day with clear consciences.

The next day was baking hot. Karenza drove through a shimmering, dusty landscape, with those enormous Kentish fields spreading treeless and hedgeless as far as the eye could see. They made you all the more grateful for Lady Preston and her surprising patch of nature.

Our target was a caravan, not on an official site, but one of about fifty in various states of dilapidation in an ordinary field: they were there to house the migrant workers picking fruit. We made our way through them, heading for the furthest corner on the advice of a gap-toothed old countryman who seemed to be some sort of watchman. Despite the occasional gusts of hot breeze the whole area smelt foetid, with occasional gusts of raw sewage.

Karenza pulled a face. 'It's like a prison I had to visit once – full of unwashed men and unwashed clothes. The only thing that's missing is the yellow-painted walls.' She shuddered. Clearly she didn't want me to ask what had taken her there. She rushed on, 'The caravan we're looking for is supposed to be in the corner near an oak tree. This one, perhaps?'

The caravan she pointed at was larger than most of the others, with its own Portaloo fastened by a large padlock and a line of washing between the Portaloo and a tree. It shouldn't, on a day like this, take long to dry. The upper half of the door was open: we could smell cooking and hear not very tuneful singing.

Karenza tapped on the lower half, calling out, 'Mrs Popescu? It's Karenza Yeo from the school. I've come to meet Georgy.'

I suspected the child might be a Gheorghe, but wouldn't have dreamt of correcting her. If Mrs Popescu was tempted, she certainly didn't show it. She emerged from the caravan interior smiling a welcome and opening the lower half of the door. A child of about five, serious-faced but sturdy and almost unnaturally clean, held her hand. Another, a toddler minus any garments below the waist, started to come towards us but was sharply rebuked, returning to his potty. Mrs Popescu could clearly teach Mrs Carnaby a thing or two. Georgy ducked away and returned dragging a cardboard box, which he parked by his mother's feet. Parked is the right verb, incidentally: someone had drawn wheels on it. Suddenly I was back at my grandmother's, whose oft-repeated view was that the best toy in the world was a box, preferably one big enough to sit in or sit under.

Karenza was down beside him like a shot.

'No tea. Try please?' Mrs Popescu was handing us mugs of what smelt seriously alcoholic. Fortunately there was only about half an inch of liquid in each. 'Palinka,' she said with a smile.

We raised the mugs and sipped, spluttering in unison as the fire hit our throats.

'I make!' our hostess said with a smile. 'And make chec.'

This turned out to be a wonderful rich chocolate cake, not, as I later found out, simply a mispronunciation.

Our conversation was sadly limited, but I got the clear sense she wanted the best for both her sons. 'Not pick fruit like this!' she said, looking around her. 'Doctor. Teacher. Real job.'

'We'll do our best,' I said earnestly. And I was sure Karenza would too.

But we wouldn't be doing anything educational for a while: when we got back to her car we found some helpful person had let down all the tyres – so much for the watchman.

To my amazement Karenza merely shrugged and burrowed in her boot. I thought I was prepared for most things, but I didn't carry a tyre pump operated off the car battery.

Neither of us really wanted to do any more work in the baking heat, but we decided to update our visit files before we gave up for the day so we headed back to Wray Episcopi. She pulled up in the shade where mine waited about twenty metres from the school, which didn't have its own lockable car park. Sadly I didn't see how we could create one, either, without taking land from the already cramped playground.

Once we'd done all the paperwork, I sent Karenza home. As for me, I would go and visit not another family but the Great House estate: it was time I bearded Matt Storm in his den.

I followed the huge yew hedge around the outside of the estate, wishing with every pace that I'd opted for the air-conditioned luxury of my car. But I'd started so I'd finish, and I plodded on. I only stopped when I arrived at the gates – serious ones, with an entryphone on my side and a couple of dogs roaming free on the other. They seemed friendly enough, but then they were on their territory and I was still on mine. They nudged up to the gates with curiosity on their faces and very tense tails as I pressed the top button and waited for a reply. None came.

Wrestling with my conscience – surely there was work I could do while sunning myself in the garden – I'd got perhaps fifty metres back down the lane when a quad bike shattered the rural silence. Mounted on it was a very pretty young man – so young I wondered why on earth a battle-scarred woman like Lady Preston would have chosen him over an equally seasoned candidate, assuming anyone else had applied for the job, of course. Unless she'd fallen for his looks: he'd have looked well as a rustic hero in a soft-focussed adaptation of *Under the Greenwood Tree*. All the flesh you could see – and for some reason he'd chosen to wear an old-fashioned shirt, with sleeves rolled up and buttons undone to the waist, so there was a lot of flesh to see – was beautifully tanned; his hair was bleached to a Scandinavian blonde. And he was slowing down, saluting me and exposing more white teeth than anyone except an American is entitled to.

'Matt Storm,' he shouted into the sudden silence as he cut his engine. 'And you must be our new village headmistress.'

'That's right,' I said breezily. 'And you're Lady Preston's right-hand man.'

What had I said to bring a slow flush to his chiselled features?

'She says you want me to mow the wild flower meadow so the kids can trample all over it.' He sounded as possessive as if he'd been caring for it for the last forty years.

'Not exactly. I said the grass was too long for little legs to run on, and that I thought we'd do more good by analysing the flora and fauna at a suitable time of year.'

He walked towards me. 'Did you indeed? Do you fancy

stepping inside my office? I make a good coffee. Don't worry about the dogs. You'll be all right if I'm with you.'

I was. But their faces were much more alert and their bodies readier for action than they'd been when I was safely outside.

He switched on his computer before he turned on the coffee machine, which made the standard disgusting noises and produced an excellent Americano. Very quickly we agreed that March would work, much as I'd have liked to look at what autumn produced. We noted how many children would be there, with what supervision, and what was to be achieved in what length of time. But when we got on to the risk assessments so vital to any educational enterprise, he became bored to the point of brusque. If I insisted, we'd walk the site a month beforehand to clear everything with Lady Preston and the governors. He was careful, I noticed, to avoid precise dates. I was ready to leave when I raised something that should have been keeping me awake at night.

'I don't suppose you've got on file any reproductions of her ladyship's pictures?' I asked. 'I can't find them anywhere in the school but I thought if I showed photos to the older staff it might jog some memories.'

'Pictures? Not my bag. But there may be something on the computer.' He looked long enough to make my coffee drinkable. 'No. Nothing.'

'Thanks for trying. I know it was a forlorn hope: they may have been donated a century ago. She's not been very precise,' I added.

'So why does she want them back?' He leant back in his chair and stared at me quizzically.

I grinned. 'There's an *Antiques Road Show* at Leeds Castle soon, isn't there? Perhaps she wants to discover she's sitting on a fortune.'

'Except it's not her sitting on anything. It's the school.'

'Or the lawyers,' I said, not quite joking, 'unless we have proof that someone actually gave away the pictures, and didn't just lend them.' It was time to go: we both got to our feet and moved into the yard.

The dogs, which had been lying peaceably in the small patch of shade afforded by the gates, pricked up their ears but looked far from ready to be patted. 'Would they like some fuss?' I asked.

'Rumour tells me you've lost enough skin recently,' he said.

I shot a look at his entirely serious face and said nothing. From serious it became unaccountably angry. I froze – but I could see nothing amiss, and all I could hear was the sound of children's voices the other side of a high barn wall.

'Her ladyship's grandchildren?' I asked.

But he was talking to the dogs, making them move from the gates with more violence than strictly necessary, and pointing at them while he ushered me out. Only when I was halfway out did he smile. 'See you around.'

I was peaceably listening to Radio Three on my way home when a traffic announcement cut in. Maidstone Services were closed because of an incident that the police were attending. Such bland language always alarms me. Sometimes I think officialdom would do better to spell out what the incident is: an armed robbery? A suicide? I'd rather know and face my fears than have murky grey anxieties swilling round my

60

imagination. But at least Maidstone Services were nothing to do with me: all I had to do was inch my car into my parking space and go and perform what for me was a small miracle: with Simon in Durham jail I could safely fling open every window in the house.

Couldn't I?

At least those well above ground level.

'It's disgusting, showing that sort of stuff on TV. Poor little Wystan couldn't eat his lunch!'

The rustic wall that separated my holiday cottage from the one next door might be artfully covered with creepers that gave a total sense of privacy, but it wasn't soundproofed, of course. I had overheard all sorts of holidaymakers' secrets I'd rather not have been privy to and, should Pat ever come down here again in any capacity whatsoever, I'd make sure we had any important conversations indoors.

Meanwhile, the woman next door was continuing to give her unheard interlocutor – she must have been on the phone, of course, going outdoors to get a better signal – tantalising bits of information about what was on the news.

The scenes I saw when I switched on to see for myself were indeed awful. The media had obviously hired a helicopter to take intrusive shots of the so-called 'incident' that was still happening just up the road in Maidstone. Some incident! The emergency services were loading bodies of all sizes and shapes into ambulances, while some – were they the luckier ones or were they even more seriously ill than the others? – were being carried off by the air ambulance. The words across the foot of the screen told the story in the baldest of terms: between forty and fifty people of unknown nationality had been found in a frozen food lorry coming in from the Continent. It was only as he approached Maidstone that the driver realised something was amiss and called the police, who had been there first as a hostile reception committee and then as desperate first-aiders, fighting hypothermia. Men, women, children. The death toll wasn't clear yet – but it could be high, even allowing for the usual media exaggeration.

Even the drinkers in the Jolly Cricketers were more subdued than usual. There were one or two less sympathetic souls, or course, suggesting it was time everyone went back where they came from and that we should pull up the footbridge and fill the moat with piranhas.

'I daresay they'll be flooding into the village school any time now,' a man said. I craned my head but couldn't identify the speaker. 'Talking all these foreign languages. What chance will our own children get? Send them home, I say.'

'Back to Syria?' someone asked.

'Their problem, not ours. It's our kids I'm worried about. Not that Her Nibs'll turn them away. The more kids in the school, the more money heads get. So she'll be fucking quids in, won't she?'

Diane's voice cut in before I could say anything. She raised a finger in a gesture no one else would register: I was to leave this to her. 'And if she is? Look how she's turned round that place. After all that terrible trouble in the winter, too. Her results are as good as anyone's in the county.'

The man didn't react to the dangerous quiet in her voice.

'But that was before any of these illegals went to the school, wasn't it? They say there's a whole lot going to schools round Maidstone and Canterbury, so we'll get a load here, you can bet on it. Lock up your sheds, that's what I say; Tom Bird had a ride-on mower nicked last week, didn't he? Them illegals, that's who did it, though the police were too mealy-mouthed to say as much.'

I had a bizarre vision of sad and weary refugees piled on to the mower to head up the M20. I kept it to myself.

'You can't blame the illegals for wanting to get here,' another man said. 'Not the way the people smugglers paint the place. Streets paved with gold, all that shit. Have you seen some of the places where they're sent? Up north?' he added, as if it was another country, not a part of the UK I'd lived in and loved. 'You wouldn't live in a house like that five minutes. Someone even painted the front doors a different colour so everyone knew they were different. But when they set out, they're told they're coming to heaven. Imagine it, herding those poor bastards into a refrigerated truck: it's like telling people they're having a shower and shoving them in gas chambers, if you ask me. Crime against humanity, that's what it is.'

'And a whole lot more drowned in the Med, they say. Three hundred last weekend, they reckon.'

The first man made a bad mistake. 'At least they'll not be coming here.'

Diane spoke. 'Sam Wood, if you can't think clearly, I'd say you've had enough to drink. I don't serve drunks here. So I'll thank you to leave us in peace. Now.' She waited.

Perhaps I'd expected a chorus of protest: it was within his rights to say what he was saying, vile or otherwise. And in their hearts a good many of the older men agreed with his sentiments, if not the way he'd expressed them – I was sure of that. But there was just an uneasy silence, the sort you get in a classroom when the other kids wait to see what will happen to the boy that cheeked the teacher. It was only broken when Sam Wood headed off to the naughty step outside, and Diane stepped forward with a poster.

'There's not much an ordinary person can do in the face of such suffering, is there?' she said, as she blu-tacked it to the wall. 'But we can all spend half an hour at the village hall next week giving our nice British blood to whoever might need it.'

CHAPTER SIX

I stirred my breakfast coffee meditatively. Would it help if I actually knelt before the builders I was going to phone this morning, to implore them to take on my rebuilding work? Should I fix a Skype session so they could see me in the act? Or should I just go round and take some photos of the cottage in the kind morning light so it wouldn't look too big a task?

Before I could decide, the phone rang. I pounced, as if it were a live builder likely to escape if I gave him a moment's chance. But it was Lloyd.

'I'm just down the road, Jane, and I wondered if I could pop round for a second. See you in five?'

I'd barely had time to stow the mug and the rest of the breakfast things in the dishwasher before he arrived.

'It's not you I want, so much as your bicycle,' he said.

'And good morning to you, too, Lloyd, and yes, it is

another lovely day, isn't it? It's in the garage,' I said, although, in fact, the car and its new little friend lived opposite the cottage in an upmarket carport in the row built in the old stables. Something to do with looking more rural, maybe. No doors. You had to trust everyone or lock everything in place. Guess which I did. I reached for the key to the industrial-grade cycle lock.

Wystan's mother – there was no sign of his father – was busily loading their mega 4x4, as if anxious to dust the refugee-sullied dust of Kent from their feet. Or perhaps, more prosaically, it was changeover day. It was all too clear that whatever the reason for their exit, it would not be done quietly, as Wystan had his own vociferous ideas about what he wanted to play with – now! – and what could go into the luggage space. Clearly he had been profoundly traumatised by the sight of all those people being rescued yesterday. Or not.

So far there were only three deaths, but nine people, four of them children Wystan's age, were still in intensive care.

Had Lloyd not been there I might have approached my erstwhile temporary neighbour: the wardens had opened up the church as a receiving centre for clothing and toy donations for the suffering families. In fact, why should Lloyd's presence stop me? He didn't need me to hold his hand while he checked out the cycle.

At first I might have been talking Chinese, but eventually she paused in her irritated pushing at intractable carrier bags long enough to look at me. Surely that was a look of low cunning spreading across her face – it spoilt a set of really good features, come to think of it. She grabbed two polythene sacks. 'Here. You can take these. It'll save me having to wash them. And this old thing – it's time he grew out of it.'

The old thing proved to be a battered bear.

'Thank you very much,' I said, taking the sacks. I even held the bear for a moment. 'But I can't take this old chap. It can,' I said in the serious, brook-no-argument voice I save for troublesome pupils, 'do terrible psychological damage if you lose something like this. It can cause major and prolonged bed-wetting problems.'

Narrow-eyed, she seized it. 'But it's filthy. And it smells.'

'Maybe if you asked him to help you give it a bath? What do you think, Wystan?' To be honest I didn't think much of the creature's long-term chances of survival, but it settled loosely under the child's arm.

I wandered into the garage – as chic in its way as the cottage, security apart – to find Lloyd staring accusingly at the bike.

'It's very clean.'

'Harry and Doreen – the people who rescued me – left it absolutely pristine. Then it got another polish when it was repaired. Were you expecting to find traces of my life blood?'

'I was hoping to find flakes of paint or even plastic from the guy who ran into you. But it was a long shot.' He straightened.

'And, come to think of it, strange that they should clean it for me. Their car looked as if you could plant seeds in it. Maybe there were some sprouting in the back footwell, come to think of it.'

'Then they suddenly clean a complete stranger's bike. You didn't think it odd?'

'Funnily enough, their house looks just like my parents' when they took us on our summer holiday. Mum practically spring-cleaned the place. And she made Dad clean the car. Every year. I think her rationale was that if we were all killed by a Cornish earthquake, the grieving relatives would know what a good housekeeper she was when they came to fight over all her belongings. So although I thought it was odd, I just thought they were behaving like Mum, and being kind with it. After all, they were very sweet to me when I was on that hedge. And afterwards.'

'You don't think that they were deliberately removing evidence?'

'When it was they who wanted me to call the police? No, I didn't. It didn't even cross my mind.'

Wystan was just being coerced into his child seat when we emerged. But he wouldn't put up a lengthy fight: one thumb was heading to his mouth, though there was no sign of the bear. A brand-new dinosaur was on his lap. Dinosaurs! After all these years working with kids obsessed by them I still couldn't see the fascination. 'Thank you for your donation,' I said, gathering up the sacks.

'I told you: just old stuff.'

I waved her off and headed with Lloyd back into the cottage.

Lloyd might have been grumpy with me but he offered to drop the stuff as he passed the church: it was only a small diversion, after all.

'Let's just see what she's donated,' I said, opening the first sack and touching the side of my nose in a conspiratorial gesture. And then, holding it melodramatically, I tipped the lot into the washing machine. 'Puke,' I declared. 'And worse!' The sack went straight into the dustbin. I came back in and scrubbed my hands.

And there was still the other one to deal with.

Lloyd had filled and switched on the kettle. He was pondering my more exotic teas. 'That reminds me of when I was younger,' he mused, 'collecting for some campaign naively entitled Bread for the World. You know the system: you drop envelopes through folk's doors and collect them up a couple of days later. And what did I find in six or seven of them I retrieved? Mouldy crusts.'

We sucked our teeth and shook our heads in unison. He chose a rose-petal-scented jasmine green tea, and dunked the bag first in one mug then in another. Then he dropped it in the recycling caddy. All very domesticated.

We adjourned to the patio. 'I don't think you'd be looking for paint or whatever if you didn't have something to compare them with,' I said. 'Would you?'

He laughed. 'I suppose I wouldn't.'

'And you also find the very absence of obvious paint or whatever suspicious.'

'I suppose I do.'

'And I don't suppose you're about to tell me whose bike it is you can get samples from.'

'Not yet. OK, maybe never. But make sure your car insurance is up to date, won't you? Just in case they have another go at you.'

Nosey practically wrung his paws with grief and anxiety at the sight of the little boy's bear hanging on the rotary washing line with Wystan's laundry. What was to be done with it? Should I accept that it had now been replaced by that revolting stegosaurus or whatever it was? If so, I could take it up to church to find sanctuary in a refugee child's arms. Or should I go with my instinct, that it was still precious in his eyes? We agonised together over an early lunch and a glance at *The Guardian*. In the end I decided to text James Ford, who worked for the letting agency running Brian Dawes' properties. He was a relatively new father, and inclined to panic until he heard about the mother's cavalier attitude. Then – and he was such a mild man he surprised me – he raged, heaping imprecations on her unfeeling head. He would phone her at once.

Meanwhile I had to address myself to work, the Preston pictures in particular. I had a meeting with Hazel Roberts, the Wray Episcopi chair of governors, and Colin Ames, the secretary. It took place very pleasantly in Hazel's old-fashioned garden as we sat in wicker chairs round a table laden with China tea and home-made cake, but it was serious enough in tone to suit a coroner.

'I'm very much afraid that Lady Preston is threatening legal action,' Hazel said, adjusting the angle of the sun umbrella. 'I've known the family for nearly seventy years, Jane, and Cassandra in particular. She once laid a girl's shin open to the bone with her hockey stick and showed no remorse, even solicitude, whatever. Now she may be less physical but she'll be tenacious. There'll be media coverage – her niece works for TVInvicta – and probably letters from her solicitor.'

'And probably more personal visits, too' Colin added, accepting another slice of cake with a gracious nod.

'Not without invitation, surely – or at least permission,'

I objected. 'Random strangers can't just turn up and demand entry.'

Colin's gentle, kindly face expressed extreme distaste. 'Young Matt Storm happens to be my great-nephew and though he's not local he has at least blood loyalties, however much diluted. He tells me Lady P claims that her family, having kindly donated and endowed the building, still owns it. There will be, somewhere deep in the council's archives, appropriate documents proving council ownership – or possibly, one fears, disproving it. There might even be a record of what happened to her ancestor's paintings, but I for one would doubt it.'

I was about to offer a commiserating but slightly smug smile: this wasn't my problem, but the governors'. The old hands who'd held legally responsible posts for years, not an absolute newcomer who'd not even sat in her new office chair. But the looks coming my way told me without words that there was something I didn't know about. And it wasn't going to be good.

'She claims she has seen in her muniments room a letter declaring that the school and all its contents are the responsibility of the head teacher. As soon as we have sight of the paper in question, we can take legal advice of our own,' Colin said.

'I wouldn't if I were you! Because if I'm proved to be responsible, then you as trustees are in the clear.'

'My dear Jane, that is not the sort of advice we want from our solicitors.' Hazel placed her thickly veined hand over mine. The diamonds on her rings could have done with a thorough clean, but their very size was impressive. 'The woman is a bully. The only way to deal with bullies is for everyone to stand against them.'

71

To my amazement, I turned my hand over to squeeze hers lightly. 'Thank you. At least the council have to provide us with legal advice – that doesn't have to come out of the school budget.'

'I don't believe the paint and furniture for your office came out the school budget, did it? You're a naughty girl, Jane. More tea? I think we deserve a fresh pot. Green gets stewed so quickly . . .'

The setting was so idyllic I almost expected a butler to materialise, but she got up herself, not without a little difficulty, though she did not use the stick beside her chair.

'I understand that you have been doing most wonderful things with your little cricketers,' Colin said. 'But I don't see you being able to do the same with the Episcopi children, not with the size of their poor playground.'

'If we could get the PTAs of both schools to raise funds for a minibus, there'd be so much we could do. But – forgive me for asking and for changing the subject so violently– are you related to the great Les Ames?'

'I wish I were! And I'm afraid I wasn't named after Colin Cowdrey either. But I do love my cricket. I had the honour of having my windscreen smashed by Kevin Pietersen once, you know, when I was parked on the boundary at the St Lawrence Ground and he hit the most glorious six . . .'

Hazel returned, pouring fresh tea, and offering more cake, which it was an effort to decline. 'Have you managed to run Maggie Hale to earth yet, Jane? I don't remember the pictures being there in her tenure, but you never know – she might have an idea. No? Well, the woman's entitled to enjoy her retirement without checking her emails every day.'

* * *

My route home was very circuitous, via Ashford, in fact, so it was after five when I pulled up outside the cottage. Who should be waiting but James Ford, the letting agent. The heat was by now so intense I showed him into the garden, where he could scarcely miss the washing on the whirligig.

He unpegged the bear and looked at him quizzically. 'Mrs Adams says you're surplus to requirements, my lad. But having had an interesting night when my William lost his cuddly cat, I doubt it.'

'Quite. Will you look after him or shall I?' I asked, unpegging the clothes and stowing them in clean sacks.

'You're not going to take him along to the church? Mind you, I'd have thought bears would be in huge demand right now. Those poor kids . . .'

'I'm with you on Wystan's wanting him. I reckon you'll get a call at midnight demanding you take him up to London – probably in the front seat wearing a seat belt, of course. Meanwhile the refugee kids won't go lonely. If you don't mind helping me with this sack, I'll show you what's in my car.'

James placed the bear carefully on the hammock.

'No, you take him! I'm not going on the Pony Express run.'

'I'm afraid William will kidnap him if I do.'

'Not if you lock him in your boot.'

'That'd be cruelty to dumb animals.'

'No worse than leaving him out here on his own.'

Laughing, we walked to my car, the bear on James's shoulder like a baby wanting to be burped. James stared. Round eyes stared back. 'Just how many teddies are there in there?'

'Eight. I cleared out the Oxfam shop. The volunteer assured me they'd all been washed.'

'You know what,' he said, as he stowed the bag of clothes in the footwell, 'I'll see what I can organise at work. It's one thing being sorry for people living so far away you can't make a difference, but another when they're here on your doorstep and quite desperate.'

We drove off in different directions. I was still smiling when I reached the church. Carol, the churchwarden, was obviously just leaving, but turned back to unlock it for me, and solemnly arranged the bears on a pew. I suspected that their fixed gaze might disconcert the preacher.

'We're going to have a brief service of blessing before we take all the donations off,' she said. 'Eight-thirty. You will come, won't you, to wave your friends goodbye?'

For the first time, I felt at home and wanted in the village, and tootled home without a care in the world.

Until I saw the blue Ford Ranger with tinted windows parked in front of my house. Just the sort of vehicle Doreen and Harry said had aimed at me.

CHAPTER SEVEN

Fight or flight? There was enough adrenaline, cortisol and norepinephrine sloshing round my system to float a battleship, assuming the UK still had one to float. I was about to slam into reverse and head for the safety of the pub – anywhere. But years of therapy made me breathe deeply and relax. That was better. The red mist was clearing. There were plenty of great ugly SUVs on the road: this one didn't have to be my assailant – he might be just an ordinary guy with too much money and not enough taste.

He might even be Ed van Boolen, who'd recently decided he needed just such a monster for his business – possibly.

It was Ed.

I slotted the car into its stable, getting out and greeting him with a smile as I zapped it locked.

Considering the loveliness of the evening, he looked decidedly grim. He greeted me with a mere flap of the hand.

'Problems?' I asked brightly.

'Yeah. Work stuff.' Very occasionally you could pick up his Netherlands origins – there was the tiniest hint of a *sh* sound instead of a pure *s*. 'Thing is, I may be away for the Oval match. Not sure yet. But you might want to think of having someone on standby, so to speak.' The *sh* was very much in evidence.

'Of course. But it'll be sad if you can't go: it promises to be a good match.' I didn't want to invite him in. Not till I'd thought a bit more about the coincidence. Though of course it could have been a black SUV with tinted windows, or just a plain ute. The trouble was, there were no Doreen and Harry to ask. And there are lots of other makes besides Fords – Mitsubishi, Nissan, Honda . . . Why pick on this?

I wanted to walk slowly round inspecting every inch of the vehicle, but I confined myself to asking, 'Is this new? I don't recall seeing it before.'

'It's a mate's,' he said dismissively. 'While my van's off the road.' Suddenly he produced his familiar grin. 'Poncy great thing, isn't it? I'd rather be White Van Man with a rickety trailer any day of the week.' He looked round, as if checking no one could overhear. 'Just to warn you, Jane, there might be a bit of trouble brewing at Wray Episcopi. The PTA noticeboard. I hear you took it down.'

'So I did. I didn't think being able to read the F and the C words on an official noticeboard was going to improve the children's education one iota,' I said, more crisply than I intended. I tried to soften it with a grin. 'I know the kids have to start with short words, but not those. And not in school.'

He returned my smile. 'Quite. I agree with you. I'd hate

to have my nephew and niece seeing anything like that, anywhere, for that matter.'

'So you're an uncle? I didn't know that. How old are they? And no, I'm not touting for business, though it would be nice to have ready-made cricketers in one of the schools.'

'I'm not good on ages. And I don't see them very often. Sort of fallen out with my sister, cos I don't get on with her husband. Anyway, it seems that someone is spoiling for a fight.'

'Not the PTA people?'

'I just thought – you know, a word to the wise . . .'

'Fancy a cold drink?' I asked, surprising myself.

He did. We sat in the garden sipping lager.

'This here noticeboard,' I began. 'It's all nonsense. I wrote to the PTA three times asking them to get rid of the graffiti. No response. I tried cleaning it up myself, even tried painting it over, but the words were so deeply incised that made it worse. I asked them to remove it. No response. What else could I do but take it down? It's still locked in my office, complete with Rawlplugs and screws, awaiting their response.' I was about to pour out my troubles with Lady Preston and her missing pictures, but decided, as ever in this village, that discretion was the best way of dealing with possibly feudal sensibilities. I allowed myself a low groan, my head in my hands. 'What is it with people? Speaking of which, how's St Luke's Bay's stroppy batsman?'

He shook his head. 'That crazy idiot Dennis Paine? It's weird. He's as sweet as a lamb half the time, and then – whoosh! He just loses it. And – this is why I'm worried about the PTA business, Jane – the PTA chair is none other than Dennis's brother.'

'Of course! Why didn't I work it out?'

'Worse than Dennis for temper. He's a member of English First.'

'I take it we're not talking about people who care about the purity of our language?' I asked ironically.

'Gerry Paine? Purity of language?'

'Actually, he probably uses a lot of Anglo-Saxon words.' It took him a moment to pick up my allusion. We shared a laugh.

'It's a nasty little right-wing group. Full of nasty little Englanders. The sort that want me to go home.'

'Like England First? But that's died out, hasn't it?'

'It might have died nationally, but they're giving it mouth-to-mouth resuscitation down here, even if it's under a slightly different name. Not just anti-immigration but anti pretty well anything. Women. Especially good-looking women with power. Sorry. But you need to know.' He drained his glass and looked at his watch. 'I'd best be off – thanks for this.'

'More to the point, Ed, thanks for the warning.'

'Take it. Please. If his brother wants to beat up an umpire, think how much more fun Gerry could have smashing a head teacher's face. See you at the match?'

'Of course. I just hope I'm watching, not wagging my index finger in the air and annoying stroppy batsmen!'

I annoyed someone else before that, of course. Not the people who welcomed me at the little service they held to send prayers with the toys and clothes, which we loaded into three or four big hatchbacks – none of which, to my relief, were threatening SUVs. Not even either of the Paine brothers.

It was Maggie Hale, my predecessor at Wray Episcopi.

As soon as the short service was over, I headed over to the playground there. By ten I was emptying flower tubs into the sacks I'd brought along. Once the tubs would have been a credit to the school, but all had died long before I'd arrived on the scene. Half of me wanted the children who'd originally planted them to deal with them to learn about the complete cycle of the growing year. The other half wanted a nice tidy clean environment, with the tubs and planters ready for the children to fill with spring bulbs. The tidy half won. How could anyone object to that?

But something had certainly enraged Maggie, who erupted from her Mazda MX-5 – at least inasmuch as it's possible to erupt from a sports car, even one with its top down.

She confronted me from the far side of the school wall, arms akimbo. 'What I'd like to know is what on earth you think you've been doing.'

'Good morning, Maggie – how nice to see you too. Did you have a good break?'

Unkindly I moved slightly so that to look me in the eye she had to squint and shield her face from the gorgeous sun.

'Break? With that constant stream of emails you bombarded me with? Some break! Let's get something straight, Jane. I have retired. I am no longer working here. The school is no longer anything to do with me. I do not wish to have any further communications from you about the trivia you seem to think will interest me – especially when I am away, not just on holiday but also on an important course. In fact, I do not wish to have anything to do with you or with the school. Is that clear?'

'Absolutely. I quite understand, and I'm sorry I importuned you. Especially when you were on your creative writing course. How did it go?' It was a genuine enquiry: after all, we'd been on the best of terms when the negotiations had been in train.

'That is not what I came to talk about.'

In other words, she'd not quite got in touch with her inner Jane Austen.

'Of course. And I assure you that I'd have respected your privacy if I'd had the option. But it seems Lady Preston is considering legal advice to get her family pictures back, and though I've searched high and low I simply can't find them.'

'Not my problem, Jane. Yours. Or the governors'.'

'I quite agree. But it would help us all immensely if you could tell us if you'd ever seen them. If not, I can simply report back to the powers that be and leave you to enjoy your lovely new wheels.' I stepped forward, opening the gate. 'May I have a peep?'

Disarmed – who'd have thought either of us would be petrolheads? – she started extolling the pretty little car's virtues. 'I had to wait till I retired, of course: you can't get full-size nativity scenes in this!' Suddenly she was the woman I'd really liked. Her tan suited her; her hair was sun-bleached – she looked ten years younger, too, especially when she smiled.

This week's beauty tip: give up teaching.

We were looking into the boot, for some reason, when she said, out of the corner of her mouth, 'There were never any pictures in my time. But you mustn't quote me on that. Can I have your word?'

'What about your predecessor?'

'Mrs Derricott. Nearly gaga. In an old people's home in Folkestone. Somewhere on the front. Trouble is, I don't know the name of the place and with data protection you're not going to be able to turn up out of the blue and ask. But if you keep my name out of this I'll make some enquiries for you.'

'Not for me, Maggie. I could go to the Old Bailey to swear on oath I've never seen the things. If Lady P or the governors are that desperate then they can do the enquiring. But thanks all the same.' I hesitated awkwardly. 'I don't know how you feel about coming back here as a visitor – but you know you're welcome.'

'I'll steer clear for a bit. It's your baby now and you need to look after it your way: I had old Mrs Derricott peering over my shoulder and criticising for years, and I wouldn't wish that on anyone.' She pressed her car zapper. 'So thanks, but no thanks. And this conversation—'

'Never happened,' I finished for her. 'Take care,' I added, conventionally.

'It's you who must take care, Jane. But I didn't say that either.' She eased herself into the driver's seat and drove swiftly away.

I coveted those wheels, all right. But it was true I needed a hatchback – and to prove it incontrovertibly to myself I started to load the sacks of detritus from the planters. Slowly. I was more preoccupied with the – classified – information that Maggie had given. How could I use it without giving her away?

Then a text arrived. The regular Wrayford umpires were both unavailable again. The good news was the match wasn't against St Luke's Bay, but against Churcham, a seaside village close to Rye. No Paines there, I hoped – with or without a capital letter. Ed added that Churcham were a well-behaved side, and that in any case any hint of dissent would be dealt with by their umpire, an ex-soldier. Oh, no, it wouldn't. It would be dealt with by yours truly. If necessary.

Perhaps my jaw was a bit more set than usual when Lady Preston hove into view, her horse appearing to share her contempt as they both looked down on me. 'Well?' she asked.

'Good morning, Lady Preston. Fine day, isn't it?' Actually, that sounded a bit yokelish. Any moment I might be tugging my forelock or dropping into a curtsy.

'My pictures or my solicitor, Miss Cowan. Which is it to be?'

It was time to ask the obvious question. It was only my wretched experiences with Simon that had made me so stupidly deferential and prevented me from asking it before. I took a breath my therapist would have applauded. 'When did you last actually see your pictures hanging on the school walls, Lady Preston?'

'I'm not interested in that: I want to know where they are now.'

'You'd have to ask someone who was here when they disappeared, then, wouldn't you? Mrs Hale? Mrs Derricott? If you fear that a theft has occurred, you could even report the matter to the police. Though I suspect in these days of extreme cuts, they'd want precise details.'

'Are you telling me how to do my job?'

'Of course not. I'm merely trying to do my own.' And

wishing I didn't literally have to look up to her all the time. I heaved another sack into the car, spending time to arrange and settle it in place. And then I returned to the playground to get another.

The gate swung shut. Before I could put down the latest sack and open it, she'd got off her horse. Looping its reins over one arm she marched towards me. She didn't bother opening the gate. Quite deliberately – and amazingly, given her age – she swung first one leg then the other across. Soon we were chin to chin, the horse adding a worrying chorus to her actions.

'A little respect from you, young woman. Open that door.' She pointed with her whip.

I had a bizarre vision of her horse following her round as she searched each classroom. Or did she expect me to stand there holding the animal's bridle?

'On grounds of health and safety I can't admit any visitors,' I said, almost truthfully. 'There are still paint tins and dustsheets all over the place. If you wish to visit the place, you're very welcome to make an appointment.'

'How dare you damn well deny me entry to my family's property?' By now the whip was pressed against my breastbone. When Paine had treated me like this other people had come to my rescue. There was no one now. 'Swanning round as if you owned the place!' she added, with a small but distinct jab.

'It's neither yours nor mine, Lady Preston, but the property of Kent Education Authority.' Until proved otherwise, of course. But that wasn't my problem, was it? 'Now, if you'll excuse me, I need to carry on with my work. I'll bid you good day.'

'I've not finished yet, believe me. With the school or with you.' One last jab and she was tearing open the gate and returning to the horse. No mounting block. I certainly wasn't going to – what was the term? – throw her into the saddle. Let her walk ignominiously home.

CHAPTER EIGHT

I didn't like having made so open an enemy, but I consoled myself with the knowledge that it was better than having a covert one. Possibly. Actually, three enemies, of course: not just Lady P but also at least one of the Paine brothers. And that was before we'd started the new school year.

The interviews for the new deputy head for the Wray Episcopi site would take place next week. Fortunately I was well into my preparation for that, and this time I was comfortable with the governors with whom I would share the interviewing. Meanwhile, I had emailed my new colleagues inviting them, a euphemism if ever there was one, to a short staff meeting to discuss any problems that might arise as we prepared for the new intake; at Wrayford School, Tom Mason, the deputy, was organising a parallel meeting. A tall, broad-shouldered man in his thirties, he'd completely shaved what was obviously a balding head and could actually look quite threatening; however, he'd turned out to be a very loyal colleague, all the more laudable in a man who'd actually had his heart set on my job. He'd never want to play second fiddle for long, however, and we both knew that his upgrading was no more than a stepping stone to his first headship at another school. Especially as he'd just parked his car in my spot.

'Next thing you'll be trying my chair for size,' I laughed, flinging open the office window as he started photocopying. Today he was in male macho mufti, flip-flops and shorts, which revealed the slightly bandy legs of a man who'd once played a great deal of tennis. His career had been cut tragically short by a long-term wrist injury; now he was a brilliant coach for our aspiring Andy Murrays and Jo Kontas.

'I'm sorry. I was in a rush.' He patted the pile to be copied. 'And now the bloody stapling function seems to have died.' He pointed to a pulsating red light.

'You group the paperwork together, I'll use the old-fashioned stapler.'

We worked together in silence for a while, achieving a good rhythm. I was quite pleased, however, that none of the children could see us: him being cleverly technological and me doing the comparatively menial work. It was generally assumed that we'd simply move an extra desk for him into my office, but suddenly my reservations sharpened. I'd seen all too many women sidelined by visitors of both genders who automatically assumed that their male colleague, who might indeed be considerably their junior, was the one in charge. But he had an ego too, so I couldn't possibly leave him in the cramped staffroom.

The answer came a few minutes later, as we discussed plans for a school council – a grand name for the small group of staff and elected form representatives, which could recommend changes but had no executive powers – over a cup of coffee. Full marks to him for having brought in fresh milk.

'I thought,' he was saying, 'we should have a dedicated school council noticeboard in the hall, where everyone could see it, with the names and photos of the kids' reps. Give them a bit of kudos.'

'We could add staff ones too. We'd have to laminate them all – we'll need to replace the laminator, won't we? – so that they won't curl. Come to think of it, why not have staff photos on all the classroom doors, so any new kids can see where they're supposed to be heading and know who to speak to if they have to take a message? And our mugshots on our office door? Remind me, I need to get a new plate made for you: Tom Mason, Deputy Head Teacher. Or would it give you a bit of a kick to sort that for yourself?' These days I knew him well enough to give him an impish sideways glance.

'It would! Absolutely!' He gave a mock swagger. 'We're having a barbecue on Sunday, Jane. Very informal. Fancy coming over?'

'Love to. So long as I'm still in one piece after the cricket match I'm due to umpire tomorrow . . .'

I was. And I was at another post-match party, with a glass of fizz in my hand. I could learn to live a sybaritic life like this. The host was a trim man in his forties: Justin Forbes, the Churcham umpire who, as Ed had forecast, had taken no nonsense from anybody. Over mid-match tea and sandwiches he seemed to have taken a bit of a shine to me. Now in what should have been the cool of the evening, but was actually oppressively hot, he was insisting on showing me the glories of his garden. Like Marcus Baker's it overlooked a bay. For some reason this was a less fashionable one, with very few pleasure craft moored within the breakwater, Justin said. On a clear night we should be able to see the lights of France, if not with the naked eye then with his outdoor telescope. But tonight, with the cloud cover almost brown it was so thick, he conceded it was unlikely. He escorted me solicitously to what he called, managing to make the whole idea quite filthy, his promontory – but then, we'd both drunk enough for it to sound funny. We didn't spend long *à deux*, possibly to his regret and definitely to my relief, because we were joined by his brother, who needed an urgent word. In private. I stayed where I was. For a few moments. Until the first flash of lightning. It lit up the bay like a heavenly spotlight. There were the few boats he'd mentioned. The thunder came almost immediately. After all the heat a storm would almost be welcome. But not for another half-hour – it would cut the evening short, and we'd all been enjoying ourselves. Another flash; one boat was moving purposefully in, unlit. It was towing in another. The thunderclap was almost painful. It was time to move; if I'd been an umpire I'd have cleared the field without a second thought.

I didn't have that authority here, I wasn't even the

host for goodness' sake – and where was he? What I was doing was the far side of rude, come to think of it – but nonetheless I ran towards the others, making herding gestures. 'Ed? There you are! I think we ought to get everyone on the minibuses, don't you?' To prove my point there was another flash of lightning, forked this time. The simultaneous thunder threatened to drown out what I was saying. 'Too dangerous in the open air!'

Everyone had the same idea, encouraged by the huge, heavy raindrops fizzing on and extinguishing the barbecue. In the chaos, someone pressed something into my hand. A piece of card. I slipped it in my pocket. It was only when I got home I realised it was an ordinary business card. Justin Forbes'. A message was written in an elegant script on the back. Would I care to accept an invitation to dinner? If so, would I telephone him?

Maybe. Well no, probably not. A bit of a tipsy flirtation was one thing; calling in cold blood to arrange a date with an ex-soldier with whom I had nothing in common but cricket was quite another. If anyone were to find their way into my affections, it could be someone more like Ed – solid, kind and in his own way quite sexy. But I didn't throw the card away. Safe in my cottage I dropped it on the pile of papers I called my pending file.

Although the electrical storm became as intense as any I'd ever seen in France, and according to my computer there were flash-floods in villages in the very south of the county, in Wrayford there was hardly any rain. Just enough to clear the air. And certainly not enough to spoil the next day's party at Tom's.

The Masons' house was a modern detached in a village

of largely older houses. The one next to it, a cottage complete with Kentish peg tiles, was obviously undergoing restoration, with scaffolding bristling from every wall. Despite the throbbing heat, despite it being a Sunday and presumably double-time, a team of workers was swarming over it. No doubt the plastic sheeting covering most of the framework would have made it intolerably hot to work under, and great rolls had been looped back. Now they were being rolled down again, and firmly clipped into place. Occasionally the person in charge would dart up to a particular area and check, sometimes summoning the original workman to do a better job. Not work*man*, however. The team was all-female. PACT, according to the standard issue workwear they all sported. Excusing myself from the party I nipped round to speak to the leader, a woman who might have been anything between thirty-five and fifty.

'Paula,' she declared, shaking my hand firmly. She listened carefully while I outlined my problems, occasionally asking a pertinent question. 'Very well, it sounds like the sort of thing we could tackle. We should be finished here by the end of September at the very latest. There's always a waiting list for our services, but it sounds as if you have more priority than some would-be second-homer who wants me to tear down a decent vernacular dwelling and make it into *Homes and Gardens*-lite. Give me your number and I'll text you to arrange a site visit. And here's my card, so you can check our website.'

This one didn't drift on to the vague pending file. It sat on my laptop until I'd noted every detail – twice. A new emotion started to fizz in my heart: optimism. Even if the PACT team's actions did suggest some bad weather in the offing.

Sure enough, as I settled down for the evening the skies darkened again, and the wind got up. I'd always loved storms, even those that cut the electricity supply as this one did. The whole village was in darkness, though the occasional householder must have run some candles to earth: wavering lights appeared in their windows. My eyes used to the darkness, I was content to sit, tumbler of whisky in hand, and watch the pyrotechnic display, though Nosey shuffled up beside me, as did the mauve bear who still didn't have a name. On the other hand, I'd not been able to give it away when I sent the others off to the refugee children, so presumably he was here to stay.

Now was not the time to give naming a bear my full attention, however. The rain came, sluicing noisily down. Closing and locking the windows, I prowled round the house, checking by scented candlelight that there were no obvious leaks. And that everything was tightly locked. For the first time in weeks, I felt uneasy. But I told myself it was just the atmospheric pressure that was making me wonky, and settled down with my laptop to check out PACT. The website looked as impressive as Paula and her team had. There were professional details of all the women: most had completed formal apprenticeships; some had taken specialised courses. Excellent.

Now the bears and I could settle down for an evening with Classic FM.

Classic FM and a number of saucepans, now placed

judiciously around the upper floor. Exquisite though the cottage might look both inside and outside, it wasn't as weatherproof as this storm demanded. Nor was my neighbour's. At nine, soaked after even the short dash from her front door to mine, a bedraggled woman was imploring me to do something. Anything.

The obvious thing was to drag her inside while I speed-dialled the letting agency's emergency number. Engaged. Well, obviously. So I texted, listening to her tale of woe, which included a ceiling threatening to collapse and a stream coming under the patio doors. Couldn't I do something? Anything!

Even as I grabbed a torch and locked up behind me, she was screaming at me to hurry. 'Go ahead and grab a kitchen knife,' I yelled above the thrumming of water cascading over the gutters.

She must have heard because as I slipped through her open doorway she practically stabbed me.

'Which ceiling?'

She just pointed upwards – not helpful.

Grabbing the knife I took the stairs two at a time. My torch showed the problem: there was a great bulge over the bed in the master bedroom.

'Help me strip this. Come on! I'm going to have to punch a drain hole in that.' I even managed to persuade her to help me pull the mattress off: we propped it on its side out of the way. 'Washing-up bowl. All your saucepans. Quickly.'

We didn't catch all the cascade I caused when I knifed the ceiling, but most, at least. The phone signal was poor up here. I ran downstairs and waved the mobile around in the kitchen. This time I dialled James's home number and got through. Thank goodness he was friends with farmers ready to lend tarpaulins and, more to the point, bring them round now. As for the stream through the ground floor, could I roll up carpets and block it at source?

With help I could. But my poor neighbour was getting hysterical.

'Please, please pull yourself together. You know you're supposed to slap people when they get like this and I truly can't.'

Reason just made her worse.

At which point, as I was on my knees with my back to the front door, doing my best to roll the sodden carpet into a sausage I could use as a barricade, I heard a resounding flesh-on-flesh wallop.

Silence.

But not in a good way. As I looked round, I rocked back in horror.

The eyes I found myself looking into were those of one of Simon's best mates.

Josh Talbot didn't recognise me. Not surprising, I suppose, considering the scene was lit by just a couple of dinner table candles, fluttering in the gusts from the door he'd left open. At least the stream now had somewhere to go. He was quick to join me on his knees, rolling with a will. As if a spring had been released, the woman started to help too. I still didn't know her name, of course: we'd both been in too much of a rush for introductions. More to the point, she didn't know mine. And I quite wanted to keep it that way.

As one, we stood up, easing our knees.

'What now?' she asked me, as if I'd become the leader.

I stepped back into the darkest shadows. 'In your place I'd cut my losses and go home. Your things'll be wet, but not ruined, with luck. I know the agent: I'll stay and sort things out. My place isn't uninhabitable. This is.'

Josh spread his hands. 'But leaving you—'

'Is fine. I know your break is ruined – or you could find a hotel if you move quickly. Before other refugees from the storm head for them!'

'She's right, Josh. And if she doesn't have to worry about this place she can take care of her own better.'

'Come on, Morag, she's helped us – we should help her. OK, you pack up and I'll help . . . ?' He looked at me quizzically. Fortunately I was still in my nice dark corner.

'Honestly I've got things under control. I've got a friend coming round any moment now: they can make themselves useful.' I always tried to avoid *they* and *them* as singular pronouns, but to hell with pedantry circumstances like these. And, come to think of it, to hell with veracity as well.

Morag was already halfway up the stairs. Josh shrugged and followed.

As I dashed back home I ran straight into James, who gripped me by the arms and steadied me. 'Jane, are you OK?'

'Deal with them first. But don't tell them my name! Please. It's to do with my past.'

He stared and then nodded slowly. By now we were both dripping.

'Just get them on their way home. Then I'll feel safe.'

To my amazement he hugged me, as he'd hug a child. 'I'll do my best. Then I'll look at your place. OK?'

Nothing more OK in the whole world.

I'd had more house moves than most in the past year, and was more than relieved when James's farmer friends got the tarpaulins over the roofs of all the cottages, anchoring them firmly. The roof next door was far, far worse than mine, they assured me – no wonder those London folk had taken off. The other one . . . they made rocking gestures with their hands.

'In other words,' James said, sucking his teeth, 'the whole row of cottages will have to be reroofed before winter sets in.'

'That means my moving out, doesn't it?'

''Fraid so, Jane. But maybe your own place will be habitable by then. Oh!'

The lights had come back on.

'I've got a firm called PACT to take a look,' I said, determined to sound more positive than I felt.

'You can't do better than them. They never advertise: just word of mouth. But they'll cost – they don't do cheap jobs.'

'Is that why no one recommended them to me?'

He pulled a face, possibly because the lights flickered alarmingly. They stayed on, but were no longer very bright. 'They're not really from round here, which is a big minus – you know how parochial a village can be. And, well . . . some of the older guys don't like them, because they don't think women can be builders full-stop.'

There was no point in arguing: why couldn't people like

Ed have mentioned them? James himself? Some lurking resentment that this was an all-women group, somehow excluding male workers? Who knew? And at this time of night, who cared?

'Are you quite happy to stay here overnight?' James was asking.

'I've not got a London pad to high-tail back to. What about the other visitors?'

'They'll stick it out till morning, they said. When they heard what you'd been up to they were most impressed. So—'

'How did they hear about that?' I wasn't happy.

'Oh, from the Talbots: they were telling everyone who'd listen you were a cross between Joan of Arc and Superwoman.'

'Bugger.' I could have added a lot more. 'It's to do with my ex, James,' I added, as his eyebrows shot up. 'Talbot and he were best mates. And you know what another friend of Simon's did earlier in the year. Simon will have heard about that; I don't want any more information to reach him. He's locked up, but after what I went through I doubt if I'll ever feel safe from him.' Ever feel safe at all. But I had too much pride, even after my unguarded confession, to admit that.

Embarrassed by the stupid tears in my eyes, he looked away. And then pounced. He poured me more whisky than I drink in a month. 'There: get that inside you.' He patted my shoulder awkwardly, while I could have done with another hug. But I suppose that's inhibited ex-public schoolboys for you. 'At least you'll sleep tonight,' he added helpfully.

Curiously, I did. But only after I'd emailed Paula to tell her what had happened to my present place, and had a wonderful reply: *I could look at your new place at 8.00 on Friday morning. Can you be there?*

I could. And with a very steady hand I could pour nine-tenths of the whisky back in the bottle . . .

CHAPTER NINE

Despite everything, I was up bright and early the next morning for the Wray Episcopi interviews, which took the best part of the day. I'd rather have seen the candidates in the classroom, pretty well standard practice these days. But given the time frame this wasn't possible and at least we got a result. Frustrating though it was to have to wait till January for the woman we appointed, the governors and I were confident we'd got the right person, even if our choice was too much of an incomer to be a guaranteed popular choice: she came all the way from Yorkshire, with an accent to boot. But she was a literacy specialist, a huge bonus.

Meanwhile on Tuesday morning the staff meeting I'd called went well, though not all the news was good. Karenza's home visits had brought us briefings on ten new pupils, a big intake for a school this size. Apart from a couple with major language issues, who would require specialist input, at a cost to our very small budget, there was one child with behavioural problems who might require a full-time assistant's attention. There was growth in the intake at Wrayford, too: nineteen new pupils, a huge leap. At a time when nationally small schools were going to the wall this was excellent news. Unless the funding crisis got really serious, when simply merging schools still wouldn't produce enough pupils, of course . . .

My Episcopi colleagues seemed to approve of their clean, smart surroundings – I might have had a tantrum if they hadn't – but none of them had heard of the missing paintings, let alone seen them. As for the PTA noticeboard, I had another warning of Paine's likely reaction.

'He's a terrible bully, Jane,' Karenza said.

'But he's never responded to my letter.'

'A man like that doesn't always respond with written communications,' she said dryly. 'Tell you what, I know some of the mothers on the committee: I'll approach them. They wouldn't want their kids to see words like that.'

'I don't know,' Elsa, the science specialist, said. 'You should hear women in football crowds swear. F and C words all over the place.'

'But you can bet they wouldn't blame themselves if we told their children off for swearing here – and if they swear at home they blame us too!'

'Not jaundiced at all, are you, Karenza! And we haven't even started the new term yet!' I said with a grin. 'OK, I'll minute the gist of the discussion, if not the detail.' Donna, the school secretary, was on holiday, with minuting a meeting a poor second to the delights of walking in the Apennines. 'Next item: school council representatives. Is that an idea you approve of and if so, can I take it to the governors . . . ?'

'Why don't we look in the roof space for those pictures?' Elsa asked, as her contribution to AOB. 'I've never been up there, and surely with two people to hold the ladder and a third poised to call an ambulance we'd pass a risk assessment!'

'If anyone's going up there it had better be me,' I declared. 'I've still got my painting overalls in my office: I'll go and change while at least two of you put the tallest stepladder by the hatch. Carefully. Not pinching your fingers. Not dropping it on your toes. Are we clear? Or Elf and Safety will send me to the Tower of London.'

'I'm good at baking cakes,' Elsa declared. 'We'll get a file in to you somehow.'

Whatever Health and Safety would have made of it, it was an excellent – and free – bonding exercise, I reflected, shimmying into my overalls. Producing my emergency torch and one kept in the secretary's office, I joined the other women. 'Geronimo!'

Part of the roof space had been floor-boarded; tongue and groove, no less. It would surely take my weight, and that of heavy objects such as storage boxes or indeed huge frames holding the missing masterpieces. But – apart from me – it was bare. The rest was simply insulation, and pitifully thin insulation at that: another obvious call on our budget. There were some birds' nests in one corner, and the now-redundant chimney urgently needed pointing. There was no sign that any part of it had ever been used for storage and, specifically, no sign of any pictures, wrapped or unwrapped, propped anywhere. The only really good news was that there was no sign of any storm damage, either.

I was about to descend with exaggerated caution when I heard voices. Female – my colleagues; male – unknown. The latter was demanding to see me. The women assured him loudly that I was unavailable at the moment, but that I would contact him as soon as I was able to.

'Contact me? She already has, stupid bitch.'

'This is a school,' Karenza's voice said clearly. 'We do not tolerate bad language here.'

'I don't see any pupils.'

'Pupils or no pupils, we insist on politeness and respect.'

In my mind's eye I could see her standing with implacably folded arms, tapping one set of fingers as she obviously awaited an apology.

There came what sounded like a very muted apology.

'What was it you wanted to see Ms Cowan about? Perhaps we can help. The noticeboard, perhaps?' Elsa, very cool.

Rumble, rumble.

'Let's go and get it, shall we?'

Their footsteps receded. It was my problem: I should be there. Coming down the ladder rather faster than I went up, I stripped off my overalls in the boys' lavatories, stooping to the mini-basin to wash the worst of the dust from my hands and face. Looking like an old-fashioned sweep was no way to present myself. By the time I reached my office voices were raised again. If I interrupted it would undermine these very competent women. But I would lurk, to take responsibility if necessary.

'Look here, if you don't like this, and it's nothing but the truth, mind, why not rub it out?'

'I think you'll find that we have tried. But the words are cut too deeply into the cork.'

'There's enough paint around here, by the smell of it. Someone could have spared a bit to dab on it, if they cared that much.'

I edged close enough to see Elsa shake her head. 'They did: see? I often find if you paint something, the marks show through. And painting actually seems to have made the words more obvious, doesn't it?'

It was time for me to bring the discussion back to the point. 'Good morning, Mr Paine. I'm Jane Cowan, the head teacher: how do you do?' I offered my hand.

He ignored it. 'You're the one causing all the trouble, then.'

'No, Mr Paine. Whoever wrote the graffiti did that. All I've done is remove the board and keep it in a safe place until you or one of the other PTA committee members could collect it. I could have binned it but it's not my property, or the school's – it's the PTA's. Oh, and you'll find the screws and Rawlplugs taped to the back here.' In victory I could afford to try magnanimity. I smiled. 'It's good to meet a representative of a very generous group that's done so much good for the school. I hope we'll be able to rely on you all in the future.'

His eyes narrowed. 'You can rely on me for something, that's for sure.' Clutching the board, which looked like a jotter in his enormous hand, he turned on his heel and left.

Elsa's eyes widened. 'That was a threat, Jane. We're witnesses. You ought to report him.'

'It might be a bit nebulous for the police,' I said cautiously. Then I nodded. 'You're right. I'll have an unofficial word with a friend who's an officer. Just in case. Very well, team: lunchtime. I've booked a table for us at the Jolly Cricketers at Wrayford to celebrate our new collaboration. My treat.'

On impulse, waving the women off, I went to visit my own house, the one no one except PACT would work on. Could I possibly live in it as it was? The roof was in better shape than the one I was living in now, but I knew that indoors it would be just as dispiriting as when I'd last been in it. The garage, however, had now collapsed completely – it was just a pile of wooden panels. Should I burn it *in situ*? Or would it be greener to have it taken away in one of the skips the builders – any builders – would need? As for the garden, it had been overgrown before, as you'd expect when it had been owned by a housebound old couple, but now it was like a young copse. A combination of the thunderstorms and lovely warm weather today would make it burgeon even more into a positive rainforest. There was no way I could tackle it on my own, and in any case if Ed van Boolen was going to deal with the whole garden it was going to be his problem, not mine.

Like a child, however, I wanted to stamp my foot and demand it was done *now*. In fact, I expressed it in exactly those terms when I ran into Ed on my way home.

'I've an idea I'm going to have to move into it well before it's ready,' I said by way of explanation. 'But I can't face the jungle at the bottom of the garden. Would you be able to simply grub out all you can and flatten everything you can't? The storm's done some of the work for you. And could you dispose of the poor old timber garage too? Don't worry about any reconstructive work yet.'

I couldn't read his expression. 'It's not quite as easy as that, Jane, is it?'

'I absolutely don't mind what state you have to leave it in. There's a funny smell about the place and I'm wondering if I've got foxes or something. One of those Dartmoor big cats could have emigrated and taken up residence in it without anyone noticing.'

The joke didn't work. Frowning, he scrolled down his phone. 'You'll have to give me a little . . . I suppose we could say ten days' time?' He must have seen my face because he added, 'Sooner if I can sort out some other stuff, though that might not be easy. Within the next two weeks, anyway.' He frowned – looked quite uncomfortable, I thought.

'That's fine,' I said, though it was a huge struggle not to let disappointment drip from my voice. After all, he must have a really full diary. And I knew in my heart I couldn't move for ages, not unless Paula worked some sort of a miracle.

That evening I invited Jo, Lloyd and their kids to join me for a meal at the Mondiale, a hotel that had offered me refuge in the past. Jo and Carys were shopping for goodies in the spa shop; Lloyd, Geraint and I waited, menus on the table before us, in the bar. Lloyd took a long, hard pull on his non-alcoholic lager. It seemed he was trying to persuade

Geraint that you could look cool in front of your mates and still not break the law. From his occasional winces, he was also trying to persuade himself that it might be possible to get to the bottom of his glass.

'How long does that James guy reckon before that holiday cottage is safe again?' he asked.

'A few days only. My roof is only missing a few tiles, but next door lost a huge section – and it means anyone with cheek and a few climbing skills can get into mine with very little effort. A few bricks here, a bit of mortar there – then I shall be safe—'

'As houses.' Geraint finished my sentence for me. 'Oh, yuck.' He shoved his fingers down his throat as if to make himself vomit. 'That's really gross, Ma.'

Jo came towards us flourishing a bikini she'd just bought in the spa shop. It seemed Carys had bought one too but she was too canny or too embarrassed to show her brother – or perhaps her father, who might have views on how much flesh a girl of fourteen should expose.

A waiter sauntered over: somehow the implication was that he didn't care a toss what we ate, so long as we ordered and headed off to the restaurant out of his way.

'I'd like to order in some drinks for these two first,' I said. 'Put them on my bill, please. Thank you. Now, avert your gaze, guys – I want to see what Carys has bought.' It was a bikini, of course, but in just her colour. I grinned at her approvingly.

'If she keeps stuffing her face with burgers she won't be able to get into it for very long anyway!'

'I always wanted a brother,' I chipped in dreamily. 'Now I'm not so sure. OK, Lloyd: before we eat, a bit of an update, but the moment we get to the table it's just family natter, right? It seems I've managed to annoy not just one man called Paine, but two. One, Dennis, is a talented but very aggressive cricketer who plays for St Luke's Bay; my umpiring got his goat so much he's had a written warning – though I gather it's becoming a habit, with solid male umpires being threatened too. And now I find his brother Gerry is the chair of the PTA at Wray Episcopi. The only really interesting thing with Gerry is that he's a member – maybe the only member – of a right-wing group called English First.'

'Sounds like Dad telling me to get on with my homework,' Geraint put in. 'Actually, I've come across them myself. Not necessarily them – one of them was a totally Essex girl woman, if you see what I mean.'

'Gross,' Carys agreed.

'They were leafleting outside the school.'

'And I can tell you that their name doesn't match their prose,' Carys said coolly. 'Neanderthal. Tell you what, Hani writes better English – and she only came here from Somalia eight months ago. Legitimately, before anyone asks. The whole family were officially granted asylum. Mind you, some stupid toads still call her an illegal.'

Geraint nodded seriously: it seemed as if for once he and his sister were in agreement. 'The head said he'd call you people in, Dad, if they didn't go away. I think he may have called them anyway – inciting race hatred, stuff like that. Pretty homophobic, and not very nice about women, which made it odd that a woman was involved.'

Lloyd produced a wry grin as he jotted the information on a drinks mat he then pocketed. 'See, Jo, they can talk and think when they can take their eyes off a screen for thirty seconds. Well done, kids.'

Jo, seated between them, put an arm round both and squeezed their shoulders.

'If ever you want them adopted, I'll take them, no questions asked,' I said.

'And have you annoyed anyone else?' Lloyd asked. 'We have two very good detectives here to help if you have.'

It was my turn for a dry grin. 'Actually, I've pleased someone I'd rather not have met. During the storm. I did my good neighbour act. Fine. Only it turned out one of the people I was helping was one of Simon's drinking friends. Josh Talbot. I only recognised him as he slapped his wife.' I took a gulp of my G&T. 'Actually, he was probably, in the circumstances, doing the right thing: she was so hysterical I'd told her I ought to but I couldn't. Then he comes in, and doesn't hesitate. So the jury's out.'

Jo took my hand. 'You knew him: more to the point, did he recognise you?'

'I don't think so. I've worked on my voice and accent, of course, and my hair's changed colour, and I took care to stand in the shadows – we'd only got a couple of candles to light a whole room, so I may have got away with it.'

'You've still got me on speed-dial if – well, just in case?' Lloyd asked. 'Excellent. Anyone else whose toes you've trodden on?'

'Only the Lady of the Manor's. But that bloody waiter's hovering again – I hate to say this but maybe we should order?'

'And don't even look at burgers, Car, or you'll be the size of a house before you know it.'

'That's enough, Geraint. While we're eating, Jane, you can fill me in on the Lady Preston affair. Steak for me, please, rare.'

CHAPTER TEN

The route back to the Mondiale from Wrayford School took me close enough to my putative new home to justify a diversion just to see that it was still there. Just a couple of days after I last looked at it: sad or what, as Geraint might have said. It was, and, as I feared, the garage was just as flat and the garden was even more overgrown.

'You don't know who owns this, do you?' A woman's head appeared over next door's hedge, which was trimmed to within a millimetre. Actually, so was the woman's hair, in a very expensive cut, suited to the Merc that lurked in the block-paved drive. And even for an over-the-hedge chat she was well made up and neatly manicured. I'd put her in her late sixties, maybe even early seventies.

Clearly when I moved I would have standards to maintain. Meanwhile, I needed to respond to what seemed a question heaving with criticism. 'I do, as a matter of fact.'

She might have misheard me. 'Well, you can tell whoever it is that the place is a disgrace. There's no excuse for this. Look at it. And the smell! I shall be complaining to the council if something isn't done soon.'

She was right: the animal smell still lingered – might, if anything, be worse.

'There are two problems: the builders who were supposed to be bringing it up to scratch went bankrupt, and the person contracted to do the garden has simply been too busy, but has promised to attend to it within the next two weeks. That should get rid of the garage and the foxes or whatever. I'm afraid, though, that things are going to get worse for you: building work and landscape gardening involve skips and mess, and probably a lot of noise, too.'

'Humph. Who is it? Some weekender?'

'No, it's me, actually.'

'You look quiet enough, that's one thing. I'll tell you, you'll want to lock your stuff away. There's been some thefts in the village.'

'Really?' My surprise was genuine. 'I hadn't heard.'

'Oh, yes. Power tools. It'll be the migrants, you mark my words.'

Stealing ride-on mowers and now power tools! Clearly these poor wanderers were versatile. To my shame I said nothing, however, because I was going to have to rub along with her for as long as we were neighbours, and so far she'd had very little reason to like me. 'I'll warn the builders. I'm Jane Cowan, by the way.'

'Mrs Penkridge.' We shook hands with no little difficulty. 'Ah, you're the headmistress. You had some trouble at the school, didn't you? You're sure it's safe to send children there now? Quite sure? I told my daughter I wouldn't want anything to happen to my little granddaughter. Charlotte. Charlotte Bingham.'

Charlotte Bingham? Not one of mine. Or not yet, at least. 'Pretty little girl,' I improvised. 'Bright? Didn't I see her with her mother at the open morning for reception children?'

Crisis averted. Perhaps I had, perhaps I hadn't, but Mrs Penkridge wasn't going to argue with anyone calling her precious grandchild pretty and bright.

We embarked on the usual manoeuvres to end an encounter. As I withdrew to my car, she had the last word. 'Don't forget, you want to do something about that smell.'

Seven-thirty on Friday saw me outside soon after seven: not for anything would I antagonise Paula by being late. But she was there before me. Nor was she alone. Another hard-hatted and yellow-jacketed woman was already checking the front of the building, making notes and taking photographs. She turned out to be the architect, a laconic woman called Ann.

Before we could do more than shake hands, however, Mrs Penkridge shot out, already beautifully dressed and made-up.

'I told you that you needed to be more security-conscious! I told you! And what have I just seen but some yobs running across your garden. Probably migrants, of course. So I shouted and they ran away. But they'll steal your bricks and mortar, that sort. I called the police but they said it didn't sound like an emergency and to dial 101 or whatever it is. And they'll get someone on routine patrol to offer some advice. I ask you, advice! You need to get some barbed wire in that hedge of yours: that'll make them think.'

It had certainly made me think.

'I'm really grateful. Thank you so much. This is my builder; Paula, Mrs Penkridge. We're just going to discuss what she's going to do.'

'A woman builder! So why did you get rid of the others?'

'I told you: they went bankrupt.'

'So you did. But I told you I've heard men's voices and thought . . . Well, they had one of those trucks. Silly me. But a woman builder!'

Quite. 'She comes with the very highest—' I was talking to thin air. Just when I ought to have been asking her about the sort of truck they drove. Was she the sort of woman to protect her house with CCTV? Because there weren't a lot of cameras in the average hedgerow, as I'd found to my cost at the start of the holiday.

In the face of considerable provocation, Paula and Ann had managed to preserve a professional demeanour, and actually looked as if they might be doing some work.

'I don't usually invite the architect along at this stage,' Paula said, 'but it might speed things up if we can agree everything on-site. It's good to see you've been paying regular visits: that'll deter the unwanted guests your neighbour was talking about.' She pointed: the gravel approach to the late but unlamented garage, tucked away at the back, was rutted. Some of the tracks looked pretty recent.

The summer's morning went cold. 'Not my tracks; not my visits. And those youths . . . My neighbour was saying she had to chase away some youths this morning.'

'I know; that doesn't sound too good,' Paula said, who was clearly into understatement. 'We'll just make sure there's no one here now. Actually, we do it carefully – I'd rather scare someone into running away, not fighting . . .'

It was weird for me to have someone else giving the orders, but clearly no one questioned Paula. Ever, probably.

Talking with very little semblance of normality, in my case at least, we ambled round the side of the house, the other women talking technicalities about utilities and building materials.

'Apart from linking a brick-built garage to the house, what plans did you have for the garden?' Paula asked.

It felt like a make-or-break interview question. 'I've got a landscape gardener friend: I'll take his advice.'

'But you must have some ideas? It'd help us no end if we could get rid of that mess of bushes and see the proper lie of the land.'

I felt like a child needing to justify myself. 'I'm already on to it, Paula. He promised to be here in the next couple of weeks. I reckon I've got foxes or something: the smell . . .'

'You're sure it's foxes? OK. Meanwhile, I'll get one of our contractors to dispose of that garage, before some clever kids think it'd be fun to set fire to it. If we can start on an absolutely clear site it'll speed us up no end. For your sake – and your neighbour's – we'll employ our regular security team. We want to make sure no materials or tools go walkabout – not that we ever leave tools overnight, of course.' She spoke as if she was addressing the neighbours, not me; I'd not have expected her to be so informative, either.

'How soon can you bring them in? I don't like the idea

of unauthorised visitors.' I jerked a thumb at the tracks.

She made a note. 'I'll make sure they start this afternoon, tomorrow morning latest. Very well, let's go round to the front, then you can let us in.'

The house smelt rank as well as damp.

'Did the foxes get in somehow? Or,' I continued, trying not to let my voice wobble, 'have I had a human guest?'

'More to the point, have you still got one?' Ann whispered.

'No, don't shut the door, Ann – leave it wide open. Let's check out the front room first, shall we?' she added loudly.

We trooped in. I responded to Paula's silent enquiry with a nod. It was just as I'd left it. I made an effort. 'I thought a wood-burning stove in a simple modern grate: the thirties were an interesting historical period, but not in the form of a brown-tiled grate in my living room.'

'So what would you do with it?' Paula asked sharply.

'Take your advice.' I gestured to her and to Ann.

That seemed to be the right response. 'Those leaded lights aren't period – so we can change those.'

I scratched my head. 'This all seems a bit micromanagement,' I protested. 'I was hoping for grand ideas from Ann and amazing building skills from you.'

'You shall have both,' Paula declared, with a sudden warm smile that transformed her face. 'But it seemed sensible to talk about the place while we were waiting for our friend to depart. Didn't you hear the back door open and shut? No?' She turned back to the hall. I ran past her, to see if I could see the intruder. Nothing. I turned back.

'It ties in with what my neighbour was saying. Look. Can we just stand outside for a minute?' Staggering out,

I leant against the house and tried to do the breathing my various therapists had insisted on. 'Sorry. That's better. It's all to do with my having a violent and abusive ex, who used to break into whatever house I'd moved to.' I explained briefly.

Ann put her arm round me. 'I'm not surprised you're shaking. Even a mere casual burglar's enough to make me shake.'

'Not a burglar, I'd say,' Paula said firmly. 'Certainly not a violent ex. More likely to be a gentleman of the road, like our old friend Montague – he's actually a peer of the realm with a stately home to boot, Jane, but he prefers the open road and someone else's roof,' she explained. 'We see a lot of him – we often share our lunches with him because he's such an entertaining talker. So long as you're sitting to windward, not leeward.'

Ann shook her head. 'Youths, that woman said. Montague wouldn't be in anyone's company. There are a lot of homeless people around these days, of course.'

'Ann puts in a lot of hours for Shelter, the homeless charity,' Paula chipped in.

'Homeless is possible. Or – given we're in Kent, and thus close to France – it could be what the media would call illegal immigrants. I'd prefer the term asylum seekers,' Ann said.

'Or even refugees,' I added sadly. Something quite visceral made me reluctant to betray them to the authorities. 'Look, can we talk through the house changes before I decide what to do?'

Paula gave me a searching look, but nodded. 'Let's see if any damage has been done, shall we? Or anything that might be . . . alarming . . . left behind.'

Alarming? Slowly it dawned on me that my guest might not have been benign. But I didn't want to contemplate that yet. 'Kitchen and bathroom – absolute priorities, of course. After the roof. And I wondered about the greenest way to heat the place.' I was talking at random, but both women took notes. 'Oh, and if it were at all possible I'd like a secure room.'

'You're still anxious about this ex?'

'Put it another way, still scared beyond reason. Of course, I don't want to admit it's a place to hide. I want it to look like a book room or something I can be proud of, not ashamed of.'

'Survival itself is something to be proud of,' Ann said tartly. 'But I can assure you that I will never design anything ugly. Paula would never build it. William Morris might not be to everyone's taste, certainly not Paula's, but he got it right about needing to have beautiful things in your home. And about having a beautiful home.'

'I've got some ideas from the holiday let I'm living in,' I said. 'Shall I send you some photos?'

'Good idea. Well,' Paula continued, 'there's nothing incriminating here. Not so much as a sleeping bag or a rucksack. So our friend was travelling light. Let's throw open all the windows and let some of this lovely summer air in. There! Now, talk me through your dreams so we can make at least some of them come true . . .'

The sheer matter-of-factness of Paula's conversation, augmented by Ann's occasional flights of fancy – all, she insisted, possible, and not so desperately expensive either – kept me going for the next hour or so. But my mind would insist on sneaking back to what I knew I shouldn't be thinking about.

At last Paula shot me one of her appraising glances. 'You were telling us about your holiday let, Jane. Can we go back there and grab a coffee and see if we can adapt anything? Sometimes it's better so see things *in situ*.'

'The place'll probably be overrun with workmen,' I said. 'Actually, it had better be. I'm sick of hotel living, and I want to get back to what passes for home these days.'

CHAPTER ELEVEN

The three of us paused outside the row of cottages, looking up at the roofs. Mine, now patched with almost-matching tiles, was separated from its neighbour by a newly built wall, so the whole structure was secure – until work started again on the middle house, of course. The other end cottage had a similar wall, so it too could be rented out once again. I had to admire the enterprise James and the owner, Brian Dawes, had shown. Where on earth had he found builders prepared to do the work at such short notice? And why, knowing how desperate I'd been, had he never thought to put in a good word for me to encourage them to do the same for my house? But at least I had Paula on my side now, so I'd try to abandon my grumpy resentment before it got a grip.

At least I had a roof again. The scaffolding was down. Someone was sweeping up the back garden.

I offered him coffee, which he declined.

The women were prowling round inside; I wasn't sure if they were checking that it was habitable again or looking at the features I said I liked, like the chic bathroom. There was no one in the space-age kitchen. Digging in a cupboard I found elderflower cordial; the big American fridge produced ice. Perhaps that would be better than coffee. The workman agreed it would be. So, eventually, did Ann and Paula. We all adjourned to the newly spruce garden, the workman having sunk his drink in one draught. With a wave, he was driving off.

The silence between us grew. They were waiting for me to speak, and not necessarily about home improvements.

'I have to act, don't I?' I said, putting my glass down on the pretty outdoor table. 'Kids like those that Mrs Penkridge saw don't just drive here in a car with big wheels. A car that makes several journeys here. You know, I'm actually worried for their safety if the car driver finds them first.'

Paula looked at me appraisingly and produced her slow, shrewd smile.

'You're assuming they're innocent victims? I hope they are,' Ann put in. 'But I have to point out that not all Syrians or whatever are angels. What if they're ISIS operatives?'

I spread my hands. 'I want them to be innocent kids, caught up in a situation beyond their control. If not . . . I'm going to contact a friend, as decent an officer as you could find. I know it passes the responsibility to someone else, but that's how it's going to be.'

Paula nodded. 'Good. Meanwhile do I have your permission to secure the property with immediate effect?'

'Of course: it's just what I was going to ask you to do.'

* * *

I watched a couple of Lloyd's colleagues offer a cursory inspection of my humble abode. It would have been hard for them to look less interested. Ann had had to leave to keep her next appointment; Paula had stayed with me after making a couple of phone calls. Another member of the team soon joined us, a slight woman somewhere in her thirties whom Paula introduced as their historic buildings expert. Nonetheless, she was the one who would devote herself to managing all the changes I needed.

We shook hands. 'Caffy Tyler. Double *f*, not *th*,' she said. 'The C in PACT. Paula and Caffy's Team. See? And I know this isn't a historic building, but I was once in an abusive relationship too and I'm stepping in to save time. The castle I should be working on has been there eight hundred years without falling into complete disrepair and another two or three weeks won't hurt.'

Before we could say more, the older constable, a guy whose name I hadn't caught, came over and addressed himself to Paula. 'I don't think we'll be much longer. You can go ahead and get that guy of yours to secure the site.'

'Guy?' I asked her quizzically. 'I thought you only dealt with women.'

Paula answered with a straight face. It dawned on me rather late that she might not have the most active sense of humour. 'For the decorating side we're exclusively female – interior and exterior, that is. I do my best to support my gender – and I'll bet you support and promote your women staff too. But sometimes a male's the best option and I'm professional enough to want the best.'

'Actually I appointed a male deputy at Wrayford School,' I said. 'Because I thought he was the best.' My confession over, I groaned, 'My God, Paula, is it selfish of me to hope this is much ado about nothing? I really need a place to call my own. A nice safe place, too.'

'You call this safe?' put in Caffy, with her two Fs. 'You've got neighbours who must have seen or heard something but who never thought to alert you or the authorities? Lovely folk, clearly. I'll build you a nice high wall no one will be able to scale, and fit electronic gates and a key-code front door. I can even build that secure room you mentioned to Paula. But I'll also keep an eye out for a better place for you, so you can sell this at an enormous profit and find somewhere to put down roots. Sorry, Jane, if that isn't what you want to hear – but I always tell it as it is.'

'Or maybe the wall will make the neighbour move out,' I said, my smile a mere ghost because she'd put into words what I'd tried to suppress.

'I'll think of something else that might,' she said with a smile that might equally have been impish or enigmatic.

With term starting on Monday, I couldn't afford the luxury of spending the afternoon worrying about my potential home. I can't say I achieved much, but just going through the routine of last-minute preparations was strangely soothing. To my delight Tom arrived halfway through the afternoon; it was good to see my deputy taking his role so seriously.

'Losing your roof must be the worst way to start the school year,' he said with a shrewd glance at my face. 'Here, sit down and I'll make some green tea – too hot for coffee. My wife even gave me this.' He produced a lemon, cutting off a couple of slices. 'There. Nice and refreshing.'

We sat. We sipped.

'I take it you'll be going into Episcopi tomorrow?' he said.

'Have to.'

'Look, if you don't mind an early start, I can give you a hand. I mean, really early. Sevenish. Six-thirty if you wish. But I need to be away by nine-thirty absolute latest.'

'Are you sure?' A man with an overworked wife and a demanding family.

'Absolutely. Especially the prompt departure.'

My phone chirruped.

'Go on, take it.' He got up, picking up my checklist and comparing it to his.

It was only a text from Ed. More umpiring tomorrow? He was only asking because the opposition umpire was stuck in France in the midst of rioting migrants. And our usual man didn't feel up to umpiring at both ends.

I texted back: *Try everyone else you can think of, because I can only do it if you're truly desperate.*

Blow me if it didn't chirrup straight back: *We are. Pick u up from Mondiale@12.30? xxx*

Xxx indeed! I didn't think I was on those terms with him. *No, thanks – I'll get myself there. X.* Just the one.

Putting aside the Saturday *Guardian*, and gathering up my belated breakfast things from the garden table, I was just thinking that it might actually be quite pleasant to spend the afternoon umpiring my favourite game, even though rain was forecast for later. A lot of it.

A phone call from Paula broke my cheerful mood.

'You need to get out to your new place, Jane. Now. I'll see you there.'

End of call? Just like that?

I wasn't the first there. Three police cars were parked in the narrow lane, already clogged with a fencing contractor's vehicle and a PACT van. The promised security fence was in place, but someone was decorating it with police tape. Some of what had been my garage was now in a skip; the rest was disappearing behind a police tent.

Mrs Penkridge erupted as soon I appeared. 'So that was the source of the smell all along!' she said, jabbing at my chest with a venom worthy of Dennis Paine. 'Fine neighbour you're turning out to be!'

Paula inserted herself between us in the unobtrusive but unarguable way I use when dealing with warring ten-year-olds. 'Let me take you over to Will Bowman, the DS in charge here: it's not good news, Jane, but you need to hear it.'

She led me to the officer checking all the comings and goings: the area was now all too clearly a crime scene. I waited as a white-suited figure squatting by the shrubbery, now even more shambolic, of course, was summoned. He got up in one fairly easy move, and approached me with a very formal smile. He was about my age and about my height, good-looking in a rather beaky way – it was the face of an academic, perhaps, rather than a law-enforcer. He didn't appear to have spent as much time in the summer sun as most people round here.

'Jane Cowan,' I said, with a similar smile. 'I'm the owner.'

'I need to ask you a few questions,' he said without preamble.

'I'm happy to supply you with all the answers I can.'

He looked over my shoulder at Mrs Penkridge, still rubber-necking. 'My car, I think.'

I said crisply, 'Sergeant Bowman, if you want somewhere quieter and cooler, it's only three minutes' drive to my rented place.'

'When I've briefed my DI – here she is now – I'll join you. Half an hour or so.'

Bowman looked longingly at the walled garden, attractive in the sun as a French Impressionist's sketch, but I decided not to indulge him. 'That's OK if you want the workmen in the next garden to overhear everything we say. And it might be cooler inside, if I can get a through draught. Elderflower cordial with ice?'

We sat down opposite each other in the living area; I waited.

'Tell me about your house and garden.'

'You probably know more about it already than I do,' I said truthfully. 'I've scarcely been in the place since I bought it. It's not ideal, and it's not in an ideal position, but at the time it was the only one I could afford. The theory was I'd get the work done this summer holiday so I could move in before term started. However, the builder scheduled to do the work went bankrupt, and for various reasons none of the other firms I approached was able to take it on. I'm just grateful that PACT has agreed to do the work as an urgent priority.'

'And you've made no attempt to clear the garden?'

'The landscape gardener I'd booked to do everything said it made more sense to wait until the structural work was done, so that newly planted beds and so on wouldn't be damaged. Neither of us ever imagined it would take so long before work could begin properly. However, after considerable pressure from me he'd promised to do something with my jungle even before your colleagues started work on it. What did they find, by the way?'

'We'll talk about that later. One of your neighbours said she was forced to complain to you about the state of the place.'

I was about to rage at a woman who didn't deserve it. I wouldn't have wanted to live next to my place in its present state. 'Mrs Penkridge. She was. She also told me she'd seen a couple of lads scarpering across my garden. I should have kept a better eye on everything, but visiting it only made me feel more impotent and frustrated: making the house habitable was too big a job, with more radical work needed, for me even to imagine doing myself. I rather lost hope when time after time a local builder would turn down what I thought would be a lucrative gig. Plus, I have been busy recently.'

His stare was cold. 'I thought you teachers had long holidays.'

'That's what everyone thinks. What people think isn't always backed up by facts.' A fact such as Tom, who was only volunteering out of loyalty anyway, being at Episcopi by six so that he could leave on time for a last weekend with his family. I got back to some facts of my own. 'It was only when I spoke to Paula from PACT and then this place got damaged that my hopes were raised. Absentee landlords . . .'

'I learnt about them in history lessons a long time ago. So you rarely visited the place—'

'Except in the company of an occasional unenthusiastic

builder, who'd give the place the most cursory of glances and then walk away. So I never noticed that my garage had been hijacked. But I think the tyre tracks leading up to it are fairly recent. Maybe my uninvited guest or guests haven't been there long?'

'Forensics will give us more information, but probably not.'

'Just long enough, I assume, to die when the garage collapsed.'

'That's what you're expecting me to tell you?'

'It would explain the smell . . . I thought I had foxes or something. But I wouldn't get a DS and a DI and police tape for the odd fox or badger.'

He flashed a smile all the more amazing for the context: 'Not unless it had TB. Yes, I'm afraid we've found a body. I'd like to know what you think about the garage door still being padlocked when it collapsed. From the outside, Ms Cowan.' His eyes were icy again.

I could feel the blood draining from my face. 'Someone – you mean that someone locked a person . . . a human being . . . in there and left them to die?'

'Someone locked a young man in there.'

'And he—My God! In a place I own. I could have – should have – checked.'

'Why?'

'Because the privilege of ownership means the responsibility of ownership.'

He shrugged. 'I'm not apportioning blame, Ms Cowan. That's for the Coroner and ultimately the courts. I take it you'd deny putting a man we think is an Afghan in there and locking the door on him.'

'I can't think – I can't begin to imagine . . .'

'I'll take that as a negative, then. So can you *imagine*,' he threw my verb back at me, 'who did?'

It was as if shaking my head vehemently triggered a thought, not necessarily coherent yet. 'Let me just get a few things as straight as I can. An unoccupied house. A garage the far side so it's not overlooked. A gravel path.' I looked up. 'You have a colleague – PC Lloyd Davies. He'll vouch for the fact I'm not usually batty.'

He looked me in the eye. 'I met a guy called Pat Webber, too, Jane. When he was on secondment. I'd say you have a good track record.'

For a moment that threw me. But with no more than a heartbeat's hesitation I said, 'Towards the start of this *long* summer holiday, I took up cycling. At one point I was run off the road. An elderly couple – brother and sister, Harry and Doreen – helped rescue me and took me to their house. When I went to thank them it was completely locked up. It has been every time I've passed. It too was remote, though far more distant from anything passing as civilisation than mine! No neighbours, even. Detached. Free-standing garage at the rear – twice the size of mine. Deep tracks in the gravel. Probably made by a vehicle larger than a car. Oh, and there's an extraordinarily long washing line. Funny how that detail sticks here.' I touched my forehead. 'I mentioned it to Lloyd – but only in passing. They helped me, for goodness' sake. I didn't want – I don't know – to think anything odd about them. Just for them to have some flowers.'

He made a little rewinding gesture. 'The vehicle that hit you.'

'I never saw it. But from the very garbled and mutually contradictory descriptions Harry and Doreen gave it sounded like a Ford Ranger or something like it. Possibly black, possibly blue. Definitely with tinted rear windows. And there are, of course, quite a number of beasts fitting that sort of description.'

His gaze implied complete disbelief, and why not? 'Are you making a connection with the vehicle and the tyre tracks at both the houses?'

'That's the frustrating thing: I told you, I never, ever saw it. You don't see much except sky when you're lying flat on your back on a very prickly hedge. Oh, I'm wise after the event: I have a helmet camera now. Look, I'm just feeding you odds and ends because you have the resources to make connections. Possibly,' I added, 'given the state of public spending and the cuts to essential services like – well, you people, of course.'

'Quite. Any other snippets, connected or not, you may remember?'

I shook my head. 'This is a long shot, and goodness knows she has no reason to love me, but Mrs Penkridge looked to me the sort of person to be far-sighted enough to have her own CCTV system. Is it worth asking her? After all, if she has, it's just possible it may have caught the vehicles she mentioned. And I'd really like to know if one of them is a blue SUV with tinted windows.'

'We'll certainly be talking to Mrs Penkridge, and not at your behest either. A serious crime has been committed, Ms Cowan, and if she has evidence she'll be required to reveal it, even if she doesn't think her neighbour deserves consideration. We'll be searching the entire property this afternoon—'

'Paula thought someone might have been sleeping in the larger of the back bedrooms—'

'We won't be trusting to her intuition, believe me – we shall be subjecting it to a full forensic examination. Where will we be able to find you?'

'On the school field here in Wrayford, Mr Bowman. Right in the middle. I'm umpiring a match.'

'During the school holiday?'

'It's a league match. Wrayford CC against—actually, I'm not sure who the opposition are yet . . . Yes, I'm a qualified umpire.'

He looked at me with what seemed genuine admiration. 'Not just children – women too?'

'And men, as in this afternoon's match. At least it means,' I said with a dry smile, 'that I won't be spending the afternoon watching my potential garden being the horticultural equivalent of strip-searched, and the house having its DNA taken.'

CHAPTER TWELVE

The first person I saw as I walked towards the school playing field was Justin Forbes, the Churcham umpire, looking as dapper as before in a traditional straw trilby.

'What a good idea, the school and the cricket club sharing the field!' he said, kissing my hand, much to my bemusement.

'Thank you,' I said: it was nice to be appreciated.

Still holding my hand he stared; then he dropped it abruptly. 'Whose idea was it, then?'

I don't do blushing bashfulness. 'Half mine. As I recall Diane, the licensee of the Jolly Cricketers, appropriately enough, was bemoaning the loss of the original cricket field, and I was able to persuade our governors to offer Wrayford the regular use of this: it benefits both the players and the pupils, as you can imagine.'

He looked entirely nonplussed. 'I . . . I do apologise. I

thought the notion was Ed van Boolen's and Brian Dawes'.'

What a surprise; the only question was whether the two Wrayford men had claimed the idea or whether Justin, as an alpha male himself, simply assumed that only other alpha males could have had it. 'The important thing is the end result,' I said graciously, though I hated myself for being so damned appeasing. 'The downside for the teams and indeed the spectators are that the facilities are all junior school sized; the up is that there are indeed facilities. Unlike some clubs where I've had to change in someone's garage and beg to use their outside loo.'

'Does the school have showers?'

'Next year, school budget and club fund-raising permitting. Symbiosis,' I said. It was time to talk about matters in hand: 'Now, Justin, the weather forecast for this evening is awful – and I can see the clouds already starting to build.' It was, as Pat would have said, black over Bill's mother's. Sometimes I borrowed the expression, but not this time. I'd clearly shocked poor Justin Forbes to the bone. He might not survive such an onslaught on his preconceptions of what people he no doubt thought of as ladies should do – and talking Black Country was almost certainly not one of them. 'Should we have a word with the captains and see if they're prepared to play a reduced number of overs in order to get a result or if they're desperate for a meaningless draw . . .'

In the event, though both teams agreed a much shorter match and a result, the weather closed in before Wrayford, batting second, could complete their overs. Although no rain was actually falling, it was simply too dark for the batsmen to see, and already lightning was playing round the horizon. Justin and I could have done complicated calculations using the impenetrable Duckworth–Lewis method to award the game to either side, but I suggested a tactical dash to the Jolly Cricketers where the skittle alley might provide a place to decide a notional result.

For some reason, Justin insisted on paying for the players' first round; I'd have to do the same for the second. After that it was up to them. Again he surprised me: no humble half-pint for me, but bubbles. None of your prosecco, either: Diane's finest champagne. I had a nasty feeling that, after snubbing Ed over his lift offer, I'd have to schmooze up to him to escape Justin's courtly attentions. Ed might, of course, need to hear what was going on at my new place. However, when, halfway down my fizz, I turned to look for him, he was returning his glass to Diane. He managed a quick wave in my direction, but didn't pause as he swept out into the rain.

Drat. Justin was claiming my attention again. 'I was never able to show you the lights of France, was I?'

'No indeed. Only the magnificent storm. Do you get many, in such an exposed position? You're pretty much the first port of call, after all.'

What had I said? He narrowed his eyes, but only momentarily. 'Ah . . . for the weather.'

And also for those unlit boats I'd seen running for the safety of the bay. Another image clicked into place. In a similar bay, though in much more benign conditions, when we'd been to Marcus's barbecue, another boat was slipping in unlit. The night I'd quoted Matthew Arnold and succumbed so publicly to that virus.

But I ought to be saying something that didn't constitute a request for an invitation. 'It must be a heavenly place for birdwatching,' I extemporised.

'I suppose there are people who enjoy that,' he said doubtfully.

I beamed, saying with almost perfect truth, 'One of the first things I shall do when I can at last move into my new home is have a mega bird-feeder: one that will hold everything: fat balls, nuts, niger seeds, sunflower hearts – I want the lot.'

'And mealworms for robins – don't forget them.' Our huge opening bowler, the one I'd seen snogging our wicketkeeper, chipped in. Des. I could have hugged him.

'Of course. And half-coconuts.'

'Hmm. Pretty well everything has to be in squirrel-proof dispensers round here. You might want to try . . .'

Even I was wearying of his list of recommendations, but Justin's eyes were pretty well glazed over. That suited me. I ought to be mixing with the rest of the teams: most were very decent men, and even those who weren't would be less likely to yell obscenities at me if I gave what they thought was the wrong decision when we'd shared jokes and the plates of chips Diane was circulating. Even the wicketkeeper, Mike, whose vocabulary was startling – yes, the wicketkeeper I'd seen with—

'Did Des get rid of him for you?' Mike asked, his mouth close to my ear. 'Good. You did me and Des a good turn. We're just doing one for you. Right?'

I stared. 'When?'

In my ear, he muttered, 'Saying nothing about . . . that barbie.'

Not that I could have done since I'd completely lost my voice that night. But I wouldn't have anyway, so all I did was smile in what I hoped was a gently conspiratorial way.

Louder, he continued, 'Didn't I hear you'd got trouble at that new place of yours? Bad business, by the sound of it.'

'Tragic. A young life wasted. I keep thinking I should have checked the place regularly. But, you know, I got so downhearted losing builder after builder I didn't even want to see it.'

His eyes narrowed in interrogation.

'Honestly, I must have had four or five just pull out on me. No reason given.'

'I wonder why that might be. And assuming you had the funds to pay, you might be forgiven for thinking it's a bit strange. Almost as if someone had told them to stay away from the job. Not that I'm mentioning any names, Jane. And I know you're a nice discreet woman, so you won't press me to.' With a comradely pat on the shoulder, as if I'd been one of his junior workmates, he caught someone else's eye and moved away. It was a good job that managing not to look gobsmacked was one of the tools of my trade.

Whoever had repaired the holiday cottage had done a decent job, I had to admit. Nothing was leaking, despite the downpour that soaked me to the skin. I should have felt warm and cosy inside once I'd stripped off my dripping clothes and soaked in a hot bath. I certainly didn't regret slipping away from the pub and the possibility of further conversation with Justin, though many people would have welcomed a lift in his luscious Merc. But I felt truly rattled. There was no reason for Mike to have lied about the interference with my building project. His behind-the-stumps vocabulary might be hair-raising, but otherwise he was a decent man whom I'd never detected in any form of cheating – claiming a catch or a stumping when the batter had been not out. And he'd taken a risk in even referring to that barbecue.

Idly, still enjoying my soak far too much to emerge fully from the tub, I stretched out an arm to find Classic FM on the radio I kept handy. The piece was one of Malcolm Arnold's Cornish Dances, with far too lively a rhythm to relax to. Something about its deliberate naivety switched on a silly verbal earworm:

> It was a dark and stormy night
> And the brigands sat round the campfire.
> 'Say, Cap'n, tell us a tale!'
> And this is the tale he told . . .'

Not quite the quality of Matthew Arnold's melancholy reflections – if I wanted to bring tears to my eyes I only had to recall *Ah, love, let us be true to one another*. But it brought me to the clear decision that I had to contact Lloyd, late though it was. The kindest thing on a Saturday night was to send a text asking him to get in touch with me next day.

One whistled back immediately. *Why not now? I'm about to phone you!*

He was as good as his word. 'Have you eaten? Because Jo and I have just picked up a takeaway and the kids have done a bunk so you might as well come over. Jo says to bring your toothbrush, then you won't have to worry

138

about drinking and driving.' He cut the call. I'd better do as I was told then. My last weekend before term, after all.

'We order from the main menu, not the takeaway one,' Jo was saying, as she put the last plastic container on their conservatory table. The storm had already passed, leaving a clear sky with more stars than you'd ever see in a city and a huge, heavy moon dominating the horizon. 'Better quality that way – more meat, less sauce, we find.'

'You could always have frozen it,' I said truthfully, but definitely, now I'd smelt the curries, without enthusiasm.

'The freezer's heaving: all the beans and courgettes and stuff from the garden. And Lloyd said you sounded as if you needed to let your hair down.'

Lloyd produced white wine, red wine, lager, water. And four plates. I looked at him sideways – was I being set up with someone?

Only with Will Bowman! Or was it to be a business supper, like top people have business breakfasts?

Recalling the on-off charming smile, I rather hoped it would be. I like a smile that stays on, not one that's only applied when someone wants something.

Meanwhile his smile was a mocking grin. 'I'd no idea you had such a palatial pad, Lloyd. Entryphone gates and all!'

Lloyd shrugged. 'We bought the place with Jo's redundancy money; the gates were already in place. All our friends know the code.'

'So now I'm not a friend.' Will turned his mouth down at the edges and gave his shoulders a huffy shrug.

'Me neither.' My mouth and shrug matched his.

'You've not had the code initiation rites, either of you. Raise your right hand and repeat after me . . .'

We did as we were told, Will hitching up a trouser leg as a bonus. I was beginning to like the guy.

'My birthday,' I said. 'Should remember that.'

At last we all settled down round a table in their conservatory – not convenient for conveying food, but lovely in the late-evening light.

Jo passed plates. 'You have stuff to tell us, Jane, and Will has stuff to tell you – at least I hope he's allowed to tell you,' she added, suddenly formal.

Will waited for the poppadum explosion to die down. 'Why don't you start, Jane? I'm still sorting out what I can and can't make public.' He tapped his forehead.

So he could listen and think, could he? Well done him. 'As you all know by now, I had a very bad virus at the start of the holiday. The evening I succumbed I was at a party hosted by Marcus Baker, out at St Luke's Bay. I was so groggy that I passed out – I don't remember much before or after that. But I've had a sudden flashback. I saw an unlit boat slipping into the harbour under cover of night. It meant nothing to me at all – though I think I observed to Marcus that someone was driving without lights. When we played Churcham, the night of the first storm, there was a barbecue at Justin Forbes' place. He has a lookout area, complete with telescope, me hearties! Exactly what he hoped he'd see once he'd lured me up there I can't think, but the incoming storm meant that the lights of France certainly weren't on display. In fact, the only time I saw anything seaward was when a really big lightning flash lit up the little harbour there. Why is it so much less popular than St Luke's? Anyway, once again I saw an unlit vessel – one towing another, by the look of it. But by then the lightning was too close for any of us to risk being out in the open, so we all ran like rabbits to the minibus.'

Lloyd looked up from the starter he'd picked out: chicken chaat. 'You've not mentioned this before.'

'Sorry: being a landlubber, I'm not too au fait with boats and the laws governing them. You wouldn't drive a car at night without lights, obviously, but boats? It's a long time since I read *Swallows and Amazons*.' I helped myself to some of the chicken chaat too. 'But today's events, plus the storm, of course, brought things back to the forefront of my mind. The kid that died – the kid you thought might be from Afghanistan . . . Lloyd, Will – do you think I saw people-smugglers? Actually at work?'

Jo shook her head. 'Surely the coastguards – sorry, Border Force! – would have picked them up. You can't just sail into someone's territorial waters and pull into the nearest port. Wouldn't a harbour master be involved?'

Will sighed. 'Lloyd and I think we're stretched: it sometimes seems to me as if the nation's protected by a couple of old guys in a rowing boat. It's not, of course: the Border Force is a highly professional group.' His face was as straight as he could make it.

Lloyd sat to attention and saluted ironically. 'Up for interview, are you? Come on, mate, you know they only got to someone the other week because a load of pensioners surrounded an inflatable and wouldn't let anyone leave. If the kids on board hadn't been half-dead with seasickness and cold, and the pensioners armed with blankets and hot coffee, it might not have had such a happy ending, of course.'

'If only you'd alerted us at the time, Jane,' Will said, apparently thinking that having no voice and passing out at one's host's feet was a pretty poor excuse for inaction. Then a storm severe enough to drive me from my temporary home. What a wimp I was.

'If only,' I agreed dryly. 'Actually,' I added less combatively, 'I should have thought of it when all those asylum seekers came over in the chilled lorry. Poor devils.'

'Oh, Jane, those kids . . .' Jo's eyes were flooding. 'I was wondering whether to volunteer to teach them – or any others. Not full-time: I wouldn't let you down, I promise.'

I squeezed her hand. 'Thanks. Actually, I'm wondering if the county will ask us to take any being fostered locally.'

'That'd knock a hole in your budget,' Will observed, 'with all the extra language teaching – they don't all come talking like Edward Said, you know.'

'I don't think I've ever met an officer who introduced Said into the conversation,' I observed, trying not to widen my eyes in a move that could be construed as flirtatious.

'We're not all yokels, are we, Lloyd? Though some are, God help us.'

'Didn't you start a PhD on Said and Orientalism, Will?' Jo put in.

He didn't look pleased. 'In another life. Anyway, Jane, our non-yokels tell me that there is evidence that your house had been used. It's a good job your predecessor left the water connected, isn't it? And the power?'

'What a daft thing to do!' Jo said.

'So we shall be telling them, when we run them to earth.'

I shook my head. 'Sadly the earth is where you may find them: when they moved out he was suffering from advanced dementia and she had inoperable cancer. So I imagine she had more important things to worry about than the utilities. I'll contact them all myself and pick up the bill, don't worry.'

Jo was collecting the starters' plates; I gathered up the plastic containers, all empty. I returned from the kitchen with large plates almost too hot to carry: I dealt them out like playing cards. Lloyd moved with alacrity, putting two restaurant-type night-light hotplates in the middle of the table.

'We're going to take a long time working through all the food: we might as well keep it warm,' he said, busy with extra-long matches.

I waited till Jo had returned with more than I could imagine us all finishing and we'd all served ourselves before I continued. 'How long have I been operating an unofficial dosshouse, Will?'

'Hard to tell. We'll know more when we've viewed Mrs Penkridge's CCTV footage – a good guess there, Jane. Someone will be on to it right now, with luck.'

'Mrs Penkridge,' I mused. 'Isn't it weird that, in these days of almost mandatory informality, we refer to her like that? She must have a first name – why don't we use it?'

'Because of her basilisk stare, I'd say. She reminds me of Hyacinth Bucket, in that old TV series,' he said aside to our hosts. 'You know, I actually believe her name is Joy: how about that for a misnomer?'

'Is there a Mr Penkridge?' Jo asked.

'Yes. He makes model boats and sails them in competitions all over the place – he's in Cornwall this weekend, apparently.'

143

I felt my face go stiff. 'A woman in her sixties or seventies on her own next to a place the police have been raiding. I know there are big fences up, courtesy of PACT, but even so – have you got officers guarding it?'

'A security firm. Latest policy – cheaper, apparently.' For the first time his voice lacked confidence. He looked curiously at me. 'Do you often manage to give orders without so much as opening your mouth? Excuse me a sec, Jo – I'd better make a call.'

'We'll save you some of that Peshwari naan,' I promised. Even though it wasn't, like the rest of the food, as good as that I used to get in the Midlands or Yorkshire.

He mimed measuring it to the nearest centimetre, and left us to it. It was as if we'd made a tacit agreement not to mention crime until he returned, so Jo – with much eye-rolling from Lloyd – brought me up to date with the kids' latest exploits. But I reckoned I knew a good youngster when I met one, and listened with an indulgent auntie's smile of disbelief.

Will's return stopped our laughter as swiftly as if he'd pressed a mute button. 'Mrs Penkridge is fine, apparently. Her nephew and niece and yappy dog are staying with her for company. In fact it was the yappy dog that alerted our noble security workers, not unreasonably sheltering from the downpour in their nice warm steamed-up van, to an intruder. Not before someone had managed to decorate the place though, I'm afraid, Jane.'

'What about that fencing – and the police tape?' Jo asked, sounding more outraged at the thought of Law and Order being summarily dismissed than even I could have managed.

'Both intact. But now with the addition of a home-made banner.' He waved his phone, but pocketed it.

Back in school-mode, I simply held out my hand and waited. I was rewarded with a reluctant shake of the head and a photo of the banner: MUDEREI, scrawled on a sheet with spray paint clearly running out.

'Daft not to make the banner first and then string it up,' I observed, as dispassionately as I could. I returned the phone, but a flick of his thumb and it was back in my hand. There was a similar banner staked in front of the holiday-let.

'You know what I think?' I asked rhetorically. 'I think it's more a case of someone wanting to show they know where I live than anyone making serious accusations.'

Infuriatingly my fork rattled against the plate as I tried to pick it up.

He nodded, clearly not dismissing the idea. 'But it could be someone who's heard the news and thinks you were responsible for the lad being on your property in the first place. Which brings me to something I really didn't want to mention at the supper table. Prints have been found on the padlock. We'll need to take yours to eliminate them.'

'You can do a gob-swab too,' I said, 'with my express permission. I can also provide you with a list of people who've come to the property with my permission. What I can't do,' I admitted, furious with myself, 'is bloody well stop crying.'

'Get this down your throat,' Lloyd said gruffly, filling my glass with a week's worth of alcoholic units. 'And—'

Whatever he meant to say next was drowned by what sounded like machine-gun fire. It was only hail, of course, but such hail: we could see stones the size of sugar lumps already carpeting the lawn. As one, we gathered the remaining food and carried it through to the kitchen. By now the hailstones were more like golf balls.

Somehow Will manoeuvred me to one side as our hosts dealt with the leftovers. 'There's actually something more positive I meant to tell you first, Jane. Mrs P's CCTV shows one vehicle, which makes several visits to your place. Looks like the sort of SUV that you believe ran you down. My colleagues will analyse what make it might be tomorrow, because, guess what—'

'It always arrived at night with the lights switched off before it got within range of her camera. As did tonight's?' At last I had a positive thought. 'Is it possible to determine the dates it came? To see if any of them have any correlation to the nights of the two post-match parties?'

He smiled and passed me my glass, raising his. 'Welcome back.'

'Welcome back?' I must have sunk too much already.

'To the Jane who uses her brain, not her emotions.'

CHAPTER THIRTEEN

Somehow the little mauve teddy bear had found his way into my overnight bag. He might not have been much of a conversationalist but was a very fine listener indeed. And he empathised: his ears pricked as much as mine when the kids came home, obviously trying to stifle whispered laughs. Did Jo worry, as I did, that the boy with Carys might not be Geraint, or the girl with Geraint not Carys? That, at least I told the little bear, was not my problem. He did not argue. Instead his tacit suggestion was that he'd be better off with a name, and it would be an infinitely better use of my time to consider possibilities, in alphabetical order. I'd got as far as H, I think, before I fell deeply asleep. He was still unnamed the following morning.

My hosts – the older two, since the younger ones wouldn't, I was assured, surface before noon – didn't argue when I slipped off early to go to church. Carol, the warden, was leading a clergyless service. She had promised to pray for the new school year, and it would have been churlish not to be present, even if I wasn't quite sure what the Almighty, no doubt busy with Middle Eastern chaos and drowning asylum seekers, would feel able to do. He'd not yet found us a new vicar, a matter of at least as much moment as local education. But I found it incredibly moving to be mentioned by name, not just as the head of two schools now, but also as one whose new home had been violated with violence. I wasn't too sure about the combination of the words, but if God could be all-forgiving, I could too.

A lot of people hugged me at the end of the hour. One kind woman even wiped away a smear of my mascara.

It was time for my prints and gob-swab to be taken.

Not surprisingly, when shopping in Canterbury called me, I responded to its summons. I'd been misled by the gorgeous summer into forgetting about autumn clothes. Normally I shopped online for my clothes, but a real trip to actual shops seemed an attractive way of passing my last afternoon of freedom, and taking my mind off a process I associated with criminal suspects.

The place was unexpectedly busy, and parking tricky, even in the fairly capacious Whitefriars Centre multi-storey. But park I did, and shop I did. I even had a very civilised lunch at Fenwick's – the last civilised midday meal I'd enjoy for a week. It was only as I left the Whitefriars Centre and hit the high street that I understood the source of the problem. A rowdy march, led by a familiar face, was heading my way, with a larger number of vociferous people of all types objecting to their presence – and why not? Anything led by

Gerry Paine and his English First chums was anathema to decent people, and I'd have loved to join those protesting. But the news media were swarming around. If I'd told the media what I thought and if they used the footage, I might be recognised by Simon's mates. A lot of ifs, I know, but all the same I supinely slipped away. Yet I was so angry with myself that I couldn't enjoy the luxury of shopping.

While I'd been idling, Paula and Anne had been working. Waiting for me in my in-box was a series of neat freehand, not technical, drawings of what they thought could be done with my house. Caffy had appended a couple of comments, condemning the dullness of one idea, but worrying that another far more imaginative one might not get planning permission. Given, they said, that the place was still a crime scene, they couldn't even walk round it with me to explain their vision, but it would be really helpful to have my immediate thoughts. I suspected that when Paula wrote *immediate* she meant *immediate*, so I almost flung my shopping on to hangers and into drawers and sat with a hastily made mug of tea to obey her instructions.

Wisely, while they'd not touched the frontage at all, they'd risked increasing the footprint to the rear, where even Mrs Penkridge wouldn't see any extensions, with the addition of a garden room. They'd reduced the number of bedrooms by converting the box room to a delectable en suite bathroom. The other room would have to use a bathroom I was sure they'd update. They would floor the loft properly, and insert Velux windows. Rather than leaving it as a dumping area for junk, they would make sure there were plenty of storage units, some of which

149

could be pulled down for seating. In other words, the loft could double as a secure room, with an emergency ladder as part of the extensive kit.

It would be easy but not, I thought, advisable to gush. The women would prefer a measured, considered response. Hang the last minute prep for the following day: I'd already made a sheaf of preparatory notes and had enough teaching under my belt to wing it, surely? A niggling voice warned me that I'd never been required to be in two places at once before. I sent my comments with the heading, *First Thoughts*, promising to send any further response as soon as I could. And then I printed out my admin notes and took them to bed with me. Nosey and Lavender – yes, he suddenly declared he had a name – were not impressed. Beds were for sleeping, they declared. The best thing was to put them down – very well, with a pencil beside them for those three a.m. moments – and set the alarm for fifteen minutes earlier.

I didn't need any alarm. I was awake at five, at my Wrayford desk by six. Tom and my Wrayford team, all arriving well before eight, assured me that they could deal with any hitches, and despatched me to Wray Episcopi.

Here everything seemed to be running smoothly. All the staff there were early too, running their private checks – I'd always had my own rituals so didn't disturb any of them. Donna the secretary, who had been conspicuous by her absence during the holiday (in fairness she was paid not very much by the hour), was looking as caring and efficient as Melanie Pugh, my mainstay at Wrayford, though Melanie would never have countenanced that dress and those sandals.

And at last the high point of my year, the arrival of children for the new school year. Everything was geared to this, all our nerves stretched for it. And yet, when the parents and children started to arrive, to an impartial observer it would all have seemed so ordinary.

There was Mrs Popescu: an unnaturally clean Georgy, in a home-made shirt the same gingham as the girls' summer dresses, was bouncing up and down beside her. The shirt should have been plain blue, but I wasn't going to argue. The other son was hitched on her hip. No tears from Georgy, who, having waved his mother a confident goodbye, marched straight up to a bunch of other children playing with a ball and joined in. Ms Carnaby had driven Robbie in my least favourite type of vehicle, the sort that had apparently run me off the road all those weeks ago. Hers was an immaculate silver, however. Posh car notwithstanding, she – but not Robbie – was in melodramatic floods of tears. A silent young woman, whom I presumed to be the potty-training nanny, hugged the little boy and, dropping a kiss on top of his head, pushed him gently towards Georgy's group. He hesitated, and ran back to the nanny. Karenza saw what was going on, and summoned all her new charges round her, like a tall mother hen. Soon there were no tears; not that many smiles, because the whole business of your first day in any school, even a tiny one, is pretty daunting, but an air of purpose and confidence.

It was a perfect start to the school year.

Except for the extra pupil.

Karenza knocked on my office door at the start of the lunch break. 'Did you enrol a new child this morning?' she asked doubtfully.

'If I had I'd have told you,' I said. 'Tell me more.'

'He turned up after break,' she said, collapsing on to a chair. 'He was holding Georgy's hand. I asked Georgy who he was. "My friend," he said. But he didn't actually know anything about him. Not even his name, which he himself can't or won't give. They'd been playing football together, that's all, according to Beth, who was on duty outside.'

'How odd, turning up halfway through the morning. Did Beth see anyone bring him?'

She shook her head. 'She can't say either way. You can't blame her – you know what it's like until the kids get used to playing nicely together.'

'I'm not blaming anyone. Playground on day one is like one of the inner circles of hell, especially with litigation on the cards if anyone gets hurt. I'd have been out there myself to help except for Sophia's nosebleed.'

'She's not still getting them! I thought her mother said—'

I shook my head. 'This was self-inflicted, I'm almost sure. Anyway, this here anonymous friend of Georgy's. Sadly we can't just let kids turn up and join us, much as we'd like to. What do you think we should do?'

She grimaced. 'That sounds like the sort of question you get at interview.'

'Not at mine, thank goodness. You're an experienced teacher, and we're part of a team. But I get to take responsibility, blame, whatever, for anything we decide – that's my role.'

'Plus mastering the art of being in two places at once. OK, Jane: unless someone's come to claim him – and several of the real tinies are only doing half-days this week, as we agreed – I'd like to keep him for the rest of the day and make sure he gets fed. Before that we sluice him down and give him some clothes from the emergency basket – he really, really pongs, to be quite frank. And at the end of the day we tackle his mother or whoever, and give them a letter outlining the application procedure.'

'Perfect in every way,' I said. But it was clear from her face that it wasn't.

'Except for one thing. I don't think he speaks any English at all. At a guess I'd say he came from the Middle East – but the holiday Arabic I learnt when I worked on a cruise ship didn't elicit very much.'

'Poor little bugger,' I said sincerely, but rather forgetting the vocabulary appropriate to the job. 'OK. Where is he now? In the playground, properly supervised? Well, we'll wash him, so long as he doesn't object too much, and sort out some clothes. Then we'll feed him. It may seem cruel, Karenza, but we'll call it motivation.'

'Or simple bribery,' she said, with a twinkle.

'Quite. Meanwhile I'll organise that letter. And we must make sure you have some uninterrupted time to grab your own lunch.'

Organise a letter I did, but there was no one to give it to, either then or at the end of the day. There were many cheerful reunions of children separated from their mothers, and somehow in the bustle Georgy's new friend disappeared. Not with Georgy or his mother. Mrs Popescu was adamant that she knew no little boy like that – and subjected her son to a torrent of rapid questions. His shrugs didn't need translating.

'Now what?' Karenza asked at the end of the staff's working day. She looked as tired as all her colleagues did:

153

it doesn't matter how well you prepare, the first day always comes as a shock to the system.

'We go home and shower and use anti-nit shampoo – right? Actually, we can't do any more. The education people have promised to look into it. But they're short-staffed and frantic—'

'And we aren't!'

'But I have extracted a promise that if he turns up tomorrow they'll send someone out, probably with someone from Social Services. And a translator.'

'What if he doesn't come back?' Even as she scratched behind her ear, there was a catch in her voice.

'It'd make our job a lot easier, and our budget happier. But for all that, I hope he does. Oh, the poor little mite. What if he's been separated from his parents? You know some parents are so desperate to get their kids a better, safer life they entrust them to people smugglers and may never see them again. Dear God, can you imagine doing that?'

CHAPTER FOURTEEN

As I'd promised I called into Wrayford School on my way home, though I suggested holding the short briefing in the open air, lest what I hoped was merely psychosomatic itching proved to have real causes. Tom was curiously self-effacing, making sure all the other teachers had their say – very short, mercifully – before adding his own brief appraisal. He lagged behind the others on the way to the car park so we could talk privately, I thought. But apparently all he wanted to do was confirm that everything had gone as well as could be hoped.

'No extra pupils?' I asked, trying to sound upbeat, but failing. Quietly, I explained what had happened down the road.

He shook his head emphatically. Then he frowned. 'But someone was telling a tale about being frightened by goblin children on their way here. By the layby at the entrance to Glebe Wood. I just put it down to too much holiday reading. I wonder . . .'

'So do I. Where did they say they'd seen these "goblins"?'

'I'll try and find out tomorrow. But what do I do if they can tell me? Real children, Jane?' It sounded like a genuine question, not a rhetorical one. 'Leave food for them? Call the police? Or should it be the Border Force? I know it's not an adventure story, with kids helping out other kids, all *Swallows and Amazons* or whatever, but I wish it was. I'd hate to see kids, any kids, thrown kicking and screaming into a detention centre.'

'I don't think they do that with children. And there might be protests if they tried – think how well we all reacted when those destitute kids were found at the motorway services.'

'And have we heard what's happened to them since? Of course not. OK, I know Social Services are involved. I know this county's overwhelmed – overwhelmed enough to ask the government to spread the load. Load! What sort of term is that?' He stopped abruptly and backed away, as if fending me off. 'Jane, did you know you were scratching your head like nobody's business?'

Our anonymous little boy was back next morning, merging with the Breakfast Club kids this time. Actually it was a breakfast lady, a middle-aged woman called Pam, who got his name out of him. A name, anyway – Zunaid. Or Junaid? Hard to tell. He liked his cereal, and drank the milk remaining in the bowl, she said. And did the same with his second bowl, she added with satisfaction. It was clearly her ambition to get him back to a healthy size.

Karenza was devastated not to have managed that

degree of communication with him. 'Georgy or one of the other kids must have got through to him yesterday,' she said, clutching her coffee mug during our brief pre-school staff meeting. 'Or why else should he turn up so early?'

'Perhaps he just didn't want to risk talking to an authority figure,' Donna suggested. 'Do you think that when any of us start asking questions we should see if Pam could hold his hand – literally or metaphorically?'

'Excellent idea. I'll ask her. Meanwhile, it's time for registration. Do you think Zunaid would like to ring the bell? I bet Georgy would help him.'

I was braced for the arrival of officialdom but got Lady Preston instead. Donna kept her in the minuscule reception area till I arrived.

'My pictures.'

'Good morning, Lady Preston. How are you?'

Her glance at Donna dismissed her from our company.

My glance insisted she stay. 'How can I help?' I looked at my watch ostentatiously – some might say insolently. 'I have to take assembly in three minutes.'

'The pictures, of course.'

'I believe you've put the matter in the hands of the police. In view of that, I'm not sure we're allowed to talk about them.'

'Haven't they searched the place yet?'

'Not while I've been on the premises. But I'd have thought you should be asking them, not me.'

'I've a good mind to search the place myself!'

'Not with the pupils present. They'd find it very disruptive and disturbing. And you have my word that despite emptying and cleaning every single cupboard in every single room I have found nothing. As a matter of interest, when were the pictures hung in the school? Would there be anyone around from that period who might be able to help?'

'Bloody hell, you're expecting someone to recall something from seventy years ago? To be alive even? You're out of your mind.'

The mind in question was busy revising a lot of preconceptions. Only seventy years? I'd somehow assumed we were talking about heavy Victorian oils, donated by a paunchy bewhiskered old man. Not that it made any difference, of course, when I had never so much as glimpsed a frame.

Absent-mindedly I was scratching my head. She shot backwards. 'I saw something jump in your hair!'

'Probably a head louse or something. The new term's intake.'

'They said you had some illegal migrants' children here. All filthy, no doubt.'

I found myself clenching my hands to keep outwardly cool at least. What on earth could possess her to say that? 'That's a very unpleasant allegation, Lady Preston, and one I'd prefer you didn't repeat here or anywhere else. As it happens, nits love recently shampooed hair.' I scratched again. Heavens, I didn't want her to meet Georgy or Zunaid, with or without Pam, or any of the team who would be bringing the might of the law on to the poor child's head. 'Now since, as I told you, I have to take assembly, I can't talk here with you any longer. I assure you I will co-operate fully with the police when they arrive.' I held open the front door; she skirted it and me as though I was carrying the plague. Some evil impulse made me scratch once again as she passed.

'There's still no sign at all of the cavalry,' I told Karenza as we wandered into the staffroom for our packed lunches.

'Good – because Pam's busy at the servery. Jane, Zunaid's such a bright kid. Georgy's lovely because he's trying to teach Zunaid, but actually Zunaid picks things up so quickly he hardly needs help. I think he's starting to trust me too.' She glowed, as teachers can when their pupils succeed. 'I thought of getting him to draw some pictures. You know, of where he comes from and of his mummy and daddy.'

I was ready to tell her what a great idea it was. Then I thought of the terrifying power of unburied memories: what if we unleashed some genie that needed the control of professional therapists to pop back into its bottle?

She read my face. 'Problems?' she prompted.

'It depends on whose theory you prefer. One of my therapists was all for digging up memories, so I could deal with them; another, saying that the past was the past, thought it was best to plan the future. Let's see what Zunaid volunteers. If he's happy being in class and eating and playing football, I'd say we let him get on with them till the social worker teams get involved.'

I'd barely eaten my first forkful of couscous salad when there was a tap at the staffroom door. Pam.

'We've got another, Jane. Another little boy. Seems he's a friend of Zunaid's. Bilal. In fact, Zunaid's already shared his lunch with him and has dragged him off to the toilets and started to strip him off.' She gave an affectionate laugh. 'Zunaid more or less told me to tell you – kept pointing at the door and saying, "Tall lady – clean pants." Or it could have been, "Tell lady."'

'Not such a bad thing to get a reputation for,' I grinned. 'I'll go and find some clothes and see what between the three of you I can find out.'

But I was too late. Zunaid was on his own in the boys' loo. Taking my hand, he pointed at the door and, clearly disapproving, mimed running. He also held his nose and pulled a face.

'He took some food but wouldn't wash?' I said slowly, miming as I went.

'My food. No wash.' As if to make the point he washed his hands as thoroughly as if he was about to perform surgery. Had he seen someone do that somewhere?

'Good boy. Now, Pam has some more food. Would you like some more food?'

'More food. Pam. Please. Thank you.' He tucked his hand in hers and led her out.

I didn't usually get sentimental about children, having had every opportunity to grow a carapace of cynical disbelief, but I nearly wept as the unlikely duo toddled purposefully away.

I told myself all afternoon that I was too busy to do anything about our unauthorised pupils, but when I'd waved the last child and teacher goodbye, I couldn't use that excuse any longer. I had to tell our governors. Hazel Roberts was interested, but not overanxious: after all, I'd notified the authorities and was providing a place of safety. A call to Tom back in Wrayford established that he'd had no unexpected enrolments. However, some of the children who'd complained about Glebe Wood goblins had admitted that they were probably real children, just different, whatever that might mean.

'I'm afraid we're not very multicultural down here, are we?' he added. 'In a city probably no one would turn a hair if a bunch of people of Mediterranean appearance turned up. But a derogatory term for travellers was the best description I could get.'

'Taking their tone from English First, I suppose.'

'Precisely. I'd love to put into practice what I talked about yesterday – leaving food out for the kids. But that's not the solution long term, is it?'

'No. We were due a visit from the education department today, but no one came. So the only brains we can pick are each other's, Tom. My advice, for what it's worth, is to involve the police. If there are children hiding in the woods, someone needs to find them and feed them and give them shelter and clothes. And discuss the socio-political implications afterwards.'

Tom was silent. Then he said flatly, 'You're the boss. So it's your bloody call.' His phone went silent.

Ouch. It had taken me long enough to build bridges with him and I seemed to have destroyed them with one decision. Which I'd better implement before I changed my mind.

Lloyd's phone was switched to voicemail. No, I didn't want to leave a garbled message, did I?

Next option, then.

Will sounded surprised to hear my voice, and was inclined to resume his Saturday night informality. But he was dead serious when I told him what I feared – and, to do him credit, agreed with me that kindness was the best approach at this stage from everyone involved.

'So no blues and twos?' I prompted.

'Not if I have anything to do with it,' he promised. 'Not if there really are only kids. I suppose the kids didn't see any adults lurking nearby?'

'If they did they didn't tell Tom – and I think they probably would have done, since we din into them every day the importance of reporting suspicious strangers. So I'm afraid – Will, I'm very much afraid that they're on their own, poor little mites.'

'You know this is beyond my responsibility, Jane.'

'Absolutely.' I added something true if unwise in the circumstances. 'But I reckon good people usually know other good people.'

He snorted. 'Flattery will get you everywhere. Actually, my DI's just come into the office: Elaine Carberry. I'll pass you over to her.'

I explained as succinctly but as urgently as I could,

'If it's migrants, it's definitely my bag, Ms Cowan,' she said. 'I'll get on to it now.' She must have put her hand over the phone. I could hear her muffled voice giving brisk orders. 'Camping in the open's OK when it's fine, but the forecast's not great, Jane. I'll meet you there in an hour. OK? Here's Will again.'

'You know they're talking about the first Atlantic storm heading our way,' he said.

'A storm? They could have forecast a plague of frogs for all I know: it's been all systems go and a bit more here,' I explained.

'Sounds as if you could do with getting it off your chest. Go and do your stuff with Elaine. Then, tell you what, let's make it a nice informal debriefing and eat at the same time. I'll collect you from yours about eight.'

He'd ended the call before I could refuse. Not, perhaps, that I would have done.

Meanwhile, I'd better go and meet this DI Carberry and pray she was as compassionate as she was efficient.

When I turned up churning with anxiety and guilt at the lay-by Tom had indicated, he wasn't there. Was I surprised? A little disappointed. But he had a lot of family calls on his time, so perhaps that was the reason, not a professional strop. But I wasn't there alone. A whole gang of people hung around, all trying to look casual, as if gathering round a layby on a secondary road was part of their usual day. I was greeted – by name – by a middle-aged woman who introduced herself as DI Elaine Carberry, Will's boss.

'I'm in charge of your Afghan body, as you may know,' she said, 'but I'm betting there's not too much to suggest you're responsible, unsafe building apart – and God knows enough buildings were proved unsafe that night. So let's get started with this, shall we?'

She might have to work hard to meet the police standards for physical fitness, but there was a kind honesty about her homely face that made me warm to her. To my amazement I seemed to be part of the senior team, which included a couple of the elusive social workers the education officials had promised to bring to Wray Episcopi and several police officers. There was also a hijab-wearing woman of most extraordinary beauty who was introduced as Yasin, our interpreter. Headscarf apart, she was dressed in jeans and a long-sleeved loose top not unlike my own workwear after my hedgerow incident.

Soon she was equipped with a hand-held loudhailer, the sort I associated with idealistic demos in my youth. 'So I go round the woods telling the kids I've got food? So where is it?' Her accent was pure Bradford. 'No food, no deal. I won't lie to them.'

A woman after my own heart.

It seemed someone was collecting a load of sandwiches from the nearest supermarket. 'Vegetarian, before you ask,' Elaine said, earning instant brownie points. 'We wouldn't risk any meat in case it wasn't halal. Milk. Biscuits. Water. I wouldn't ask you to lie. When they've eaten we'll invite them into the minivans. Over there, Jane, where no one can see them. I don't want the kids to take one look and bolt. OK, Yasin – off you go.'

'I've seen kids like that a thousand times on TV,' I said, my hands still shaking, though I tried to keep my voice under control. I tugged my bathrobe more closely about me. 'Thin – emaciated really. Heads crawling with lice. Dirty. Not just grubby because they'd been playing outdoors. Filthy. Some of them ill. Some dressed in the remains of some parent's idea of best clothes. Some with little bundles. Some with nothing. Some even with something tattooed on their wrists. Turns out it was their parents' phone number or whatever. But here? In the Garden of England? No, I don't think I want to eat, thanks, Will.'

'Tough. I've got a table booked at my local. And so we can both drink I'll organise a cab back for you when we've fed. OK?' He looked at his watch. 'Time to go. Or do you want to dry your hair first?'

Subtext: dry your hair and get some clothes on. I'd been having a prolonged attack on my nits and had been almost hypnotised by the force of the shower into losing track of time. Obediently, I got to my feet, keeping my bathrobe decently together.

'Does it make it better or worse that that kid who's joined your school – Zunaid? – wasn't in the woods?'

'I don't know. I want him safe and sound, with a roof and clothes and food. But I want to keep him in our manageable little school, where he's already made a friend. And where he tried to befriend a child called Bilal I never even got to see. I'm sorry! I'll go and dry my hair.' And my tears. 'I'm sorry!'

And there I was, being wrapped up in his arms and comforted. That was all. But with a great punch in the stomach I realised how much I was missing physical affection. OK. Put it another way, how much I wanted sex and, even more, post-coital intimacy. With Will? He'd have to rebuff me, whatever his instinct, because in theory I might be a suspect in a case he was investigating. If he didn't, it would destroy him in my estimation. Heads I lose, tails I certainly don't win. Breathing out firmly, I disengaged myself and retreated to the bathroom.

Will lived in a village to the south, much nearer the coast than Wrayford, but not close enough to the sea to have the fabulous views offered by St Luke's Bay or Churcham. The pub he called his local was quiet, but heaved, he said, at weekends. The food would never win awards, but he'd never had a bad meal, whatever time he turned up.

So far, so good.

Until I excused myself to go to the loo. Two of us found ourselves using the same outer door, me pushing, the other woman pulling. Usually there'd be one of those silly after-you-no-after-you moments. But this time, after a second's delay, the other woman thrust past me, giving me a look of such intense loathing that I almost staggered. Who? Why? What had I ever done to her to be treated like that? So instead of going into a cubicle, I turned and followed her. Not to confront her. Just to see if I could place her, because by now I realised I knew her from somewhere. I was too late to see her face again, but did see something else from the front door: a huge SUV, blue, with tinted rear windows, driving stupidly fast out of the car park.

'Problem?' Will asked, as I stared after her. He got up and closed the door for me as I returned to our table.

I managed a bleak laugh. 'Not now. But I have this crazy notion that it was the woman I just met who—'

'The one who stormed out then?'

'That one. I've an idea she might have been the person with the SUV that ran me off the road at the start of the holidays.'

CHAPTER FIFTEEN

Goodness knows why I said such a stupid thing. Regretting it, I sat down and took a long sip of my drink – the local beer that Will had recommended, as opposed to the wine which he couldn't. 'Forget it. My mind's off kilter.' I gave a rueful smile. 'And now I really have to go and use that loo. Sorry.'

I stared at my hands as I washed them as thoroughly as Zunaid had washed his. Not that I was seeing them. I was seeing the woman's face. I examined it feature by feature, trying to imagine it without the undiluted loathing. Yes, I'd certainly seen it before. I prided myself on never forgetting a face, even when a child I once taught reappeared before me years later wearing adult plumage. But the answer wouldn't come, and Will was waiting.

Not just waiting, but with information that suggested that he'd taken what I'd just said at face value – even if the information was negative.

'Tess – that's the landlady – doesn't have CCTV, I'm afraid. But she says she's seen the woman here a couple of times before and if she remembers anything about her she'll tell me.'

'Let's forget it,' I said. 'Sorry: thank you for asking her but let's forget it.'

'I wish I could. But if she drives an SUV, then there's a possible connection with an SUV that makes regular visits to your house with its lights off.'

My eyebrows shot up. 'Or not. Tenuous to the point of non-existent. Sorry. That was uncalled for. There is one odd thing, though. Now, remember my past. You know I have every reason to have a sort of selective amnesia.'

'It's best to forget some of the stuff Simon did: that's the theory?'

I couldn't blank out, of course, the way he knew about that: through conversations with Pat. 'Yes,' I said, perhaps inadequately. 'Any road up, for all the hoo-ha just now, there was a serious bit of remembering going on.' I explained. I managed a grin as I added, 'Surely I'd remember anyone I'd annoyed as seriously as that?'

'*Any road up*,' he repeated. 'Pure Black Country.'

'Oh, ah,' I agreed.

'Absolutely. You've got the idioms: can you do the accent too?'

''Course I can, me luvva.' We exchanged a grin. But soon I was serious. 'Just for the record, Will, I'd much rather not talk about Pat. He's back where he's supposed to be because I'm fine these days,' I said firmly, overriding something he tried to say with a question: 'Tell me, how are my fingerprints shaping up?'

'No match except where there's supposed to be a match. DNA? – unless you go round spitting on bolts, that seems a waste of money.'

'I can promise you I only ever spit on bolts if I've already dabbed my fingers all over them first.'

'You did dab your fingers on something, though, earlier. It really intrigued me. When we were leaving your place, you seemed to pat your door frame.'

My laugh was genuine. 'Just touching wood, Will. OK, touching a strip of Sellotape on top of the wood – from the door to the door frame. If it's torn when I get back I can see that someone's got inside. I thought I'd grown out of the habit, but I just did tonight – something subliminal.'

'Jesus. That's what living with an abusive partner does to you, is it? Will you ever feel safe?' Both the shock and the concern sounded genuine.

'My new place is having a safe room, just to make sure,' I admitted.

He shook his head gravely.

Just as the food arrived, my phone whistled to announce a load of texts. If it was a choice between what Will assured me would be a perfect steak and the texts, I'd put manners first and the phone second. I'm not a big meat-eater, but I have to admit that he was right.

By the time I'd finished, the whistling could have been coming from an aviary. With an apologetic glance at Will, I checked quickly. Tom apologising; Elaine thanking me for my part in the rounding-up exercise; one of the social workers involved, assuring me that the kids were having medical checks and would be settled as quickly as possible: I shared that one with Will. Three – no, a fourth was arriving – from Ed van Boolen? Because of the language involved, I didn't share them. He wanted to start work on my new garden but couldn't get adjective clearance from the adjective police. And he needed an umpire for Saturday. Was I still OK for the ODI at the end of the month because he might be able to free himself up after all? Lastly, it was ages since we'd met for a drink. No need to share that, either.

Pam: could she offer Zunaid a home?

The dentist reminding me of an appointment at five tomorrow night.

Justin, inviting me for a drink at his place. That surprised me, though not very much: he'd seemed to be heading that way on Saturday. But just now I didn't do drinks at anyone's place, not on my own.

Paula: when could she have further access to the house?

My library books were due back.

Was I happy with my phone network?

And, finally, to my genuine amazement, one from Brian Dawes, who didn't usually favour such terse means of communication as texts: he was suggesting dinner, to catch up after his prolonged absence.

Why, when I had no time to spend on anything, was I suddenly flavour of the month?

And why did I want to dump it all on Will, who despite what he'd said earlier had confined himself to half a pint and was now on mineral water? If you want to tell someone stuff you shouldn't, it's best to ask them about stuff they don't want you to know. And though Will had come, one way or another, to know a lot about me, I knew virtually nothing about him.

'Sorry,' I said belatedly, conscientiously switching off the phone without attempting any replies. 'A couple more of them actually involve you, as it happens: my landscape gardener wants to start preliminary work and Paula needs access to the house again.' I spread my hands. 'I've waited long enough for something to happen, so don't think I'm going to nag you to do what they want.' I took a deep breath and a risk. 'But I will tell you one thing. Someone I was talking to in the bar on Saturday reckons that pressure has been exerted on all the builders I approached not to work for me. He didn't know who and he didn't know why. I'd rather not tell you who gave me the information. Thank God for PACT. And now, Will, let's have a normal conversation? As if we'd just met?'

He looked totally bemused. 'Don't you want me to tell you when we're likely to have finished at the crime scene? Because I'd have thought your gardener and builder could start this time next week. The builder could certainly have another nose round the house any time she wants, subject to obvious precautions.'

'Thank you. That's great news.'

The landlady arrived with the dessert menu. 'Not even coffee?' she asked as we shook our heads and declared we couldn't manage another morsel.

I flicked a glance at my watch. 'I daren't, thanks, not at this time of night. But if you want to, Will . . . ?'

He shook his head, asking for the bill. 'I'll settle up – you can pay next time. When we have that normal conversation.'

Which seemed quite a big assumption, but for some reason I didn't argue.

The forecasters were right: it was blowing up a gale, the

rain coming in squalls, and small branches bowling across the car park.

'In this weather,' I said, 'I always think of that hymn asking for help for all those in peril on the sea.'

'Right. The Royal Navy hymn. My father was a captain,' he said. 'My mother was an old-fashioned services wife, oozing loyalty and devotion.'

It sounded from his voice as if he was doubtful that his father deserved either, but I could scarcely ask directly about that.

'How did he cope with your ambitions to study Edward Said? Whom, incidentally, I've never read,' I added, as his face showed quite clearly that that was too personal a question.

He managed a grin. 'Shame on you. I can offer you two whole box-files of the preliminary notes for my PhD. Do you have a finished thesis I can read?'

'Heavens, no! I enjoyed uni, but I'm not an academic. The language they have to use. All the passive voices. And the footnotes, of course. Give me cats on mats any day . . . So what takes a genuine footnoting scholar into the police?'

'Apart from failing to be a genuine footnoting scholar? Probably the same motivations that took you into teaching. A desire to make other people's lives better and the temptation of a halfway decent salary with a modicum of job security. And Kent Police called. Except we're so closely linked to Essex, in the interests of efficiency, of course—'

'Otherwise known as saving money—'

He gave an appreciative snort of laughter before continuing, 'that we're pretty well merged. Essex and Kent Police. Essex only being separated from Kent by a great dollop of water known as the Thames estuary. Much of what I feel now is something else you'll share, I'm sure: a huge frustration with the country's leaders who seem hell-bent on destroying vital services. Still, it could have been worse, Jane: we could both have been prison officers . . .' He put the car into gear and pulled out of the car park.

The route he chose took us very close to Harry and Doreen's bungalow. On impulse I told him – perhaps because somewhere deep down I really didn't want to acknowledge I was enjoying his company and wouldn't mind prolonging the journey back to my piece of sticky tape.

'The weird couple who helped you and then beat it? OK. Shall we go and have a look?'

It might not have been such a good idea after all. Parts of the lane were already flooded. At one corner I had to nip out and clear a couple of branches. But he pressed on.

'There!' I pointed. The moon briefly broke through the cloud, allowing us a glimpse, no more.

He stopped to look. 'Shame! No bats! No swooping owls!' he lamented in a ghoulish voice. 'A Gothic night like this, that bungalow ought to be a turreted house – castle, even,' he declared.

'What are you doing?' It was obvious, actually: he was pulling on to their drive.

'Just thought I'd take a look.'

I never thought I'd get to say it. 'What if you're messing up a crime scene?'

He threw his head back and roared with laughter, but reversed to a nearby field gateway.

He'd unclipped his seat belt and was checking his door mirror, obviously about to do his inspection on foot, when he suddenly lunged my way and enveloped me in an embrace. 'Someone's coming,' he muttered. 'Act passionate.'

Only act? Hmm. What the hell were my hormones doing?

'And keep your eyes open.'

I did. 'He's cut his lights and driven straight on,' I whispered.

He pushed himself upright, and then turned, cupping my chin and dotting a kiss full on my lips. 'Back to work I'm afraid,' he said, almost before I could respond, pulling out his phone. As he dabbed at the keypad, he pulled his seat belt back on. His conversation was short and to the point. We were after a suspicious vehicle and backup was required.

'Rough drive ahead, I'm afraid. And can you be i/c communications?'

A rough drive it was, especially since he didn't want to use his headlights and he was driving rather faster than conditions ought to have permitted. It might have been exciting, but I had other things on my mind. A lot.

No time for quiet reflection. Time to answer Will's phone. And to put it on conference.

I didn't understand all the lingo but I did get one thing all too clearly as we bucketed along, Doreen and Harry's lane having been built more for trundling bikes than for speeding cars: we had lost the target vehicle. Will sprayed some foul language around, surpassed by a woman colleague of his who was homing in on the area.

At last he put his headlights on and proceeded in a

northerly direction with considerably more decorum.

'Gone, gone – and never called me mother,' he said mournfully.

'It's "Dead, dead", isn't it?'

'Pedant.'

As we drove past my house, looking terribly dejected behind its fencing and its fluttering police tape, he pulled over. 'Caffy Tyler – the PACT woman – says she can't ever imagine my living here,' I said casually.

'Can you?' he asked sharply.

'I don't want yet another holiday rental because someone's feeling sorry for me – and moreover thinks that offering me a chic roof will earn him goodwill in the village.'

'Ah, our friend Brian Dawes. Get on with him all right, do you?'

I trotted out my usual spiel. 'He's an excellent, conscientious hands-on governor. I couldn't have managed without him during the worst of last year.'

'You can take that tongue out of your cheek. Pompous prick, I've heard him called.'

'You can't possibly expect me to agree. Seriously, he was a total pain at the start of my tenure, but he did show a better side. Funnily enough, one of the texts I got was from him, asking me out to dinner.'

'Will you go?'

'Only if he wants to talk shop. I'm wary of making friends with governors, as I'm sure you are of making friends with senior officers. But I wouldn't want to make an enemy of one: they can fire as well as hire, you know.'

He set us in motion again. It was only a couple of hundred yards to the holiday cottage. It seemed he was going to see me in, or at least check the adhesive tape. 'And security at the rear?' he asked curtly.

'Anyone wanting to get into the garden would have to scale the wall. And the patio doors have a triple-lock system.'

'All the same.'

I was to let him in. And then what?

Going ahead of me he ran lightly upstairs. He returned more slowly. 'No one under the beds. Or in them.'

'Two teddy bears apart,' I corrected him. Foolish. I was trying to avoid comments like that. Trying to avoid eye contact.

'Work day for both of us tomorrow,' he said, stating the obvious but including, I suspected, a subtext. 'I shall be glad when this case is over, Jane. You know as well as I do, I should imagine, about officers and victims of crime.'

'Or even officers and criminals.' I added brightly. 'You haven't tested that DNA yet.'

We laughed but the tension was palpable.

He had his hand on the front door. 'See you around – right?'

'See you around.'

What if he turned back and kissed me?

What if I'd called him back and kissed him?

CHAPTER SIXTEEN

Because I'd got to be pretty good with make-up, covering bruises and disguising puffiness, it was possible that my colleagues wouldn't notice that I was pale, with dark circles under my eyes. If anyone did, and asked, then I could tell them that it was the sight of all those poor children – there must have been fifteen – summoned from the woods as if by the Pied Piper. Pam had obviously had a bad night too, her eyes reddened by even the thought of not being able to foster Zunaid, she admitted, stifling a sob. Wherever he'd spent the night, he was back with her this morning, helping clear the tables after Breakfast Club. And the education department and social services were coming today: their email was quite definite, though they couldn't commit to a time yet. I emailed back: they must avoid lunchtime because then I'd be in Wrayford, maintaining a presence at my other school, and I considered it essential that I was in Wray Episcopi when they came.

One thing a school is judged by, rightly or wrongly, is its attendance rates, so it's a matter of great concern when two children from the same family go missing without any notification from their family. At this stage of the term, too. Donna popped her head round my office door to tell me she'd adopted the standard procedure: she'd texted, left a phone message for and emailed the parents, with no response.

'The thing is,' she added, 'it's not just any pupils. It's Joe and Nicky Paine – Gerry Paine's children. PTA noticeboard Gerry.'

'And English First march Gerry. Hmm. I don't like this, Donna. I don't know why. Just something twitching in my thumbs.' For her sake, I lowered my shoulders and straightened my back. 'But you've done all you should – couldn't have done more. Thank you.'

'Actually, there is one thing. Mrs Hale always said that if there was any doubt at all about the children's safety, we should notify the police.'

'And is there? Any doubt?'

'He's a big man, Mr Paine. Very strict.' What was she implying? But that was a big conversation for another day. 'So it is odd they're not here.'

'Who usually brings them?'

'They walk. It's only three hundred yards, four maybe. They don't have to cross any roads.'

'OK. Good parenting on that at least, I'd say. Tell you what, Donna, go through the whole absentee procedure again – a couple of times, say – and I'll have a word with their class teachers. Then we can make up our minds.'

But our minds were about to be made up for us.

I heard the noise before, looking out of Donna's window, I saw the cause. It didn't quite constitute an uproar, but was horrible enough: nine or ten large, loud beer-gutted men with home-made placards with deeply offensive messages were occupying the pavement right by the playground and yelling racist slogans at the top of their voices. The children in front-facing classrooms couldn't help but hear.

She picked up the phone and was already dialling. 'You can't reason with that type, Jane: I'm calling the police. To report a hate crime.'

Was it officially a hate crime? Whether it was or not, I wouldn't quibble. 'Excellent. Tell them to polish up their best smiles – because they're going to be on TV. Look, there's the first media van arriving! Paine must have notified them himself. And call Hazel Roberts and Colin Ames: ask them to tell the rest of the governors.'

Before I did anything else I must warn the class teachers to keep the children in at break: they'd have a wet-day play in the hall. Between them they must make up some exciting game involving darkness, because I was going to draw the blackout curtains. I didn't want any telephoto shots of the children.

But I did want some of my own – of the men. I snapped away through the window.

Only then did I go out and confront them.

'We're not on your land: you can't make us do anything,' Gerry Paine declared before I even opened my mouth.

'As the head teacher, Mr Paine, I'm asking you to tell your friends to put down all your banners, and I'm inviting

179

you to come into my office to explain your grievance.'

He repeated my words so that all his mob could hear. 'My grievance? My grievance, woman, is your letting filthy children from God knows where into the same school as decent white children, spreading disease and stuff.' He jabbed at my chest, his spittle reaching my face.

His mates clustered round him, emphasising his words – there were more in his splenetic utterance than I've recorded – with jabs of their banners. It would have been easy to be scared: I'm tall, but the shortest of them was a good three inches taller than me. On the other hand, if a camera was busily recording all their actions, they might draw the line at actually hitting me.

'I repeat, Mr Paine, that this is not the way to deal with any difficulty. Tell your friends to put down those banners and go away. And we will discuss in private anything you have to say.' Teachers can make themselves heard from one end of a playing field without raising their voices. I made sure that all my words would be recorded.

In fact, I turned to the reporter alongside the camera. 'These people are disrupting the education of all the children in the school. I am asking them to leave immediately.'

Mistake.

'Is it true that you've got illegal immigrants in the school?' the reporter asked.

I should have seen this one coming. 'The authorities are aware of all the children here,' I declared.

'Have you seen their passports? Their parents' passports? Is it true that you've got completely unidentified children running wild here?'

'I don't see anyone running wild, do you? All the children

180

are in classes supervised by excellent highly qualified teachers. All the children except for two unauthorised absentees.' No, I mustn't name them. It wasn't their fault. It might be illegal, too. But I looked meaningfully at Paine.

Someone came and stood beside me. Hazel Roberts. Leaning heavily on a stick, she looked frail but redoubtable. As if we were at some social event, I introduced her formally. All TVInvicta's viewers would know her next time they ran into her in the supermarket. Waitrose, if I knew Hazel.

'Ms Cowan is an excellent head,' she declared. 'She has the unreserved backing of myself and the rest of the governors. We have every faith that she will transform a good school into an outstanding one.'

Too much information. Now they'd know I was a new appointment. Fortunately there wasn't time for the reporter to make any capital of it. The police were here – one guy on a motorbike.

I suppose we were lucky we didn't have to wait for him to ride all the way from Essex.

The poor man. One versus ten. And two women hoping – if not quite expecting – that he'd be able to do something. Actually he did. Something very useful. He spoke to the TVInvicta crew. 'I don't think your presence here is very helpful. At the very least you're aiming to give airtime to what I believe is an illegal organisation. It'd be a good idea to show it to your legal department before you broadcast it. OK?'

As they packed up, he turned to me. I introduced Hazel, just as I had for TVInvicta, then myself. 'The gentlemen object to the presence of two non-white children in the school attended by Mr Paine's son and daughter.'

'Do they indeed?' He turned aside to speak into his radio. As he did so, one or two of the men decided they had previous engagements. Then another couple. Soon the only ones on the pavement were him, Hazel and me.

As one we adjourned into school. Donna, already at the coffee machine, greeted us with mimed applause.

'All the same,' he said, 'I do need to know about those children he was talking about.'

'One, Georgy Popescu, is entirely legitimate – his parents work for the fruit farm down the road. Their paperwork is in order. Georgy has been officially enrolled. But there is a possible problem with Zunaid. He arrives and departs on his own, eats like a horse, works incredibly hard at his English. But no paperwork, no nothing. And he keeps coming back. We know he appreciates personal hygiene, because he tried to help another little boy who turned up out of the blue, but this kid didn't like being washed and so he just pushed off. He's not been back since. And I didn't see Zunaid or his little protégé amongst that batch your colleagues and the social workers flushed out of Glebe Wood last night.'

Perhaps he hadn't known about it. But in a big organisation, why should he? 'An illegal, you reckon?'

'A refugee, let's call him. Yes, Donna?'

'Looks like the education people are here, Jane. Just two of them, though.'

Turning to the still-anonymous officer, I shrugged. 'You want to stay and join the party? At least you wouldn't have to hear it all second-hand.'

It seemed he'd prefer the edited version later. If at all.

* * *

There were two notable absences from the party, however. An interpreter and Zunaid. There was no sign of him. Nor, significantly, of Pam. I edged Donna to one side. 'Phone her and tell her to get them both back here now. At once. If she wants to foster him, she's got to be like Caesar's wife, above suspicion. Just tell her – breaking the law's the last thing she should even imagine doing. And she'll need a really convincing excuse for not being here on time. Go on, I'll make the coffee.'

She nodded and, mobile in hand, headed into the playground. 'Shall I tell the teachers it's all clear, by the way? The kids can go outside?'

'As soon as you've located Pam. Oh, and tip Karenza off too. We shall need her.'

'Shall I sit with the class? I've done it in the past.'

'You're an angel.'

Even without the policeman, my office looked as overcrowded as I'd hoped: the shorter the meeting the better. Actually I was wrong: I might need to prolong it, mightn't I? Until Donna had located Pam.

I suggested we adjourn to the library, an ambitiously named windowless room. But there were books aplenty there, and enough seats – if on the small side – for everyone.

'What happened to the interpreter I understood would be present?'

The incoming professionals exchanged a glance. In it I detected an instant sticking together, an agreement to sing the same song whatever happened. 'Unavoidably detained,' said the social worker, Marina Foster, a woman whose clipped diction belied her homely appearance. 'But I'm sure we can manage without her.'

I caught Karenza's eye: I was far from sure.

'Let us start by laying out some facts,' Education Man, Robert Plumley, said, sounding sweetly reasonable but probably deliberately obtuse.

'Excellent,' I declared, hijacking the meeting. 'Karenza – can you begin?'

Karenza outlined the situation so far; I briefed them about the English First incident – and finally, finally, but in fact as if on cue, Pam and Zunaid appeared, both tearful. Pam said Zunaid had enough English to know that bad people wanted to be rid of him. I wasn't at all sure about that, but let her continue with her narrative, which involved Zunaid running to her for help as soon as he saw them and her taking him for a little walk to calm him down. Zunaid simply clung to her leg until she sat down, when he scrambled on to her knee, burying his face in her shoulder.

'You know,' I said truthfully, 'in the continued absence of an interpreter, it seems unnecessary for Zunaid to stay. I think he might be a lot happier playing football or helping Pam lay the tables for lunch. Don't you, Pam?'

At first she went to carry him, but he slipped down, took her hand and walked out with her.

'She reminds him of his grannie,' Karenza said. 'He drew this picture of her this morning.' She held it up: actually, there was a surprising likeness. She took a deep breath. 'As his class teacher, I strongly request that any arrangements you propose involve Pam. Formally or informally. He likes me and he likes Jane, but he loves Pam.' She flushed bright red and stared at her lap. It seemed that Karenza, who could control a class of hyperactive monkeys with the quietest of words, was like many teaching colleagues I'd known: shy in front of other adults.

Marina Foster trotted out predictable verbiage, stressing that she had a range of experienced foster parents at her disposal, all trained in the particular expertise needed in dealing with children from such exceptionally difficult backgrounds; Plumley outlined his own ideas for Zunaid's future, including schools with staff who were qualified to teach English to young non-English speakers. They both sounded humane and sensitive, but I could see that Karenza shared my reservations.

'He doesn't need specialist linguistic help,' she declared. 'He has a gift for languages. Couldn't he be fostered by someone living locally? So he could keep coming here? And still see Pam every day?'

The professionals exchanged glances. 'As far as I know, there's no one on our register who lives locally. And being a foster parent doesn't just happen overnight, you know.'

'Of course. But—'

'In any case,' Education Man Plumley corroborated, 'if those racist yobs come to the school again, won't they cause him further grief? Besides which, Jane, your language budget would be bound to suffer if it turns out you need a specialist teacher – or at least classroom support. There wouldn't be that problem in a larger school geared up for handling migrant children. Plus, if he was admitted here there'd be complaints from local parents whose children weren't given a place and now see a stranger getting preferential treatment.'

'We can overcome those difficulties. The only reason I can see for taking him away from us,' I said flatly, 'is Paine's racism. But why anything so morally offensive and in any case illegal should prevent a child having the love and care he needs I don't know.'

'I understand his children are pupils here,' Education Man said. 'Isn't that an issue?'

'*They*'ve never made any racist remarks,' Karenza said.

'But perhaps they've never encountered a suitable target until now,' Education Man said reasonably. 'It seems obvious to me that the child should be removed to a place of safety, have his health checked and be found a suitable school. So we are all agreed?'

'Actually, no. There's just one thing that we have all omitted from our theories,' I said. 'Zunaid comes from somewhere every morning and goes back there. Voluntarily. If you just take him away – even if Pam takes him under her wing, for that matter – he won't be able to get back to whoever might be waiting for him. Maybe even his mother.'

'Or more likely a people smuggler,' Foster said tartly. 'You don't want us to leave a child sleeping rough where he is for another night, do you?'

'He may not be sleeping rough. We need to know. We need to ask him where he's living. For that we need an interpreter – who was supposed to be part of this discussion, as I recall.'

It was hard to tell whether their faces were red with anger or red with embarrassment.

Education Man spoke first. 'Are you suggesting that someone *follows* the child at the end of school? Spies on him?'

'Not unless there's no alternative. An interpreter would obviate the need. Until then, we should maintain the status quo.'

'I can't agree. In any case, the Border Force have to be involved. If we don't take him, I should imagine the school can expect a visit from them. It'll just take a good deal longer to get everything resolved – and a good deal more unpleasant for the child – and, I should imagine, for the school.'

I spread my hands, epitomising sweet reasonableness: 'All you have to do is bring an interpreter here and you can prevent it happening. Until then, Zunaid remains in my care – and you will recall that a head teacher is *in loco parentis*.'

CHAPTER SEVENTEEN

If it all sounds clear-cut, it wasn't. I don't know how many times I reiterated the need for Zunaid to be questioned sympathetically, or how many times I was subtly depicted as a monster. But I stood my ground. No decisions without that interpreter. 'Let's reconvene this afternoon,' I said reasonably, 'when you've had a chance to locate another one if the first choice can't manage it. Two o'clock? There's an excellent pub in Wrayford, just a couple of miles down the road, where you can get a sandwich.'

It was clear I wasn't going to Wrayford myself: my meeting with Tom at the school had to be put back till tomorrow, something he sounded harassed enough to be grateful for. I wouldn't budge: I didn't trust my so-called fellow professionals not to come back surreptitiously. Neither, for that matter, did I entirely trust Pam not to spirit Zunaid away again. So, having phoned Tom apologetically,

I made myself very obvious indeed, prowling round inside and out like a marauding tiger. All present and correct.

It was time for afternoon classes to begin: I had forty-five minutes before the scheduled return of my visitors.

Coaching was far too grand a word, but I was going to put the upper years through their running paces. Back at Wrayford running before morning registration was becoming a normal part of the day, but life at the smaller school was still pretty sedentary, playground football apart. So here I was, in my lightweight sweats and trainers, teaching warm-up stretches, warm-down stretches, to everyone, including the class teachers, bless them. The kids were in PE kit, the women also in a variety of sports gear, with various degrees of modesty. I had three separately labelled asthma sprays in my pocket. We managed two circuits of the playground before the first child started fading.

And before Lady Preston and her horse appeared at the railings. 'Well done! Keep going! No, don't give up. You can do better than that. Don't be such a wimp!' She beamed down as she waved at me. 'So that's what we were talking about the other day. Whole-school running, eh!' Her eyes narrowed. 'But not quite the whole school, surely?'

If she could make an effort to be civilised so could I. 'Not the little ones. Not yet. I want to do a lot more confidence and indeed muscle building before they start. Some of them are still brought to school in pushchairs, would you believe?' I spotted an excuse to end our conversation: a child starting an asthma attack. 'Your spray's over here, Mark! Stand tall. That's it. Breathe out. Harder, harder, harder. Now press the button and IN!!! And again. Good boy. Now you can help me count how many times round they're doing. Sorry, Lady Preston – I have to get back.'

My visitors – three of them this time – were pushing at the gate. So they had found an interpreter, which gave round one to me, even if I was at a disadvantage in my sports gear, not a suit. I slipped on my hoodie as if that was a mark of respect.

We trooped back to the library, without Karenza, who really needed to be with her class. Magnanimous in my minor victory, I ordered coffee all round, and sent for Pam and Zunaid. The small talk we made wasn't exciting, but it was good to get a sense of the interpreter they'd found: a young man called Dawud who looked mild enough, but whose eyes burnt with a baffled anger. It transpired that he too was from Syria, and had seen his family drown in the Mediterranean in one of the first tranches of escapees.

A frantic knocking at the door heralded the arrival of Karenza, with Pam almost tripping over her. 'He's gone!' Pam shouted. 'Gone. He told me he was going straight to class, but—'

'Never made it!' Karenza shouted. 'And Georgy – he said he wanted to go to the loo and he never came back. They've gone, Jane. We've checked every room in the school. Every last hiding place. Gone.'

'We should have taken him when we had the opportunity,' Marina Foster declared. '*In loco parentis*, I think you said.' Her sneer became more obvious. 'And three grown women have contrived to lose not one but two small boys.'

'Donna's called the police and Georgy's mum, who promises to organise a search of their caravan site,' Karenza said, ignoring her with aplomb. 'The police are already checking the roads round here. And Glebe Woods, where they found the kids last night.'

'Excellent.' I put my head round the door and called to Donna, 'Can you keep the phone line free – just in case? Thank you.' I turned to my visitors. 'So one kid is scared into escaping and his best mate offers to go with him. That'd be my scenario. Now, you are welcome to stay here – Dawud, you'd be more than useful to reassure Zunaid when we find him. Or we can simply reconvene when we've found him – and Georgy, of course. Karenza, can you ask all the staff to cross-question every last child? Reassure them that it isn't snitching and no one will get into trouble if they have to own up to something. And ask them to renew their search of every last corner. I'll get Donna to text and email all the parents to enlist them in the search at least of their own and their neighbours' premises. Pam, does Zunaid know where you live? Get there now. Keep your mobile on: I'll call the second I hear anything, good or bad, I promise.'

At this point the visitors left, though it was clear that Dawud would have preferred to help us. He needed a lift, however, so had to fall in line.

And what could I do? Tell the governors, for one thing. But that didn't involve striding round, questioning people – anything. It must have been some of that frustration that Hazel Roberts sensed. 'I'll alert everyone else on the board and start them searching too. Meanwhile, my dear, get off the phone. It's vital you keep the line open. You're the point of contact for everyone – *the still point of the turning world*, as Eliot put it.'

Where on earth could Zunaid be? When you've looked in all the likely places, it was time to look in the unlikely ones. The roof space? They probably didn't even know it was there. And how could they have moved the ladder into place – even between them? I checked: the ladder was chained safely in place. And just to make sure I checked the key was still locked in the safe in my office.

Wringing my hands wasn't going to do any good. If there was a roof space, was there a cellar – even a coal hole? I couldn't, in my panic, remember. Still clutching my mobile, as if it was an amulet, I did a circuit of the outside of the building. And yes – those heavy doors, set into the ground like those by a pub, must give access to a coke chute. But the bolt was rusted solid. If I couldn't shift it, a child couldn't. And there were no loose bricks anywhere near to suggest anyone had tried to get in that way. Once again I was ready to weep with frustration. But at least I now had official reinforcements; a police car was pulling up by the gate.

Before she was even out of the car, the driver was shouting to me. 'Are you the head that called in about missing boys? We've got reports of an injured child being taken to hospital. No details yet. I'm on my way to where we got the call – not very far from here.' She ducked back in and accelerated away.

I ran after her. Ran. How foolish and irresponsible was that? The officer's expression said it all as I caught up with her, though she did admit I must be pretty fit to shift that fast. I'd even got enough breath to ask for details.

Identifying herself as PC Fiona Berry, she said, 'We've got reports now of two little boys in hospital. But two little boys don't just get injured, so I was near here and decided to check. Skid marks, evidence of an assault – I don't even know what I'm looking for to be honest.'

I stood silently beside her as we stared at bland tarmac and undamaged verges. Shaking her head, she reached for her radio.

But then I did something weird. I grabbed her wrist and raised a finger. 'There's someone still there. In that hedge,' I added on my breath, pointing.

'Assailant? I'll call for backup.' She was equally quiet. She tiptoed off, but came back frowning. 'Fifteen minutes.'

'You've got me. Citizen's arrest.'

We separated, advancing on the source of the sound from opposite directions. She started to yell – a strong, carrying voice. 'Give yourself up. Come out with your hands up! You're surrounded!'

What movies had she been watching? I continued my silent approach, hoping she'd drive whoever it was in my direction. Crazy – it could have been an armed man twice my size.

I could hear my heart pounding. Surely whoever was lurking would hear it too. Casually I slipped off my hoodie. And edged closer.

'Now!' the officer yelled.

I dived, the hoodie outstretched, as if I were after an errant cat. And caught not a knife-wielding adult but a squirming, biting little boy.

Not Georgy.

Not Zunaid.

But the little boy who hadn't wanted to be washed.

Fiona held him in place. 'My name's Fiona.'

'I'm Jane. From the school.'

'We don't want to hurt you. OK? But if you won't lie still I'll have to make you.' She dropped her voice from

Englishwoman-talking-to-foreigner mode. 'I daren't try and drive with him like this.' Nor could she – not with a tiny bundle of fury pulling her hair and spitting at her. But how could we restrain him?

'We'll just have to tough it out and wait for assistance,' she said, calling in while I took her place at his shoulders. Her voice was tight with embarrassment. Before she took over again, however, she pulled on blue protective gloves.

With a dry laugh, I said, 'I'll summon our tame social worker. The kid's in need of tlc, not a police cell.' Standing up, I called Donna, telling her the good news/bad news. 'Marina Foster is just the woman we need right now. Here. Tell her she'll need a bin liner and a complete change of clothes from our emergency collection. And a load of paper towels. The police will supply rubber gloves. And make sure she brings that interpreter. Dawud. Any interpreter. Now! Oh, shit!'

The little boy had chosen – and I really suspected it was a matter of choice – to empty his bowels and bladder.

To do her justice Fiona clung on. 'It's worse when adults do it,' she said dourly.

'Thank goodness you've got here so soon!' I said, enthusiastically greeting Marina Foster the moment she and Dawud emerged from her car. She might have been my long-lost cousin.

'I told you children like this are a job for the experts.' Her beam was perilously close to triumphant.

'That's what I told Fiona over there. But if you need me I'll stay and help, Marina.'

'No – you have a whole school to run.'

Need she have sounded quite so patronising?

'In that case, I'll run – literally.'

'No problem. Is that more police?' she asked in disbelief.

Blues and twos? A brightly coloured vehicle spurting gravel as it came to a halt?

'Looks like it. But don't dismiss them out of hand – you may still need them. He really doesn't want to have anything to do with any of us.'

'Very well. So this is Zunaid, is it?' she asked rhetorically, heading towards the still-struggling little boy.

'Actually, no,' I said. 'This is the one who ran away because he didn't want to be washed. Are you still sure you don't need me?' Taking her temporary and possibly aghast silence as assent, I took to my heels.

Now as clean as the inadequate staff loo washbasin would get me, and looking slightly more the part, I hoped, I joined Donna in the office. She passed me a cup of tea. 'I've been fielding all sorts of calls,' she said, making one for herself. 'First of all the police. Some woman found a seriously injured little boy – you know that? With another child? Took them to hospital? 'Course you do. And since they knew we'd lost one, they thought we ought to know. So I said Pam was the one to identify him and – in the absence of any official social worker – to be with him when he was having any treatment.'

I put down my mug and hugged her. 'Well done.'

'So I called Pam, who set straight off to William Harvey A&E. It's weird – she says she's looking after Georgy, who couldn't or wouldn't say anything about what had happened. Anyway, I called Georgy's mum, of course, and she's off to William Harvey too – so she might get some sense of what's going on. Meanwhile, I've texted or emailed all the parents, and let the governors know. Oh, and I told the teachers too. Hey, what are you doing?'

'Handing you my name badge – you can run this place better than I do. At least you don't go haring off chasing little boys who don't want to be caught.' My turn to fill her in.

'So Her Nibs is having to deal with a child who's filled his pants? That's a bit naughty, Jane.'

'Isn't it just? I offered, believe me I offered, to stay. But when an expert tells you to go off and run your school, what can you do?'

'Have one of these biscuits,' she said. 'Oh, perhaps not – you're due at the dentist's, aren't you?'

CHAPTER EIGHTEEN

After all the excitements of the day, not to mention pleasures of the dentist's chair, there was still a lot of mundane admin to do, so I went back to work long after everyone else had left. Not that I did much. I didn't like my behaviour towards Marina Foster very much. No point in denying it. It came between me and everything I tried to do. At last I texted an apology.

I got a response. *Child now safe with approved foster carer. Whereabouts of Zunaid, please?*

As a response it wasn't what you'd call gracious. Maybe it was all I deserved. Some irresponsible imp wanted me to respond to her question with a flat, *No idea.* Instead she got, *Will try to find out.*

The hospital had already refused to give any information, of course, and Ms Popescu's phone had been off ever since Donna had first contacted her. I tried

Pam for the fourth time – and she picked up immediately.

'Sorry, Jane. It's been chaos here. Yes, A&E. Zunaid's been sewn back together, and Mrs Georgy's just managed to get Georgy to go back home with her – he wouldn't leave Zunaid, even when the doctors told him to.'

'Sewn back together?'

'Didn't I tell you? It seems the poor little mite – Zunaid, that is – got bitten by a dog. When a passing woman motorist saw the mess he was in, she stopped to help and bundled him into her car. But as she set off, Georgy suddenly appeared, and wouldn't let go of the car door. Seemed he wanted to be let in – or he might have wanted her to let Zunaid out, she wasn't quite clear. Anyway, she kept yelling "hospital!" and eventually Georgy came too. She's a real heroine, the police say: she insisted on staying till someone came. He was absolutely covered with blood.'

'So you're in charge of him now?'

'Only until a social worker turns up: I'm afraid it'll be that one who was so sniffy earlier.'

'I hope not. She's not very pleased with me and she might try and take it out on you. I must let her know, of course, but I'd say possession of the seat beside his bed is nine-tenths of the law.'

I had sounded much more positive than I felt. Realising I was defeated by the thought of any work, I gathered up my sports kit, doubting, however, that if it went through the washing machine a hundred times I'd ever want to wear it again. What an idiot. Into the machine it went.

It was just warm enough in the last of the evening sun to sit in the walled garden and deal with all my texts over a cup of tea. I felt very efficient as I dealt with the last, but disappointed I didn't have one more to respond to: one from Will. Insist how I might that I wanted to know what was happening with Harry and Doreen's bungalow – with my own house too, for goodness' sake – I was lying, wasn't I? As the sun dropped, so did my spirits – but there was something waiting that stopped me feeling sorry for myself, a bundle of administrative work on costing the presence of Zunaid at Wray Episcopi if we were allowed to keep him on our roll. The cost of losing him was incalculable.

To Pam, if not to me.

Work: that was the best therapy.

I had barely started number-crunching when someone else knocked at the front door. No chains, no spy-holes for holiday home doors. I froze. Before I could move, a text came through. Will! *Outside. Sorry. Should have texted before.*

'You've been crying,' he said accusingly.

'Bit of a day,' I admitted. 'And I don't think it's over yet.'

He stepped inside. 'I didn't think you ever cried.' He headed for the posh wine fridge, retrieving a bottle of New Zealand sauvignon blanc. He found the glasses as if by instinct too.

'On an empty stomach?' I said, eyeing the amount in the glass. If I could have bitten it back I would have done.

He took the empty glass from my hand, looking around the immaculate kitchen. 'You know I'm a detective? Well, I'd say you don't do much cooking in here.' His stomach grumbled massively. 'I've not eaten since breakfast either. What's your village pub like?'

'Hotbed of gossip. Good food. Unofficial headquarters of the cricket club. Haunt of Brian Dawes. Run by a kind friend of mine.'

'It sounds like the ideal place to eat,' he declared. 'No?' He pondered. 'Not if you want to eat in peace?'

'With all that's been going on? Glebe Woods last night, the business at Episcopi school, whether Wrayford school is also going to be overrun with what people will insist are called *illegal migrants* and young men asking why the hell did I say I wasn't sure about umpiring the match on Saturday.' I took a breath. 'I've got frozen stuff if you fancy something ad hoc with me? We can talk while I microwave.'

'You're as bad as I am,' he declared, inspecting the contents of the freezer. 'And they say that to stay healthy we should eat home-cooked food.'

'And go on the five:two diet. Mind you, I'm on that most of the time – a two:five diet, in fact. Meanwhile, do you suppose cooking the rice myself will make these curries any more home-cooked?'

'I know it's probably not what you want me to say, but I think the authorities are right about taking kids into official care,' he said at last. 'And I guess you do too. In your heart.'

'Of course. The next person wanting to foster might not be a decent loving woman with amazing grandma substitute potential, and all her background checks immaculate too. God knows there are enough people in the world who mask evil with an appearance of loving kindness.' I shook my head at the memory of just such a man who had died not so long ago. 'So yes to checks and balances. And yes to Pam being found a virtuous and loving woman who will bring Zunaid nothing but good.'

'Amen to that. From what you've said they should stay in touch even if the authorities can locate any of his family over here.'

'Meanwhile—' I stopped in mid sentence. 'What's that noise?'

'The chopper? There's a big search going on all round here to locate any refugees that were missed before. Lots of personnel and some dogs, too.'

'Dogs?' I shuddered. 'You make it sound like Nazi Germany. And it might feel like it to the people being hunted.'

He looked offended. 'I hope not. The choppers are dropping leaflets in Arabic and other languages and the dogs are accompanied by Arabic speakers offering help.'

'Sorry.' Putting the microwaved food on the table, I gestured him to a seat and collapsed myself.

He gave a forgiving grin. 'Now, Jane, you've been extremely patient. The news about that bungalow.'

Manners! 'Can I offer you another drink before you start? If you don't want wine I've even got some low-alcohol lager, because that's what Lloyd favours if he's driving.'

Pulling a face, he opted for water. Reluctantly, because getting drunk seemed a good option right now, I joined him.

'There's no sign of the bungalow being currently inhabited,' he said, helping himself to some of the naan I'd found in a cupboard, just within its use-by date as it happened. 'Sorry – I mean, as far as we can tell, Doreen and Harry don't seem to be living there now. But that's their business. We think. We hope. But there are plenty of signs that their garage is in use: as you suggested, there are lots of tracks, mostly left by larger vehicles than the Fiesta you said they drove. But they may have rented it out—'

'Though I can't see why, since no one lives for miles in either direction.'

'True. The trouble is that though there will be some of my team lurking in that layby this evening with night vision cameras, there's no money for an extended surveillance operation. And no CCTV coverage, as you'll recall. But if we can make a reasonable case to a magistrate that a crime is being committed on the premises, then we can get a search warrant and poke our noses in.'

'If it ties up with my house and my "accident"?'

'We'll probably have to arrest you! Only joking. There are some good connections. The habit of unlit vehicles accessing both lots of premises, which are both relatively secluded.'

'And both have detached garages. Tell me, Will, did you or your colleagues notice the enormously long washing line at the bungalow? Far longer than two elderly people would need, unless they ran a flourishing B&B, of course. And I saw no evidence of that when I was in their living room.'

He jotted. 'That sounds a bit Miss Marple-ish, Jane, if you don't mind my saying so.'

I gave an expansive shrug and we finished the Marks and Spencer meals in relative silence. However, I felt we needed something to round off the meal, and produced cheese and biscuits, with home-made quince jelly bought at the school summer fete.

'Would one more glass of wine put you over the limit? I've got a lovely soft Pinotage that would go beautifully with the Lancashire.'

We sipped and nibbled cheese in companionable silence. And then I heard a noise: the snoring snuffle of a hedgehog. We watched entranced as it approached the water meant for the birds. It drank. Suddenly Will was on his knees by the patio door, phone at the ready. It rolled up when I slid the door open, but soon decided it was safe to go on its way, rooting amongst a few dead leaves.

'Where's it gone?' he demanded.

'You see that little hole there? Apparently the architect's a wildlife buff, and insisted that there should be a gap under the walls so they can make their way through to the sluggiest garden. I've never seen it used before. What a treat!'

We opted for green tea to round off our supper, another meal that could have been spoilt with work talk. What had happened to our promise to have a crime-free meal? But, sitting opposite me in the tilting armchair, he started to talk about places and things he'd photographed, and his descriptions of his only safari – so far – took me to South Africa with him.

'It's always been one of the places on my bucket list,' I confessed. 'Second, actually. My dream, my absolute dream, is to play cricket on a West Indian beach. Preferably with a few kids who applaud when I play a cover-drive into the sea . . .'

We laughed. He set down his mug with a rueful grin.

'I have to go, don't I? Seven o'clock start latest.'

'And I'll raise you to six-thirty!'

His phone pinged. Without apologising he checked. 'Bloody hell – there's a fire at that sodding bungalow!' Grabbing his coat he was off, pausing only to dot a kiss on my cheek.

CHAPTER NINETEEN

I don't call out wimpish things like, 'Wait for me.'

Grabbing a jacket of my own, and even remembering to lock up carefully, I set off after him. Knowing the roads better than him I had the advantage.

But then my brain caught up with my instinct. What was I doing clogging up the road that might be needed by emergency vehicles? If it was my own house that was on fire there'd be every excuse, but rubber-necking someone else's disaster was pretty despicable, wasn't it? So I slowed, looking for a lane to turn in or a layby wide enough for me to do a U-turn. I found the grand drive of someone's grand house. No turning or parking. Sorry. My phone whistled. Not a rebuke from Will but an update from Pam: Zunaid was being kept in overnight. The medics had asked her to stay so as not to distress him.

Go, Pam!

The road seemed deserted enough for my manoeuvre, apart from someone coming towards me at speed. So I took his picture – several pics. Just because I could. What I didn't anticipate was the driver wrestling to do a handbrake turn to get back to me. He botched it. It looked like a ditch job. I set off briskly in the direction I'd been taking, before ducking and diving round as many lanes as I could find. Even I was pretty well lost, until I realised I was on the outskirts of Jo and Lloyd's village. Their welcoming gates beckoned. I tapped in my birthdate. They opened sweetly and I was almost safe. Jo, answering my frantic rings on her doorbell, peered at me.

'Being followed!'

'No problem.' Pulling me inside, she pressed the touch pad by the front door. The gates closed obediently. 'Got the kit, might as well use it. Lloyd? Are you decent? He's only just in from work,' she added.

So he was. Still in uniform.

'Sorry. Something or nothing,' I said, following them into their kitchen. I waved away the glass she was holding next to a wine bottle. 'No thanks. Honestly.' I gave what I hoped was a brief but cogent explanation.

'Let's see the photos,' Lloyd suggested, rubbing his face and eyes before taking the phone. 'Hmm. Send them to me, eh? Thanks.'

'I'll just go and make up the spare bed,' Jo said.

I shook my head firmly. 'You're very kind. I've got work I have to finish tonight and I have to be up and about by six. So if I can leave the car here, I'll get a cab and collect it tomorrow.'

'One other idea,' Lloyd said. 'I'll see if anyone's on a

routine patrol in the area and can escort you home now. It's only a couple of miles, after all.' He was already on the phone so I didn't waste anyone's energy by arguing. And I certainly didn't want anyone as dog-tired as he obviously was offering to accompany me.

'Result. Someone should be along in a very few minutes. And if you encounter any baddies en route you'll have lights, camera and action.'

I didn't need either. The roads were pretty well deserted. My kind escort waited while I parked and checked the cottage was safe. We waved each other a silent goodbye and, once I'd texted Jo with an apology and an assurance I was safe, it was time for me to do a bit more homework.

Will texted me first in the morning to say he'd let me know anything he could about the fire, but that they were waiting on the fire investigators for the full picture. He didn't mention the photos of the speeding car I'd sent Lloyd; on the whole I was glad. I felt I'd overreacted horribly both to the fire and the car, and rather hoped I'd hear no more about either.

So it was wonderful being able to sink into the safe routine of school, with only the predictable dramas of best friends falling out or knees being grazed in the playground. Karenza's class designed get well soon cards for Zunaid, Georgy was hailed as a hero, and I had no news whatsoever about the other little boy. Pam had taken a day's leave to stay with Zunaid, so Donna phoned a substitute whom Pam suggested; she arrived punctually and all went well.

There was a rumour flourishing amongst the children about a wild dog in the woods. Though I was tempted to say nothing, I did mention at assembly that dogs had personalities just as humans did, and it was never wise to try and pat a dog without the owner's permission. After all, they wouldn't want complete strangers coming up and patting them, would they?

I'd actually have liked a bit more information about the dog myself, as I told Tom at our postponed lunch meeting. I certainly didn't want one terrorising the playground, or attacking children on their way to or from school.

'But I'm sure the police will be following it all up,' I said eating the last bit of a pretty inadequate home-made sandwich, 'and will let everyone know what's going on.'

He checked his smartphone. 'Funnily enough, there's absolutely nothing about any of it on any local news websites. Odd really. I'd have expected something if a child's been hurt badly enough for an overnight stay in hospital. And a bit of news about this Georgy's loyalty.'

'Not to mention the child who didn't want to be looked after,' I said. 'Patient confidentiality?'

He chuntered a bit about that – seems one of his relatives had been taken ill and admitted to hospital and when his daughter phoned in great distress the GP's receptionist had first of all refused to acknowledge that he was unwell and then declined absolutely to say to which hospital he'd been taken. I had a theory I really did not want to voice: that Zunaid had been hurt by one of the search dogs that Will had mentioned. Perhaps the Border Force or whoever had started early and didn't want bad publicity. In the countryside, however, there were always dogs, including those that savaged sheep while their owners did nothing.

In the end we had no satisfactory explanation, and

turned instead to the mundane necessities of admin.

I managed to catch Jo before she went into class, to grovel for my unannounced arrival the previous evening.

She looked at me through narrowed eyes, but her voice was amused. 'There's a lot of story you didn't tell us last night, isn't there, Jane?'

'Lloyd looked as knackered as I felt.'

'So he did. But he always likes a good story, you know. So do I. Especially if it involves Will.' She looked up at me like a robin hoping a stork would drop a tasty morsel.

'That might be a long story, and I'd hate to make you late for class. Ciao!'

I got back to Wray Episcopi to find Ed van Boolen's white van parked outside. He was busy charming Donna when I let myself in, begging her, apparently, to intercede for him.

'Bended knees,' he was saying, 'just like this.' He dropped to one knee, hands lifted in supplication.

'Heavens, Ed,' I said. 'I'm sorry to interrupt your marriage proposal.'

He got up in one easy movement. 'It's more important than marriage, Jane – it's cricket. That match on Saturday. We're desperate. You may even have to do it all by yourself, since St Luke's Bay can't raise anyone.'

I shook my head. I'd only ever stood as sole umpire once before, and in an inter-church match at that. Usually, of course, you get one umpire at the bowler's end, and the other standing at right angles to the batter, at square leg. At the end of the over, the square leg umpire marches solemnly to the stumps his or her end, and bowling starts from that end. The original umpire takes up position at square leg at the far end. Every six balls, it's turn and turn about. If you really have to function alone, you just keep going to the bowler's end, with (one hopes) an honest twelfth man standing at square leg. The time I did it was the loneliest couple of hours I've ever known on the field of play. Big men tried to intimidate me, and every single decision was questioned – by one of the vicars especially. Even if your fellow umpire doesn't agree with a decision, at least he'll stand shoulder to shoulder in public, saving any criticisms for later, in private.

'I know we're not talking Test Matches here,' I said, 'but it is a league game, no matter how minor. We have to have two. Get on the blower, Ed. There must be someone floating around, even if he demands a fee.' I wasn't being anti-feminist – just realistic. Spare umpires tended to be old geezers, sometimes with less than perfect eyesight, which is why they were spare, not in regular demand.

'Come on – it's our last home game. Booze-up at the Cricketers afterwards. You don't even have to worry about driving afterwards. Pretty, pretty please!'

'You'd better kneel to Jane, Ed,' Donna said with a grin.

He was down in an instant.

'Knees or no knees, the answer is still not on my own. Get on that blower. Even an unqualified ex-player. But I'll make a few calls on my own account,' I conceded. I could have added piously but perhaps priggishly that the game had given me so much I was glad to give something back. Not just me personally either, but also the children of Wrayford School. Exercise and co-ordination, of course, but growth of self-esteem, too, and hugely improved mutual support.

'You're an angel,' he declared, all handsome charm and manliness.

So why had I never liked him less? 'Get phoning now, Ed.'

The children were just leaving for the day. Mrs Popescu was at the gate with Georgy, who was waving a cheerful goodbye to his new friends. I caught her eye and joined her. Frustratingly neither of them could summon enough English to explain what had happened yesterday to Zunaid, and my Romanian was non-existent, of course. I tried very hard to tell her how brave Georgy must have been to insist on sticking with Zunaid, but without the success I'd liked. But we seemed to part on the best of terms. As for an account of the incident, perhaps Pam would have more luck with Dawud's translated version.

The gush of children from the playground had slowed to a tiny trickle when a car approached so fast I'd certainly have a word with the parent. But it was the driver who wanted a word with me: Matt Storm, already apologising for his speed so near to vulnerable pedestrians.

'It was just that I wanted to catch you before you left,' he said.

'In that case you arrived with two or three hours to spare,' I replied dryly. Waving the last child goodbye, I turned to usher him into the school. Rightly, Donna asked him to sign in.

He raised a disdainful eyebrow. 'At this time of day?'

'It's school policy for every visitor whatever time of the working day. Which lasts till at least five-thirty,' she added, unconsciously echoing me.

The point was made further by a burst of laughter from the staffroom as we walked past.

He looked approvingly round my office. 'Lady Preston said you'd had this done up.'

'Correction: I did it up. It's not exactly the Sistine Chapel so I thought I could manage it. Take a seat and tell me how I can help you.'

'Lady Preston was so impressed by what you were doing with the children yesterday she's told me she'd like to help. The running. I think we can get permission to mow just a swathe of the meadowland short enough for them to use. I'm looking into it, anyway.'

'Thank you. And thank Lady Preston.' I got to my feet. 'Sadly there's still no sign of her paintings.'

He got to his. 'Tell you what, Jane – I've never been in a village school like this: would you mind if I wandered round?'

I would. Very much. This was teachers' private time. On the other hand, good community relations were always worth cultivating, so I turned on my most public smile. 'Let's start with the hall, shall we?'

'It's all very plain,' he said as I led the way. 'I always thought there'd be children's paintings on the walls everywhere. There were at my prep school.'

'There will be here, soon. But as you can see the walls everywhere have recently been painted, and there's no new artwork ready yet. Having your work put up has to be an honour to be worked for, not just routine. That'd make it too like their kitchen at home.' We shared a non-parental laugh.

'No photos of the children either.'

'There will be.'

He clicked his fingers. 'I could do that for you. Take the snaps. And print them off. Tomorrow?'

'Brilliant! Hang on, better make it – say – next Monday, so the parents can make sure they're all spruce in their cleanest bibs and tuckers. Do you need any equipment?' I was thinking of the backdrops and other paraphernalia other photographers had always had to drag into school.

'I'll bring everything. No problem. Nine?'

'That'd be terrific. Just one thing,' I added, as I moved him gently but inexorably to the front door, 'can you bring your DBS certificate with you when you come?'

'Sure. Er . . . not quite sure where it is.'

Or even what it was, I'd be bound. 'You could probably get a copy from the Disclosure and Barring Service,' I said brightly, 'though they'd probably want to you pay for it.'

'Surely I don't need it just for an hour's work?'

He probably didn't. 'I'll check and text you.' Why was I being awkward? 'What's your number?'

Now he was the one playing games. He made a great show of patting down his shirt and jeans. 'Look. I'll call Donna and fix it with her, shall I?'

'That'd be great. Just to warn you, first thing in the morning's always best – before cuts and bruises and torn trousers. See you – and thanks again!'

Donna, who'd have been able to hear everything I'd said, looked at me quizzically when I popped back into her office. 'DBS certificate for taking a few photos? Are you sure? Even Maggie Hale wasn't that punctilious. Not always, anyway.'

'After the stuff that went on back in Wrayford, I want

every "i" dotted, Donna. Especially when I don't know anyone properly. Mind you, even knowing someone and liking them doesn't mean they're not villains.'

'Doesn't Hamlet say something like that?' she asked sunnily.

How many school secretaries would ask a question like that?

CHAPTER TWENTY

I'd never had a Twitter account or Facebook page, lest I drop the slightest clue that could alert Simon to my whereabouts. But if ever a woman needed one I did now. On the other hand, aged umpires probably didn't tweet either, so I needn't waste time repining. Or should I do the obvious thing and get young Geraint and Carys on to the case for me? I sent a conventional email explaining the situation to Jo and Lloyd, with a further apology for dropping in on them so precipitately last night.

Before Jo could even receive it, however, she buzzed at the school door, and Donna, on her way out, let her in.

'What's all this about you and Will, then?' she asked, plonking herself in one of the visitors' chairs.

'Like Pat, he's a serving officer working on a case in which I'm involved, just about possibly as a perpetrator, but more likely as a victim. So what else can I say? I know,'

I added in response to her cynically raised eyebrow, 'that you'd love me to gush about roses round my new front door. Actually, that's a good idea – I'll ask Ed to plant some when he gets to landscape my garden.'

Her eyes rounded: 'Two eligible young men!'

'Possibly three. A fellow umpire invited me over to his place down in Churcham. Speaking of umpires—'

'Wow. And what does Brian Dawes have to say about that?'

'Would it sound terribly pompous to say I neither know nor care? Actually, he's kept a very low profile recently – maybe he's given up on me. But about umpires, Jo – I've just emailed you, first to grovel about my bedtime arrival last night and secondly to ask you to enlist Carys and Geraint in a search for one for Saturday.'

'Is it all in the email? Right, I'm sure they'll do it. You might be elderly and worst of all a friend of ours, but they reckon you're OK. But tell me about Will.'

'I like him. I'd like him even more if he told me what was going on at the bungalow after the fire last night. Nothing all day.'

'It's possible he doesn't know. There's some big meeting today for DIs and above about budgets and mergers of ranks and all sorts: he's probably doing Elaine's job as well as his. Lloyd's just glad he's lowly enough to be out of it.' She stared at a point midway between us. 'The thing is, Jane, if he ever were made redundant or anything, I'd have to look for a full-time post.'

'I don't think you'd have to look far, Jo. An experienced maths teacher on the loose? You'd be fending off a dozen head teachers at least. Actually,' I said seriously, 'would it

218

help if I found you some more hours? I could certainly justify them in terms of educational need – here at Episcopi if not at Wrayford. One of the areas the inspectors picked up on was weak maths teaching. We're doing our best. But if small schools like this are to stand a chance of surviving, we need to be considered outstanding in as many areas as possible.'

'We're OK, just now. No worries at all. But . . . What age group?'

'All! Year One and Year Five particularly. Whichever would help your CV most.'

'I'll talk to Lloyd. So really no good news about you and Will?' She looked genuinely disappointed.

It would be wonderful to be straight and honest with her. And why not? 'We get on. We like each other. But he's so . . . He seems very careful what he talks about. It's a very present tense relationship, with no mention of his past and no speculation about a future. I know I'm cagey, Jo, but I'm an amateur compared with him.'

Her face was as serious as mine. 'I could ask Lloyd for all the gossip – and I'm sure there's plenty. But I guess you'd rather hear everything from Will himself? 'Course you would. OK, I'll have to fix another curry night! Or not?'

I spread my hands. 'Not just yet. I don't think either of us would want to be railroaded into anything. Let's just wait till this particular case is over, and we'll see what happens then.'

She threw her head back in an uninhibited roar. 'Oh, Jane, I'm sure all sorts of things will happen, and you may see a lot more of Will. A lot! But you may still know nothing at all about his past!'

* * *

Pam was just letting herself into her house as I drove past it on the way home. A cup of tea was clearly on the cards, so long, as she said herself, we could talk as the kettle boiled – though most of what she said concerned the less than perfect state of her kitchen. And then the mess in her living room.

'I'm not some inspector!' Privately I thought she would have to deal with unwashed dishes and a pile of old *Daily Mail*s before she'd want any social workers to come and assess her.

At last we sat down.

'He's better. There's no need for me to stay over with him tonight, because he's agreed to stay with a really nice woman. Just for a bit, we're both saying. Zunaid and me, that is. Until I can get this place childproof, for a start. But Dawud – he had me in tears last night, after Zunaid was settled – was saying he really thought he'd be better long term with an Arab family. "Nothing against you, Pam," he said, "but round here they just don't get the culture. So he'd be fine at home with you and at school, and I'm dead sure everyone would be nice to him – but he needs to know about his roots and his religion and know about them from people who live and breathe them, not just read about them in books."'

I held her hand. 'But this would mean—?'

'In the short term, they promise that Zunaid can keep coming to this school and start staying overnight when I've got a bed and everything for him. And a social worker, not that Marina Foster woman, says she knows of a charity that might give me a small grant for that, not that I won't find the money myself if I have to. Meanwhile, they'll try and find out if he's got any extended family – is that the right word? – here in England. If he has, and they can take him in, then – well, if it's best for Zunaid, I'll just have to live with it, won't I? Because I love him.' She stopped to gulp tea. I found tissues for us both in my bag. 'Anyway, I'll make a start clearing out that room tonight, so we can make the best of it till he has to go to Leeds or Manchester or wherever.' She made them sound as if they were in deep space. 'And maybe he'll be able to come and see me – in the school holidays or whatever.'

'Of course he will. Did he say anything,' I asked at last, 'about how he came to be injured? Not to mention how Georgy came to be with him?'

'I tried, Jane, don't think I didn't try. And Dawud – he had quite a go at him. All he'd say was what we know: that a dog went for him and Georgy hit the dog with a stone and a kind woman stopped to help. And nothing more could we get out of him. He denies knowing the third little boy at all, so he's just been taken off to a ready-made foster home, if you see what I mean. Zunaid got really upset – we had to stop. And then he had nightmares about it – it's a good job I was beside him really to love him better. But someone, if you ask me, has put the frighteners on him.'

'Who on earth—? He's just a child!'

She gave a shrug a Frenchwoman would have been proud of.

'Did he say anything about his family?'

'Not a lot. Dawud and I thought he was trying to avoid answering. As if he was afraid that if he said anything they'd come to harm. Dawud said that this had

221

happened to him. If he complained about the people-smugglers, his folk back in Syria would suffer. Oh, Jane, what that poor lad has endured. Dawud, I mean. I wish I could be his granny too. People should be ashamed, treating humans like so many animals – no, worse than animals. Putting them in boats and towing them out to sea and leaving them to hope they're picked up. Terrible. And then getting here – no money, just a bare living . . . It's been an eye-opener to me, I tell you. I thought' – she glanced at the papers – 'that they were like that man Paine said, scroungers, coming here to find a cushy number at our expense. Well, if I see that bugger again, pardon my French, I shall give him what for!' She drained her tea. 'Now, this sounds very rude, Jane, but just now I prefer room to your company. I've got work to do. That bedroom.'

I thought of all the admin I had to complete for tomorrow, not to mention the food shop that was becoming quite urgent. I thought of my smart work suit and good shoes. 'Come on, I'll give you a hand.'

Which is how I came to run into Will by the chilled meals section in Ashford Sainsbury's at ten o'clock at night.

We fetched up in an Indian restaurant where Will said the food was usually respectable. Sadly on this occasion our fellow diners were not – not in their present boozy state, anyway. We didn't even want to hang around for a takeaway, so bowed out to a series of catcalls. Eventually we picked up fish and chips, which we ate in Will's car in the Vicarage Lane car park. He made a couple of calls to suggest someone might want to breathalyse the boozers, but, as he said, more in hope than expectation. 'We simply don't have enough boots on the ground to deal with every set of pissheads. Not in towns like this, anyway. And things aren't going to get any better. Not that I'm supposed to say that. Maintaining public trust and morale are paramount. No, *is* paramount. Sorry. Christ, Jane, I joined the police to catch criminals, not spout fatuous policy. And now we seem to be talking shop again, I can tell you that a lot of accelerant was found all over the bungalow site, but no sign of any bodies. Not so far. There'll be a further examination tomorrow, with luck, to see if any bodies were buried in the garden. And I have to warn you that Harry's Fiesta hasn't been picked up by any cameras since the day you went back to thank them. That's a long time. Sorry.'

'So am I. They seemed to be decent people. And they were kind to me.' I scrunched up my chip paper. 'It's too late to update you on Zunaid now, Will, but I'm happy to at a more civilised time.'

'Saturday? Lots arising from today's meeting . . .'

'Saturday's fine. Except in the afternoon I shall be umpiring the last cricket match for our village team this season. Provided they find another umpire to stand with me. I don't suppose you know any masochist who'd like to join me?'

'I might. I just might.'

'In that case you can both come to the party at the pub afterwards.'

'Deal. I'll be in touch. And before you argue, you'll find I'm tailing you home. Just in case. OK?'

'OK. Thanks. Really. Thank you.'

What if he kissed me?
What if I kissed him?
Too late. Too complicated.
To be honest, too tired.

CHAPTER TWENTY-ONE

The weekend at last. And, with no thanks to Ed and the team who were supposed to be on the case, and actually no thanks to Carys and Geraint's undoubted efforts, we had the right number of umpires. We owed everything to a police contact of Will's, who gave up chasing online paedophiles for a day to officiate with me. Not that anyone was to know his daytime job: if anyone asked he was 'something to do with computers'. Which had the benefit of being true, of course. Robin was Mr Average in everything – height, build, somewhere between forty and fifty, and with a vaguely Midlands accent. And it turned out he was Mr Elaine Carberry, the officer who'd been in charge of the Glebe Wood operation.

So the match was going ahead. And with fine September weather forecast, and the promise of a party afterwards, we expected more than the one man and his dog that often made up the entire crowd. The loos apart, the school was out of bounds, but since I had all the keys I could invite Robin to my office – Tom's office too, of course – to check all the paraphernalia umpires carry, from scissors to trim bits of frayed leather from the ball to tissues to remove flies from eyes. I counted the six smooth pebbles I always transfer from one pocket to another each time a ball is bowled: I didn't want five- or seven-bowl overs on my watch. He did the same, asking for a pencil sharpener to improve the stub of pencil for his notebook. He passed it to me to do the same. Mobile phones – just in case. Properly equipped, we could establish our general policy with regard to lbw and other possibly contentious decisions.

'What's your rule of thumb?' he asked, eyeing our wall-planner. 'Golly, you work some hours, don't you?'

'If in doubt, give not out. And the umpire's decision is final, unless my fellow umpire thinks I've called it wrong. I make a point of conferring so long as my fellow umpire does me the same courtesy.'

'Some don't, I take it? No, I needn't ask. How do you deal with dissent?'

'Tell the captain to stop it. If it's the captain complaining, then I have been known to threaten to abort the match. Just the once. Horrible.'

He nodded glumly. 'It's time cricket had the same red and yellow card system as other games, if you ask me. I had this guy grab me by the shirt collar the other week – nigh on choked me. No, no one tried to intervene. And I won't do kids' games any more, not after this parent landed me in hospital for giving his lad out one short of his fifty.'

I commiserated with tales of my own experiences: not just generally patronising language but some highly sexist behaviour alongside physical threat. 'Why do we do it, Robin?'

'Love of the game,' he said with a smile that lit up his whole face.

A lot of team members' partners were sitting round the boundary. If he counted as such, Will was sitting next to Elaine. Surrounded by cool bags, a gaggle of women – the tea crew was almost inevitably female – had set up tables near the school building, ready to lay out food and brew up. Others looked after children, many of whom were already bored with the concept of cricket and shinning all over our playground equipment, bought with funds raised by our PTA. It would be good if the Episcopi PTA could make a similar effort, because whichever way I looked at our budget I couldn't see it stretching to that sort of non-essential expenditure – but that would probably mean an unlikely truce between me and Gerry Paine. Meanwhile, of course, I had the pleasure of umpiring his brother Dennis to look forward to. At least it was someone else's job to worry about prioritising parking in our small staff car park and on the road outside. Predictably ordinary saloons were outnumbered probably four to one by 4x4s of various makes. SUVs? Yes, three of them, too. I was too far away to check if one bore the scar left by my bike; in any case, surely that would have been resprayed long ago. Meanwhile, St Luke's Bay were just arriving in three minibuses – quite a lot of support, then.

Marcus Baker, their skipper, and Ed van Boolen shook hands with each other and with us. Marcus won the toss and elected to bat first. Their opening bats trotted to the middle and took guard. To my shame I prayed that if anyone had to give Dennis Paine out for whatever reason it would be Robin. Des, our huge opening bowler, marked out his run-up.

Holding my arm out to establish all was ready, I held my breath. For an instant I felt like a conductor ready to bring her orchestra into a great opening chord. It was time. From now on I must think about nothing except the players and the ball.

I caught Robin's eye. 'Play,' I said.

As far as I knew, not many people knew that Des and Mike, whose language never ceased to shock me, were an item, so I never said anything that might hint at it. But I had to say something about the way Mike was sledging Marcus, coming in at second wicket down. As the field changed at the end of the over I caught Robin's eye again. He strode purposefully over: there was still something of the beat officer in his walk even if he now spent his days glued to a computer. Together we called Mike over. 'We're not in Australia, Mike,' I said, 'and there are a whole lot of children here. I'm not having it – understood?'

'OK, boss. But I'm right about his wife being a—'

'Enough!'

Robin's body language as implacable as I like to think mine was, he waited for me to finish what I'd started, the best sort of support. I summoned Ed, who was inclined to offer a matey smile, as if I was having a bit of a joke.

I wasn't. His eyes dropped first.

Play continued, with Marcus scoring quite freely, until Mike neatly stumped him. I gave Mike a dry grin: that was the way you made your point to opposing batsmen, with your gloves, not your mouth.

St Luke's had achieved a respectable score by the time their forty overs were completed; to my secret relief, Dennis Paine hadn't had to bat. But he still had to field, of course. The prospect didn't stop me enjoying my tea, however – a sandwich and cake feast for all – during which any animosity was traditionally forgotten. Robin and I mixed with the players, on the receiving end of banter, true, but dishing out as good as we got. Of Gerry there was mercifully no sign, though I'd seen Joe and Nicky with some other kids on the climbing frame. Soon Marcus joined me, first to thank me quietly for dealing with Mike, and secondly to tease me very publicly for collapsing at his barbecue. 'It was like dealing with a Victorian maiden!' he said. 'Like this!' He gathered me in his arms and, as he gripped tightly round my waist, I promptly tipped backwards in a mock swoon.

All very daft. It gained a round of ironic applause from both teams.

At this point Brian Dawes appeared, his smile very formal.

Greeting him enthusiastically, I spread hands to encompass the whole scene. Benches and deckchairs for the players in what would have been a pavilion on any other ground – the spot nearest the loos, at any rate. Deckchairs in little knots round the boundary. A few blankets beside them for babies. Children in the playground. 'What a good decision you governors made,' I declared in my most carrying voice. 'This is what villagers should be doing, isn't it? Gathering as a community to everyone's benefit. The proceeds of the raffle will be split between the school and the club. Ideal.'

He demurred, as well he might, knowing it was a kindly lie as well as I did. But my declaration of gratitude opened the way to a lot of other people wanting to speak to him and indeed enthusiastically shake his hand – possibly as a result of the very strong Pimm's circulating in some areas. Robin and I eased ourselves to one side, to compare notes and possibly to avoid any discussion with anyone about the stance we'd taken with Mike. Especially with Mike. He was in animated conversation with Des, who was the last man to bat. Meanwhile someone's child was having a tantrum; above the sound of her screaming and yelling, I thought I heard another, older female voice, in much the same hysterical mode.

Robin rolled his eyes. 'Let's leave them to it, shall we? Nothing to do with us, after all. Do you have a warning bell or does one of us have to go and yell? Ah-ha!' he said pouncing on the old-fashioned playground bell we used. 'Always wanted to ring one of these – ever since I was five.'

Before he could live out his dream Ed materialised at his elbow, as if he'd taken lessons from the Cheshire Cat, to say the opening batters were ready. That wasn't going to stop Robin's fortissimo venture into campanology. Despite the appalling din, however, there was no sign of Marcus, who was, after all, due to lead his men on to the field. Without him, the Bay team gathered on the boundary, having a team huddle worthy of the England squad. At last their wicketkeeper, Angus, I think, broke away to say their twelfth man would come on until Marcus returned. 'Bog, I suppose,' he said helpfully.

As I took my place, Dennis Paine was fielding as far from me as it was possible to get. But as a bowler he could soon be within spitting distance, an image I wished I hadn't thought of.

'Play.'

Wrayford had a strange innings. Ed, usually the mainstay of the side, was out for his first duck of the season – a golden one, too, since he was out first ball. Mike, in general a slogger who hit the ball as if he was executing it, played a gentle but very efficient game, accumulating runs without anyone noticing. The lad from Tonbridge School who rather expected to sign up for Kent managed an undistinguished two. One way and another, however, Wrayford got to within eleven runs of the St Luke's total with one over to go. Two wickets to spare. Tight. But with Des at the crease with Mike still in place at my end, anything was possible.

A single to third man – not what you'd expect from Mr Muscles.

Mike would want to try his luck now, surely – but another nibble with just a single to prove it. Four balls. Nine runs to tie, ten to win. Hmm. Two more twos. Then six to win off two balls. An almighty swipe from Des nearly took Robin with it, but the ball fell short of the boundary, bobbling up almost into a fielder's hands. A good throw might achieve a run-out. It fell twenty metres short, was scooped up by Marcus who hurled the ball with all his might – and suddenly I was crushed on the ground, the wind knocked out of me. And no wonder: fourteen stone of sweaty Dennis was lying on me. As he scrambled to his feet, leaving me, still spread-eagled, to follow suit, he let fly a tirade of vituperation at Marcus. The gist was that the man was an idiot to throw so badly: he could have knocked the esteemed umpire's head off. By now Des and Mike had gathered me up, and Robin was remonstrating with Marcus, in somewhat less colourful language but with equal vigour. Marcus, red-faced with anger or embarrassment, said all he'd been trying to do was run Des out. 'It was a bad throw, OK? Ball slipped out of my hand. And I'm sorry she's upset. But it was an accident.'

'It would have hit her fucking head, man – didn't you learn anything from Phil Hughes' death? Or perhaps you did!' Mike yelled.

Yes, a cricket ball was hard. A missile. One of the best Australian cricketers of his generation had been killed by a short-pitched ball.

Everyone was yelling now. I'd better take control of the match – and of myself.

Just as I did when I had warring factions in the playground, I held up both hands. 'Enough. We'll talk about this later. But we have a match to finish. Sadly I can't recall how many you ran, lads. Robin, can you?' We edged away for a confab.

'I was so concerned I lost count too. But now I really think that big guy saved your life. Whether what Marcus

232

did was deliberate I couldn't tell. Not to swear in a court of law. Either way.'

'Like I said, let's worry about that in a minute or two. Let's get this game over. God, there's going to be a fight any moment! Can you trust me on this? I don't think it's in the Laws but it's what I'd do in a kids' match.'

'You might want to tell them just that,' he said dryly.

'I'm going to, don't you worry!'

I summoned the captains and spoke to them as if they were six-year-olds. At any other time it would have been a joy to watch their faces as I told them that I was declaring the last ball dead – that it would have to be bowled again so that both umpires could give it their proper attention. 'So we're back to six off two balls for a Wrayford win, and five for a tie. And if we have any more dissent, Robin and I will abandon the match with no result. Do you all hear?' I added, to the rest of the teams. 'Excellent.'

As I handed him the ball, Dennis said, sotto voce, 'Christ, you've got fucking guts.'

I had an idea it was meant as a criticism of our decision, but couldn't be sure. Actually, perhaps it wasn't.

Any captain will tell you that in this situation his last instruction to his bowler, often given right at the end of his run-up, is not to bowl a no-ball, which will add one to the score whatever the batter does and result in another ball being bowled – another scoring opportunity. What Marcus said to Dennis I couldn't hear. But I did get a strong sense of Dennis making a very pungent response. He didn't bowl a no-ball or a wide. He bowled a very good yorker, and Mike was left fending off with some desperation.

Six off the last ball. Robin and I exchanged a glance.

As the ball left the bat we all knew it was going to be good. But possibly none of us quite expected to hear the unmistakeable – and decidedly pleasurable – sound of a windscreen being broken.

CHAPTER TWENTY-TWO

Our contract with the club covered just such a problem. The car owner, Ed and Mike could sort out insurance details. Joining the melee in the nominal team area, I was sipping what Robin told me should be brandy but was in fact champagne from the hamper he and his wife had brought with them, clearly slightly misjudging the social milieu. Will was all for making Marcus's throw at me a police matter, the concern and anger in his face as comforting as the fizz, in their way. 'And don't tell me you want nothing to do with it.'

'I wouldn't dream of doing so. Though actually it'd be terribly hard to make any charge stick, wouldn't it? Accidents do happen in cricket, as in any sport. No one was hurt. No TV umpire to refer to. And Marcus apologised. End of, probably.'

'Hmph. There's quite another conversation I might want

to have with him, actually. Wasn't he the guy from whose garden you saw unlit boats coming into the harbour at St Luke's Bay?'

'Yes. His, and then Justin Forbes'.'

'And since Forbes isn't here – is he? – then I can have a word with the one who is. Hang on – sorry.' He turned away to take a phone call.

I suppose there were a lot of things I ought to be thinking and saying, but suddenly my legs went weak and I really needed to sit down in a hurry.

A hand grabbed my elbow and steered me towards one of the wooden picnic tables that the PTA and cricket team had paid for. Another hand removed the glass. My head went down between my knees. Whoever the first-aider was I couldn't for a moment see. All I could do was imagine what that ball would have done if Dennis hadn't intervened. And I came to a sudden but deep conviction: being alive, no matter how hard it had been at times, was better than being dead. I sat up, with a genuine smile on my face. 'I'm fine. Victories off the last ball always have this effect on me.' An emergency vehicle siren? 'I do not need an ambulance!' I declared, to whoever might be listening.

'That's good because it's a fire engine,' Des said flatly. 'It's heading into the village. No, you should keep your head down.' His large hand meant I couldn't argue. 'You were right to bollock Mike, by the way. He was way out of order. Though, they say, he was right about Mrs Marcus. Grazia. We reckon she was born plain Grace and decided it wasn't posh enough. Snotty cow. Loathes her husband playing cricket. Loathes his friends. Loathes his friends' children. And – this might be the thing that

236

applies to you, now, Jane – she loathes any woman her husband might fancy.'

I snorted. 'Marcus? I can tell you it's not mutual.' I came up more slowly this time. 'Any more of that champagne? The ball didn't actually reach me, after all, so I don't have to worry about alcohol making concussion worse. Funny thing: Dennis Paine's never been my idea of a hero, but he did well this afternoon, didn't he?'

'I reckon you might owe the bugger your life. But that doesn't mean you have to like him or his brother. Nasty piece of knitting, that one.'

I nodded absently before returning to a more immediate topic. 'What's the consensus amongst the players? Both teams?'

'There isn't one. Most of St Luke's fielders were in the deep, hoping for catches on the boundary. So they wouldn't have had a good view. Most of ours were down here, cheering our guys on. The batters were simply going hell for leather for a run – heads down, ready to dive.' Then Mike scratched his head. 'I suppose if you wanted to make an issue of it, either as the one that nearly got hit or just as an umpire, then some people might have caught it on mobile phones. But it's not very likely, is it? Hello, it looks serious,' he added as two more fire engines hurtled past the school, followed by an ambulance and two police cars. 'Anyway, if you promise not to faint, I'll go and, as your bloke would say, make a few enquiries. If you don't see me again it's because I've nothing to report.' He seemed to be channelling *Dixon of Dock Green* as he walked heavily off.

My bloke, if such he was, was still on the phone, looking very serious. Before I could make my brain even consider what I ought to do next – the effects of the shock or the shampoo? Who knew? – Robin came over, sitting beside me. 'If it's OK by you, I'll recommend a written warning for Marcus. A suspension, if you prefer. By accident or design, what he did was dangerous.'

I nodded. 'Des there is trying to find if anyone videoed it. That might help. If anyone did or if anyone cares to admit it. This bubbly's good: you ought to try some.'

'I would if I could find Elaine's picnic hamper. Yes – you've already met her, haven't you? I've an idea she's joined the team washing up.'

'But she's a guest!'

'You pick up a lot as a washer-up. And even at weekends you never stop being a police officer, you know.'

'But—'

He overrode me, saying loudly, 'Nice little school you've got here, isn't it? And being able to use the kitchen's a bonus.'

'Pity everyone has to use mini loos – only the umpires get into the main part of the school,' I added in a similarly public voice.

'Ah, I noticed you used keys as if it was Fort Knox.' Another police car shot by. 'Lord, a burglar's delight: all Kent's rapid response cars in one square mile. Meanwhile, for Marcus both a written warning and a suspension? I'll sort it. But I think one of those cakes would perk you up – and sustain me.' He returned with two chocolate diabetes bombs.

No one showed any interest in whatever was attracting all the emergency vehicles, and despite myself I soon got sucked into discussions about cricketing matters – all the while studiously avoiding the subject of Marcus's throw. We talked about plans for improved changing and showering facilities, not forgetting full-sized loos, and the formation of a women's team. No, I didn't have time to coach it or manage it. Being a teacher I could mostly manage being in two places at once, but three was more difficult.

Despite my firm rejection, I had a feeling that I wouldn't hear the last of it. As a diversion, I suggested everyone should be on their way to the Jolly Cricketers, where Diane was laying on a barbecue. It was actually Ed's duty to see that all the litter was gathered up and the school and its grounds were left pristine. Then he was supposed to check that everyone had left school premises and that it was safely locked up. But there was no sign of him. I grabbed Des and Mike and persuaded them to organise a last tidy of the field. When they'd done that I'd take care of the school buildings. It seemed that Robin and Elaine weren't sure whether to go to the party: I got the impression that he wasn't enthusiastic but that she was. In fact she became quite insistent.

In his place I probably wouldn't have been keen: I knew from personal experience how unpleasant it could be when players came at you with alcohol-fuelled complaints. I just hoped that I'd get more understanding than criticism this time.

Another person I didn't see was Brian, usually efficient to the point of officious in double-checking that the premises were secure. But I was as happy with his room as with his company; bag in hand, I turned the last key in the last lock. Will was waiting. Wouldn't it be lovely if we could spend

239

an evening together without having to talk shop?

We fell into step with Robin and Elaine, who smiled at me as if I was an old friend, but said nothing about the incident.

'Like you said to Brian Bores-for-England,' Robin was saying, 'it's a nice community event – no one wants to go home.' He nodded at the knots of people still chatting on the pavement and in the road.

Will grunted: 'Some of them have strange notions of what constitutes parking cars, rather than simply abandoning them where they feel like it.'

It felt as if he was making an effort to keep my mind off other things, so I said, 'It's clearly an issue we'll have to address for next season, before the locals start to complain. Rightly,' I added, as an SUV driver attempted a three-point turn rapidly escalating into double figures. I clutched Will's arm. 'It's that woman who was in the pub – isn't it?'

'Can't see any scars on her vehicle, though.' He photographed her number plate nonetheless.

Elaine scratched her chin. 'But you can have scrapes repaired . . . Yes, Will told me all about it. And about the stuff you tackled with the paedophile here: well done you.'

'Thanks. Hey, Robin, are you all right?' I added, as I realised he could hardly keep pace with us. He stopped altogether. Not a heart attack. Please don't let him be having a heart attack. He was heaving for breath.

'Asthma. Don't worry.' He produced a familiar type of spray.

'Harvest dust,' Elaine explained. 'He's fine standing still but – There! That's better. OK, love?' They squeezed hands.

Will ignored the little incident, setting us in motion again, but more slowly. Then he paused to take a call, which didn't bring pleasure to his face. 'Look,' he said at last, 'I'll see you at the pub – right? And, Jane, please don't leave there till I arrive.'

He looked as if he might add an extra please, a pretty one.

'OK,' I said offhand, 'if it's important.'

Presumably it was. He turned and retraced his steps at a gallop.

Ed was already in the Jolly Cricketers, clean and scrubbed as if up for interview rather than just being the self-appointed Mine Host. Less cordial was Brian, also looking spruce – but then that was the norm. And there was no doubt he considered that Ed was an upstart usurper of his rightful role: he made sure it was he who had fought his way through to the bar to buy me a glass of prosecco, and didn't hesitate to provide Elaine with one too when I introduced her. But he didn't seem anxious to pursue any conversation with her, trying, in fact, to edge her out with a traditional masculine turn of the arm and body that made her step back a pace.

I moved so she could step back in. Even so he contrived to ignore her.

'Are you sure you're all right after that incident?' he asked, clinking glasses with me.

'I was shaken at the time but now I'm fine,' I assured him. 'And everyone enjoys a close finish. Very exciting, wasn't it, Elaine?'

'Absolutely,' he chipped in. She narrowed her eyes at his rudeness. 'What a splendid end to the season. Tell me, will you be coaching the new women's team?'

I tried to be as patient as if he was the first person to ask the question. 'It all depends on my other commitments, Brian. Taking on the second school has been quite a challenge, you know, Elaine.'

Again he cut across her. 'But you're not doing any teaching – we're even proposing new school signs naming you as Executive Head Teacher.'

Elaine gave something nearer a snort than a chuckle. 'If I'd known I'd have curtsied,' she said dryly.

'So you should,' I said with a grin. 'But with our budget so stretched, Brian, is giving me such a grandiose title it merits new boards a priority?'

'The Episcopi one has to be changed anyway, doesn't it? It would look odd if the Wrayford one weren't updated too.'

'True. But we shouldn't be talking shop, should we? Shall we go and see what the barbecue has on offer, Elaine?' I raised my glass in a little gesture intended to convey both thanks and an end to the conversation.

En route we came up against Dennis Paine. He spoke first. 'You OK, Umpire? I'm no lightweight, you know.'

'I do know,' I laughed. 'Thanks, Dennis – I hoped I'd get a chance to say how grateful I am.'

'Like I said, you got guts.' He looked almost furtively at Elaine, who was afflicted by a massive bout of hiccups, genuine by the sound of them. 'Has that fool of a brother of mine changed his mind about pulling his kids out of your school? They're bright, those little ones, and they deserve the best, you know,' he added ambiguously. 'I shall tell him about this afternoon, don't you worry.' He edged away.

Elaine's hiccups had stopped but she looked washed out.

'Do you want to find Robin?'

A quick glance showed that Robin was at the heart of a knot of players all sharing a raucous laugh.

'Leave him. He's as happy as a pig in muck,' she said. 'He always grumbles about having to socialise, but when it comes to it, he really gets stuck in. I think it's because his job is pretty lonely, and he thinks he's forgotten how to mix, but – hey presto! – he hasn't.'

'What about you? You seemed really keen to come. But—'

'I was. I mean, I was anyway, because I like village stuff like this. And I liked the way you worked the other night, and I wanted to see how you and Will are together, of course – and there he is gone. Pfff. But that's the police for you.'

'So it seems. But we're not an item, Elaine, much as Jo and Lloyd Davies are trying to push us that way. And now you! It's not as if we can be, is it, with everything in the air – and me not yet ruled out from having committed one of the crimes.'

'True. But it all looks very promising from where I'm standing. And there might have been another reason for wanting to come.' She touched the side of her nose. 'It's not just walls that have ears, is it? Those fried onions smell wonderful,' she added more loudly. 'I like them better than burgers, truth to tell.' She set off purposefully into the beer garden, where not just two but three barbecues were in operation, staffed by three teenagers more interested in their phones. 'Come on – you need feeding, and I certainly don't.' She grabbed some of the muffin round her waist and squeezed. 'At least fizz isn't fattening, is it?'

'Not when Brian Dawes buys it,' I mouthed, winking.

Some of the younger kids were already high on sugar, and making a thorough nuisance of themselves: dashing round, jumping, shoving. Worse, any moment now one of them might career into a barbecue, with potentially disastrous results. En route to warn Diane, the landlady, I spoke to a couple of mothers I knew from school: 'We have to move them away from here. Or at the very least somehow fence off the danger area. Any ideas?' I did have several myself, but since they involved the water butts on which Diane prided herself I kept quiet. Talking about drowning infants would not be good for school recruitment.

Diane, detailing Ed to take over the bar, hurtled out with me: 'It's not supposed to be kids doing the cooking, but a team of adults. And I showed them where to put – Jesus!' She grabbed the nearest children, more or less throwing them out of the way, and weighed in to abuse a crowd of adults who watched the chaos their offspring were causing as if it was nothing to do with them. Within seconds she and I were making a little barricade from large planters and garden chairs; without being asked, Elaine was deftly fielding kids determined to penetrate it.

One was an especial pest. Twelvish. Old enough to know better. Arms folded he was leaning against a swing, daring other kids to grab burgers directly from the griddles.

I knew him. How? He wasn't at either of my schools. Nonetheless, I approached him in head teacher mode. The gist of what I said involved him being removed from the area and sent home. 'So you'd spoil not just your evening but your parents' too,' I concluded.

'You fucking whore,' he responded sweetly. And in such a lovely middle-class accent, too.

Elaine and Diane picked him up bodily and removed him from the danger area – me, now, not the barbecues. 'Who does this child belong to?' Elaine asked. But her voice didn't carry.

I switched on my playground tones, the words almost certainly resonating as far as the bar, too. 'Whose child is this? Will his parents please come and collect him?'

A woman – no, not just any woman, but the one from Will's local who'd looked at me with such hatred – came towards me. I was already wearing my stern smile. Soon I was wearing a great deal more: a glass of red wine. A large one too. I was still wiping the wine from my eyes when I realised that the bottle it had come from, smashed on one of those planters, was coming straight for my face.

CHAPTER TWENTY-THREE

There wasn't time for me to scream. I was too busy trying to escape the jagged edges. But people were gathered so close around me, if I moved, someone else might be slashed. Dare I try a karate kick or something? All these nanosecond decisions, with everyone yelling and trying to push themselves and their children away. Not Elaine. She simply stepped behind the woman, grabbing her arm, forcing her on to her knees on the grass in one apparently effortless move. The bottle dropped and rolled harmlessly away. All those unkind thoughts I'd had about Elaine's weight, and she had moved like lightning! And now arrested the woman. Grazia. Grazia Baker – though the surname was a little bathetic after the elegance, spurious or not, of her first name. Marcus's wife.

Interestingly, though he watched from the sidelines, Robin made no attempt to help his wife. But then, officially he was just something in computers, wasn't he? Indeed, with Diane taking her orders to kneel on Grazia's shoulders, Elaine needed no more assistance. Amazingly soon, in no more than three minutes, a police car turned up, and off went Elaine and her prisoner.

'All very deft. Just like that.' Diane snapped her fingers. 'But what are we going to do now that young Master Bates – whoops, sorry! – is on his lonesome?'

'Find his father. Marcus Baker.'

Perhaps my voice was drier than I'd intended: Diane gripped my arms, looking hard into my eyes. 'The guy they say tried to kill you back there? What a sweet family.'

I shook my head to clear it – all that booze. 'There may be a daughter here as well. I think there were two kids. No, I can't remember. But any of the St Luke's Bay people will know.'

'You're not the one to ask them. Come on, into my sitting room. Just in case.' Since she left me there with a clean T-shirt, a burger, a huge plate of salad and yet more fizz – real champagne, this time – any protest I might have made was quickly silenced.

It soon got quite frustrating to know that a jolly party was buzzing away outside while I was stuck here; now I knew exactly what it was like for kids I kept in at playtime as a punishment. No. Not quite. I hadn't done anything wrong. At all. Had I?

Nothing at all, I told the part of my brain that still had the remains of Simon's nasty imprint scarring it. He'd convinced me that whatever I did was wrong, that any of his disasters had to be laid at my door.

But not this.

Time for displacement activity.

I could either read one of Diane's eclectic mix of books or check my phone. Reluctantly I turned away from any full-length works: when had I last had a chance for a nice protracted read in term time? So I ran through my emails, none of which required any action except deletion, and my messages. One. *Remember – stay at the pub until I get back. OK?*

And now another. From Elaine. The gist was the same.

Neither said anything about incarceration, however, so I was free to go and get some more food and mingle. Wrong. I wasn't free. Someone had locked me in. Was it Diane being kind or someone else being a nuisance? At least I could check the first.

Stay where you are. Marcus is kicking off about police brutality. Crap. I'll bring you more food as and when. X. And stay away from the window for a bit.

Great. Thank God for TV, and the exciting end of a fifty overs match not involving yours truly.

More food appeared, and a large jug of water: for one whose career involved people pouring alcohol down their throats, Diane was safety conscious, in this case quite tediously so. But then, I made myself admit that getting seriously drunk on your own was never a good move, however much fun it might seem when your mates were all getting silly too.

I sank a glass of water.

Someone knocked on the door. 'Ed here, Jane – can I have a word?'

It was humiliating but true: 'I don't have the key, Ed, so you'll have to yell and share the word with anyone close enough to overhear.'

'Fucking hell. Come on, just open up.'

'I told you. I can't.' I was about to tell him to go and ask Diane for the key. But a wicket fell on the TV match, and I didn't. And perhaps I was glad. She had a pub to run – a living to make – and she did not need to waste time arguing with a large man who might or might not be sober. I sat tight. Ate. Drank. Watched. But turned the sound down so I could listen to anything happening the other side of that door.

It was a very thick door.

Can u let me out? Desperate for a pee.
Use the flower vase. No. Artificial flowers. Cross your legs.
Great.

I rather wish that when Will unlocked the door my first act hadn't been to push past him and head for the ladies, but that's champagne and water for you. And since he had to wait, he could wait a few moments more while I brushed my hair and reapplied make-up.

'You great fusspot,' Diane said, as I returned. 'Anyone would think you'd been there a day, not a lot less than an hour. There's not much party left but you can come and mingle if you want now you've got a bodyguard. I hope you're a carnivore, Will – loads of burgers and sausages for the asking. And pretty well all the salad. What is it with you men and lettuce?' She bustled off.

'I think that was one of the most humiliating hours of

my life, and I'll bet you were behind it,' I told him flatly, heading towards the garden.

'Yes, I was. From what Elaine had picked up from the washing-up team, we knew there might be trouble. And Elaine was right. No, stay and listen. I wasn't here because something else was happening. Let's eat first and then I'll tell you.'

I couldn't read his expression, but it seemed to be at odds with the entirely frivolous suggestion of food. 'For God's sake – the world's ending, or something like it, and you want to feed your face before—'

'And yours.' For a moment he looked quite impish. 'I said "let's" – that included you, didn't it?'

'Don't mess me around, Will. Two attacks in one day. I've had enough.' But his face changed. He was about to impart bad news. 'No. No. Please don't tell me – not Zunaid! No one's tried to harm him?'

'No. He's fine. And what's her name – Pam? – is with him and they're having a whale of a time.'

I said nothing. Just stared at him. 'Who else are you trying to break bad news about? Pat?'

'As far as I know he's safe with his wife and—Shit! Shit! I really . . . I'm so sorry. Me and my bloody mouth.'

I might have looked away for a moment, but only for a moment. 'I did rather wonder. And don't apologise: it's best to know. And—'

And Diane chose that moment to come breezing up, just as I was about to tell him that he knew as well as I did that any feelings I'd had for Pat were pretty well past tense anyway.

'Does she need a lift up?' she asked. 'Will, you've not told her yet, have you?'

There was something else? I put my head on one side and looked at him enquiringly. 'More good news?' I hoped my smile, ironic or not, showed that the news of Pat hadn't broken my heart. Which it hadn't. Truly hadn't. 'Come on, Will, I've learnt it's better to know the facts whatever they are than to imagine what they might be.'

He looked from Diane to me. 'Do you want to sit down?'

'No, I bloody don't.'

'Told you she wouldn't,' Diane snapped.

'OK. All those emergency vehicles we heard. Saw.'

'The fire engines. Right? Except I'm sure they're not called that any more.'

'Well, the good news is the fire didn't spread to your cottage.'

'And the bad?' For all my bravado, my voice wasn't sure it belonged to me.

'The one next door is gutted. Probably arson, or less likely, an electrical fault.'

'Where does that leave me?'

'There's a room here ready for you,' Diane replied, but not really to the question I'd asked.

'The officer in charge of the incident will let me know as soon as. He'll err on the side of caution, of course.'

'Of course,' I echoed hollowly. I should have pointed out that said officer should be in touch with me directly, but I was wrong-footed by a sudden pang that told me I hoped that neither Nosey nor Lavender had been roasted alive. What the hell was I doing, getting attached to cuddly toys?

'It's not your place – OK?' He gripped my shoulders and stared into my eyes as if he was telling a young recruit not to lose her bottle.

Well, I wouldn't lose mine, either. With an airy gesture I waved away all I had in the place – pouf! Just like that. So long as Nosey and Lavender were all right. 'You're sure it's the place next door that burnt? You know what? After all the stuff fate has been in the habit of shoving my way, I suppose I'm quite surprised. Yes, I am. You don't suppose someone got it wrong, do you?' I asked.

'I shouldn't laugh,' Will said, unable to stop, however. 'Jane, you sounded just like Eeyore. "Can I have some more thistles, please?"'

'You're too kind. Next you'll be taking me on a Woozle hunt. Oh, yes – you are, aren't you? Right now.'

'What are you two on about?' Diane demanded, looking from one to the other.

'Friends of friends,' I said beginning to laugh too.

'I thought that was Pat,' she said. 'Shit.'

'No. Pooh.'

'A Bear of Little Brain. A bit like me,' Will said.

'You've certainly never struck me as a Tigger,' I said, by way of forgiveness.

'But you're as patient as Kanga.'

'For goodness' sake, shut up the pair of you. Arson is no laughing matter.'

'Of course it isn't. Anyway, time for an expotition.'

There was a black gap in the row of cottages, water and muck everywhere, and a strange elusive smell. There was also a lot of police tape.

'Police tape? It is a crime scene, then?'

Very carefully, as if wondering how often he ought to breathe, Will said, 'Yes. Possibly of a serious nature.

Very serious. But we don't know all the circumstances yet. Now,' he added, sounding more like himself, 'the reason you can't just nip into your house is that.' He pointed at the wall they'd built to keep my part of the row safe and habitable. While once it had been vertical, like any self-respecting wall, now it stood at an angle of about ten degrees from the vertical. 'Apparently for a load of reasons I don't quite grasp, a combination of the heat from the fire and the pressure of water from the hoses means it's collapsing inwards – towards your cottage. The firefighters are prepared to go in and rescue anything you treasure, because they know how to do it and they wear helmets. Right. So you make a list of what you want brought out, upstairs or downstairs, and they'll see what they can do. Actually, tell me and I'll write it down.'

There was something he really didn't want me to ask, wasn't there?

Anyway, the list. 'Nothing in the guest room. In the en suite bedroom, anything they can retrieve in the way of clothes, shoes and make-up. It doesn't matter – nothing they should put themselves at risk for. Downstairs my laptop and iPod and anything on or in my desk.'

He looked me in the eye – professional, not flirty. 'Is that absolutely all? No books, CDs, whatever?'

'There's nothing that can't be replaced. Nothing, in other words, worth risking someone's life for. But actually, and I'm sorry, I know this sounds really infantile, and I ought to be ashamed of myself and I suppose I am because . . . well, I didn't say it before. But on my bed – en suite bedroom again – are two teddy bears. You probably clocked them the other night when you were intruder-hunting. Nosey and

254

Lavender. I'd really like them. Please don't look sorry for me. Please. Or even compassionate.' I made a huge effort. 'That's Kanga's job, compassion.'

'Of course. I'll give this to Dave over there and be back.'

I hardly had time to sniff and wipe my nose on my hand before he was back. 'No probs, they say. I said we'd wait in my car. Now,' he continued, as he held the passenger door for me as if I was a lady, 'there is something else you'll learn soon enough, and it might as well be from me. In a situation like this, where the house is unoccupied and mains electricity turned off, and there's no immediate indication of accelerant – the sort of thing you'd expect with arson – the most likely explanation is an unauthorised intruder. A homeless junkie, perhaps.' He closed the door gently and went round to the driver's seat.

'In a city, yes, but surely not in a tiny village? And – no, Will, I'd have noticed. Wouldn't I?' I turned to face him. 'Next door? I'm neither deaf nor blind.'

'What if someone arrived after you left for the match? And tried to make themselves at home? Jane, they don't think the cottage was empty when the fire started. I'm sorry. I really am.'

'So the smell was burnt flesh,' I said flatly.

'I'm afraid so. Remember, death by asphyxiation is very quick.'

'And have they any clue who it was who died?'

'There'll be a post-mortem.'

'That was a very professional thing to say. In other words, you'd rather not tell me.'

'In other words, you'll know as soon as the autopsy is over. I'll tell you then myself if you want. Not because this is my case. Nothing to do with me. Someone else's problem. But you can hear it from me if you prefer. Ah, they've got stuff for you.'

There wasn't much: I hadn't asked for much. But one of the firefighters, a woman my height but built as if she used weights a lot more than I did, opened one of the black sacks carefully. 'Safe and sound. Though they may need a bath. There you go.'

Will stowed everything except the bears' sack, which he passed to me, in the boot. 'Come on, Kanga: you're tough, you know. And I'll bet you can go on being tough. Hey, late night Sainsbury's will still be open – let's go shop for you.' He started the car.

'Before we set off: you took quite a few calls this afternoon. Were they all about this?'

He stared at the steering wheel. 'Not all. Something's being set up for tonight I really am not at liberty to tell you about. And after we've shopped, you'll have to get a taxi back to Diane's. Sorry. Because I'll be part of the team.'

'And you ought to be there now, oughtn't you?'

'Actually, yes. I hadn't realised quite how late it is.'

'And actually I'm a bit tired. I'll just get my car and make my own way back to the pub.' I reached for the door handle.

'Er – Jane . . . There are drink-drive laws, you know. And they don't ignore medicinal champagne. And your car is technically part of a crime scene. So I'll do the driving – OK?'

'OK. So why not drop me back at Diane's? We can catch up tomorrow.'

He dropped his hand on mine. 'I told you you were

tough, Kanga.' He drove the couple of hundred yards in silence. As he pulled up, he added, almost as if he hadn't paused, 'Make sure you keep your phone charged. And switched on.'

'I will. Goodnight – and thanks.' I retrieved the black sacks myself and waved as he drove swiftly off.

CHAPTER TWENTY-FOUR

'My tumble dryer's got a special setting for cuddly toys,' Diane said, insisting on emptying the sacks with me and shoving the bears and my clothes in the washing machine, batch by batch. The bears went in first, on the hand-wash cycle, in, at Diane's insistence, a pillowcase so their eyes wouldn't get scratched. 'You don't want bears with glaucoma,' she said, so seriously I knew she must be mocking me, only it seemed she wasn't.

There were only a few dry-clean-only items, which would spend the night in her garden shed because she insisted they smelt of roast pork. I didn't tell her what they really smelt of. That could wait till tomorrow.

'There's no reason why we shouldn't go to Sainsbury's or Tesco or wherever,' she declared. 'I've been on the wagon tonight, what with one thing and another. I'll get my keys. Twenty-four opening,' she added as if I was dimmer than I felt.

'Tomorrow's Sunday, so it's Cinderella closing time tonight.'

'Shit. And they won't open till mid morning.'

'Not a problem. If there's anything we've not washed and dried, there's always the spare clothes I keep at school. Both schools. And what I could really do with is a glass of your knockout juice, your special insomniacs' delight, and your spare bed.' I plonked myself on the nearest kitchen chair.

'Not until I've told you my bit of news. That guy they said nearly killed you. Marcus. Husband to the delightful Grazia and father to the equally sweet little Cordelia and Atticus. Actually, Cordelia was OK. Ten or eleven. Quiet. Very, very thin, with bitten nails. Anyway, I expected the police to come back for Marcus. Attempted murder or something. To be honest, the more beer going down throats, the surer all the team were that you'd nearly had your head knocked off. Literally. Seriously, he can't get away with that. Can he? No, don't start on the rules of cricket—'

She didn't seem to be making any sense at all. Or maybe I was missing something. So I picked up on one thing I was sure of. '*Laws* of cricket. And no, I doubt if he'd be arrested because he apologised and said the ball had slipped from his hand. The other umpire's on his case, so let's forget him. And – Atticus, did you call him? As in *To Kill a Mockingbird*? The archetypal good guy?'

'Maybe another one. Pretentious, anyway. Little shit. But with parents like that . . .'

'For your ears only, Diane? Promise? I suspect that it was Grazia who knocked me off my bike. And I think I

260

might know why. When I passed out at the after-match party chez Baker, Marcus caught me before I fell. All very knight in shining armour. So I think she rather took against me. And this afternoon, blow me if he didn't grab me round the waist as if I was fainting again, which I did, very melodramatically. All very stupid. But enough to enrage her.'

'So all the time she was watching the match she was plotting something like that. It's worse if it's premeditated, isn't it?'

Much worse. 'She'll probably say my treatment of Atticus provoked her. Enough speculation, Diane. Let's free those bears from their pillowcase and pop them in the dryer.'

'On no account. Dryer yes, but in their pillowcase. Or with tape across their eyes. It says so in the manual.'

Was I convinced by her claim she'd been too busy to drink all evening? Not entirely. But I let her do as she wanted, and then reload the washing machine.

'So what was young Will doing, to drop you off as quickly as if you'd got a Victorian father waiting for you on the doorstep?'

'Work. Something he couldn't tell me about. Which is fine.'

'Fine? Well, considering what he did tell you about. What a shit. Pat, I mean. Will was just stupid. I really liked Pat, you know. Really liked him. If you hadn't obviously had the hots for each other I'd have rather fancied him for myself. But why didn't he tell you himself? Did he want to have his cake and eat it? Bastard.'

As if I was an umpire again, I held up my hands to stem

the flow of words. 'Stuff happens, Di. My situation was dire most of the time he was supporting me. He never, ever made any sort of sexual move. The only thing he did wrong was not to mention his wife – maybe he's even got a family. I did suspect. But I was so busy worrying whether I was just grateful or really loved him that I forgot to ask what he might be feeling. He saw me back on my feet and left, making no promises. Yes, he could have done better, but no, he did nothing actually wrong. Heavens, he could not only have lost his job if he'd made a move, he could have ended up in jail. So please, please forget the notion that I was a victim of a decent man as well as that louse Simon. Please.'

'I saw what I saw, Jane. And it wasn't a lot different from what I see with you and Will, to be honest. Talk about smelling of April and May.'

I couldn't place what seemed to be a quotation, but for once didn't care about literary allusions. Any moment I'd lose my temper with the best friend I had in the village. 'We'll talk about Will in the morning, maybe. Meanwhile, I need to charge my phone, and even more, I need your special knockout drops.'

'And your bears. Don't forget your bears.'

There was nothing of particular interest on my phone when I surfaced at about eight the following morning. In other words, of course, no text or voicemail message from Will. Perhaps he was still busy; perhaps his own phone was down; perhaps he'd simply fallen asleep and forgotten to call. Whatever.

The fire was mentioned on a number of news websites,

with the dead person described by a police spokesperson as a probable vagrant. So much for Will's circumspection. But *a probable vagrant* wasn't the same as *a vagrant* so I wouldn't hasten to judge him.

A shower. Clothes from Diane's dryer. A quick bite of breakfast with Diane before I set off for church. Pat had made me go because of village politics; now I enjoyed going for its own sake. Not that the remainder of the day of rest would involve much rest, because the best thing would be for me to work at one school or another. Or – and the idea was terribly tempting – I could sneak some me time with some retail therapy.

I'd just started on a week's worth of statistical analysis in the office I shared with Tom when my phone whistled. No, I would not respond to a text like one of Pavlov's dogs. I would finish what I was doing before I even looked to see who the sender was. I didn't, of course. Who would? But it was from Diane, not Will. Her lunch hosts had been let down by the original guests, there was plenty of food and they'd love to have me instead. I demurred until she mentioned that they lived in Churcham, home of Justin Forbes, the village overlooking the bay where I'd seen those little boats in the dark. What might I see in daylight? Then she added that they had something they wanted to discuss with me. Discuss? Why me? So long as it wasn't whether or not we should encourage more grammar schools . . . Actually, I owed Diane several favours, and if this was one of them I ought to agree. She dismissed my murmured objection that I had no suitable ladies-who-lunch clothes with a brisk promise to pick me up immediately so that we would have enough time to stop off in Canterbury to pick up something appropriate in Fenwick's.

Diane's friends – Robert, so erect he might have been in the armed services but actually an ex-local government administrator, and his wife Yvonne, once no doubt willowy and elegant, but now stooping into sun-blotched boniness – enjoyed a spectacular view over the harbour. They were old-school polite and welcoming, reminding me of Hazel Roberts in their desire to make me at home. Their dog – a mongrel called Tim – greeted me politely, but retired to a basket when eventually we ate, sitting in their conservatory, all windows open to welcome the sun. Lunch involved home-made soup and a fine fish pie, with vegetables from their garden. Throughout the meal I had the sense that there was some subtext I didn't know about, and since I was careful to avoid the political controversies of the day the conversation became slightly stilted. It was only when I mentioned my house development, neatly skirting round my uninvited guests, that they came alight again – and it was the name Caffy Tyler that did it. PACT had done some work for their niece: over coffee they showed me before, during and after photographs of their work.

'In fact, I was going to phone Caffy,' Robert said, as I waved away a second chocolate, 'because she has some friends in the police too. Very senior.'

I was ready to bristle: had Diane been asking them to ask these friends for a character reference for Will?

Yvonne corrected him. 'They've retired now, dear.'

'Anyway, Caffy's been known to do a spot of detecting herself. But dear Diane here says you've got a young

264

man in the police, and I wondered if he'd be interested in something I've seen. No, we didn't phone the police because they're not interested these days – you dial 101 or whatever it is and hang on ten minutes and leave a message and nothing happens.'

Yvonne put her hand on his knee. 'They're overworked, poor dears. All those cuts. And it's a long way to come from Essex.'

I forbore to embark on a long explanation of how the service was operating. Instead I smiled like one of my kids wanting the rest of the story. 'What would you like me to tell Will?' I asked. 'Did you take any photos?'

'I never thought . . .' But then Robert peered at my feet. 'I can show you, if you like. It's not too far to walk, but . . .'

'I've got some sensible shoes in my car.'

'Excellent. I'll get Tim. Oh, do you have a camera?'

'My phone.'

Yvonne and Diane stayed behind, but Robert, limping slightly, and I set off on what appeared to be one of Tim's regular walks through woodland: he left and collected messages at a dozen or so trees then, trotting ahead, struck off uphill along what was less a path than a track.

Robert clearly struggled on the uneven ground, leaning against a tree as he paused to catch his breath. When he thought I wasn't looking he rubbed and then eased his right knee. This adventure wasn't doing him much good, was it? At last he had enough breath to say, 'This is new, you see. No one ever used to walk here. Maybe the odd rabbit. Possibly deer. But, as you can see, it's quite well worn now.'

I took a couple of photos of it, and we walked on, Robert touching his lips like someone in a *Swallows and Amazons* book. Quite suddenly he stopped, pointing. Someone had hacked and dragged together enough branches to support a tarpaulin. There were litter and faeces in evidence. I took photos and backed away, nodding to Robert who was doing his best to bring Tim to heel without calling him loudly. A dog treat did the trick, and we headed quite briskly away, still without speaking. A couple of times the descent was steep enough for me to grasp his arm, as if it was me needing support. Once he slipped quite badly, and, worse, quite noisily. We froze. But no one came crashing after us, and once Robert was ready to move, we set off again quite steadily.

By the time we'd reached the path Robert's limp was pronounced, but he made no mention of it, or of his worrying shortness of breath. 'The thing is, Jane, we think we've seen people coming ashore. Dead of night, going-to-the-loo time. No photos, of course. And Yvonne's heard voices – not me, of course: too deaf.'

'My aunt is too,' I said. 'But she's had her own private miracle: hearing aids.'

'Funny thing – that friend of Caffy's, the policeman, he's got some. She says he's very impressed.'

'Small too. Hardly noticeable,' I pursued. 'She can enjoy her bridge club again.'

His face lit up. 'Really?'

By now I was working out what I should do and say. 'I do hope Yvonne can find us a cup of tea after all this. You know, Robert, if I were you I wouldn't walk in this direction for a bit. Not until your new neighbours have been checked out. And certainly not till my police friend has seen these pictures. No, there's no signal here – I'll do it the moment we get back to your house. And then I can go online and show you some pictures of Auntie Julie's hearing aids . . .'

I don't know if my casual chatter deceived him at all, but he didn't cavil. With Tim clearly happy to lead the way, we returned to the house.

Stuck at work. Can't respond just now. But don't go back.

What I'd call terse and to the point. Not quite the reply I'd expected when I texted Will, attaching the photos.

Then came another text. *Grid references? GPS co-ordinates?*

Thanks to Robert's dog-eared collection of OS maps I was able to oblige.

No acknowledging text.

Diane touched her watch: she had a pub to run and in any case we didn't want to overstay our welcome. We said our affectionate goodbyes on the broad gravel sweep of their drive.

Despite her brisk persona, Diane always drove so carefully I often wanted to offer to take over. But today her circumspection was fully justified. She nosed out into the road, ready to turn right, up the hill, like a hedgehog checking it might be spring.

And froze, swearing as someone in an SUV nearly removed her number plate as he hurtled past her.

'Come on! This is a lane, not the M26! Thirty! You know, there's a speed limit here for a reason,' she said to thin air. And blow me if she didn't heave the car round and set off down the hill after him.

I could have reasoned with her: road rage wasn't the answer. But I'd had time to see who was driving. Lady

Preston's estate manager. The man who kept vicious dogs. Maybe the man whose dogs had attacked Zunaid. The man working within earshot of the children whose voices I'd heard. Matt Storm.

CHAPTER TWENTY-FIVE

Diane was never going to catch up with a vehicle going that fast, and by the time she was approaching the harbour car park she was clearly having second, possibly third, thoughts.

'Let's just park here for a few minutes for you to catch your breath,' I said, not adding that I'd love to have a quiet, touristy snoop round. And that Diane, nervous and overextended, was not the best person to be in charge of a lethal machine.

It seemed we even had to pay on Sundays. I coughed up for two hours, though I suspected we'd be leaving within ten minutes. Churcham was not exactly Brighton, and we'd look decidedly out of place in our lunch outfits. But the place was pretty enough, in an underinvested way, with a couple of shops and a walk round the harbour wall. It was just the sort of place anyone would take a lot of photos:

boats, sea, shingle. Diane perched on a wall. Me perched on the same wall. Clothes apart, all we needed was kiss-me-quick hats and an ice cream. When I spotted Storm's SUV parked within fifty metres of the ice cream hut, I drifted us that way. I got a lot of snaps of Diane half-hidden by her overflowing cone, but a lot more she might have thought were of her but were actually of Matt in conversation with some individuals who might well have been innocent yachtsmen but equally might not have been. I made sure the number plate was clearly visible in at least one, but by then a cold breeze was bringing a sea fret in and it was clearly time to call it a day. Even an antique shop was only able to hold our attention for a moment.

'I've almost forgotten how to work the heater,' Diane joked as we dithered back to the car.

We were well on our circumspect way home when she said, 'I think that I saw the SUV that was speeding back there. I should have had a word, shouldn't I? I bet you would.'

'If he'd been a kid in the playground, yes. But not in real life. Not after Simon, Diane. Hey, fancy your friends knowing Caffy. I know this is a cheek, but I'd love to drive past my potential new home and see if the police tape has gone and she and PACT can start work.'

The tape hadn't gone. For the first time since yesterday's fire, I wanted to weep.

'Shall we have a look at your current place?' she asked, as if seeing a second disaster might brace me.

I agreed. But there wasn't much to see. A tent had been erected over the burnt-out shell, suggesting that the victim was still *in situ*. My house – Brian's, of course – was guarded with steel shutters.

As we turned dismally away, a car braked suddenly and Brian emerged, running towards us. 'My poor girl,' he declared, enfolding me in a surprising embrace. 'What a terrible tragedy. How are you coping?'

When I could pull back without giving offence, I said, 'With help from my friends. I shall be staying at the Cricketers until I can work out something else.'

'There's no need – well, in the short term, perhaps there is – because I have other properties. Not as convenient as this, of course, but not too far away. Sadly the fire service haven't been able to give me any firm idea of what happens next. I should imagine that's a demolition job,' he said, pointing to the cottage next door. 'But they seemed to think that yours could be salvaged. In time, of course. Such a shame your own building plans have stalled, though I can't imagine your ever wanting to live in a crime scene, no matter how good a job those women think they can do.'

I'd never have imagined Brian and Caffy having the same idea.

'I've seen some of their work,' I said, almost truthfully. 'I'm sure they'll transform my place beyond recognition. Meanwhile, what grieves me is that lives have been lost,' I added. 'Innocent lives.'

'Economic migrants! You'll be telling me next you think we should let everyone in.'

'I won't because I don't. But these people are victims not just of their own ambition – and over here we applaud if people want to better themselves – but of the vile scum called people traffickers.'

'Oh, you *Guardian*-readers,' he said with an avuncular smile.

Diane was checking her texts. 'I'm sorry, Jane, but I'm going to have to push off – I've got a couple of late bookings for tonight. I'm afraid I may have to ask you to move rooms.'

Brian and I bade each other worryingly courteous farewells.

'I was lying,' Diane said, as soon as she had started the car. 'I'd have hit him if we'd stayed. But I didn't want to lose you that offer of a roof over your head.'

'It's not his to take away. He and his insurance company have to find me alternative accommodation. It's part of my contract. But I shall be so glad when I'm no longer beholden to him. Now, may I ask you to drop me at the school? There are some things I simply have to get done for tomorrow.'

'Remember the chef packs up at nine, won't you? Though I daresay I could always rustle up a sandwich if you're not too late.'

'After that lunch and that ice cream, I may never eat again. But I'll call you if I'm going to be really late.'

The first thing I did was forward to Will some of the photos I'd taken, the ones I itched to see on my nice big computer screen. But I couldn't ignore the pile of jobs on my desk.

Ought or must? Which should come first?

On the grounds I was paid to do one task, no matter how much I wanted to nail anyone involved with what I was increasingly convinced was a people-smuggling gang, I turned to admin. Fortunately Tom was being a wonderfully efficient deputy head, as if anxious to prove that one or two incidents between us in the past were mere blips in an excellent working relationship. So it wasn't long before I could upload the photos I'd taken and could see much more detail.

A text came through. Ed. *R U free?*

I was about to text him back saying I was too busy or in the bath or something. But if I was either of those things I might not have picked up his text. *If in doubt, say not out,* is the umpire's dictum. A friend of mine had added a rider: *If in doubt, do nowt.*

There was no car outside to show where I was. It was the work of a moment to make sure I was locked in and no lights were showing. Then I could go back to my office and look properly at those images.

Then I picked up my phone. To text not Ed, but Elaine and – not at all as an afterthought – Will.

'You look as if you've seen a ghost.' Elaine gripped my arms and peered at my face, as Robin closed the heavy school door firmly behind them.

'Not a ghost. Someone I thought of as a friend. One of the photos on my phone. But the definition's not quite good enough to be sure.'

'No problem. We can sort that out.' She looked at Robin, who nodded.

'It's pretty well my day job, if no one else is around. If I've got the right kit. Let's see what you've got.' They peered at the images I showed them. 'It's hard to tell for sure, so don't panic . . . Yes, let's head to Canterbury nick and I'll sort those out.'

Elaine nodded. 'How many people know you intended to stay at the Cricketers tonight?'

'Brian Dawes. People who knew about the problem with the cottage would probably make an intelligent guess, so I'd include Ed van Boolen.'

'That's the Wrayfield skipper?' Robin confirmed.

'Right. And a good enough mate to ask me to a One Day International. He pulled out, and told me to give the tickets to a friend – and then said he was in again.'

'Hm. Anyone else?'

'My car's ensconced at a crime scene, so people would know I wouldn't be going far.'

Elaine pulled a face. 'Good job I've alerted Lloyd and Jo, then. Can you phone Diane and get her to put anything you might need in a bag?'

'OK. But I can't put her pub in a bag. Or her. What about their security?'

'Your room may be occupied by someone else if I can fix it. And there'll be other surveillance. Don't worry, Jane – no one will be put in harm's way. How long do you need to finish up here?'

'As long as it takes you to call Diane.'

'OK. We'll stop off at Canterbury nick first – get these images logged as evidence and take a preliminary statement from you.' She was already dialling, and was as terse with Diane as she had been with me.

I was just about to grab my bag when I stopped. 'I need to double-check everything's locked before I go. Right?'

'Right. I'll come with you,' Robin said.

We worked as a team, looking in alternate rooms. All well. Until he called me. One of the outer doors was unlocked.

'Locking up's Ed van Boolen's job, and Brian usually

double-checks, but neither was anywhere to be seen – remember? So I did it, didn't I?'

'You did. And I suspect Will was looking over your shoulder . . . Not quite OCD. Just very conscientious.' He grinned. 'OK, let's relock it, and in the absence of Will I'll personally push it to make sure you've done a proper job. By the way, did Elaine tell you you'd have to lie down in the back passenger footwell with a blanket over you?'

A civilian techie was doing even cleverer things enlarging details of the photos than I'd done, his task probably made no easier by Robin's peering over his shoulder and making suggestions.

Elaine came surging in.

'No sign yet of Marcus Baker,' I told her.

'No. Nor the delightful Grazia,' Robin said. 'But I really think I should push off. We've got a big case conference tomorrow – I need to be on top of my brief.' He dotted a kiss on her cheek, and headed for the door, turning at the last moment. 'Jane, use your common sense, won't you? No heroics?'

He was gone before I could think of a riposte.

Elaine took his place beside the techie, who, with a sigh and a meaningful glance at his watch, started to rerun the images. She watched in silence. At last she glanced at me, making space beside her so I had a better view of the monitor. 'I recognise one of the company, but I gather you don't? This one? No?'

'It must be the company you keep, Elaine – I'm just a respectable teacher, remember.' The techie moved to the next image, taken from a slightly different angle. 'My God,

275

I don't believe it! Gerry Paine! Mr English First! The guy who wants nasty immigrants kept away from his kids lest they pollute them. What's he doing there?'

'Show me. My God, I think you're right. That's weird, isn't it?'

'Assuming he's talking to people smugglers, not confronting them. Or am I making an assumption too far? You do think that that's what Matt Storm's involved with?'

'You're a witness, Jane: I can't confirm or deny anything like that. I'm really sorry. But I daren't do anything that might compromise a trial. I know I'm keeping you in the dark about a whole lot of things, but I have to.' Touching her lips, she nodded in the direction of the techie. Suddenly I remembered one of my favourite TV series. Cagney and Lacey exchanged a lot of information in the ladies' loo, didn't they?

Before I could suggest we adjourn there, Elaine pointed. Then she put her arm round me. 'Yes, Jane – I'm afraid there's no doubt about it.'

There wasn't, much as I'd fought against accepting it. As I fooled around for Diane so she could get some snaps, a familiar face was looking – appalled – in my direction. With his arm round Matt's shoulder, there was Ed van Boolen.

CHAPTER TWENTY-SIX

Ed van Boolen.

My face wouldn't move. Rigid with shock and disbelief, it must have mirrored that image of Ed's. Or perhaps not quite. I suppose I was less surprised, having fought off admitting the very notion that he could have been part of what I was beginning to think of as a gang. He was a friend. Well, better than just an acquaintance, anyway. Someone I might have considered dating. A fine upstanding cricketer, who'd given so much time to the kids at the school. A man devoted to making things grow, though I had to admit he'd been very equivocal about rescuing my garden from all its chaos. Perhaps, now I came to think of it, he had a very good reason not to want to dash in and help me: he knew more about that garden, and especially about the garage, than I did. Maybe he'd even driven the poor kid there in the first place.

I don't think the others even noticed my distress. They calmly continued to scan each face they found, from time to time muttering names I didn't recognise. I ought to say something, but my mouth was still too dry to frame any words. Some tiny part of me resented that something I'd initiated was running briskly away from me. Then I reminded myself furiously that they were the professionals. I was just a witness, a tired one at that.

'. . . that one? Jane, do you know this guy? Hey, are you OK?'

'I'm fine, Elaine. But I could do with a coffee and a loo. In reverse order, actually. No, I don't know him. You know, there are other names I'd like to throw at you. And there are questions I really want to ask. But a five minutes' break would be great.'

The techie muttered and kept his eyes on the monitor. Elaine flapped a hand in irritation, I thought, at having her concentration broken. On the other hand she didn't look well, easing her back, and now chewing Gaviscon tablets. Maybe soon I'd have to be more assertive, but for the moment I would do something more useful to them – possibly. A teacher always needs a pen to hand, at one time red until educational psychologists thought it was too demoralising for children to have their work criticised so vividly. I fished a black one from my bag and, finding a scrap of paper on the table at which I was sitting, started jotting.

News of Harry and Doreen – anything, even a burnt-out car
The corpse in the garage of my new home (always assuming I get there)

The corpse next door
The kid who wouldn't change his clothes
The bivouac in the woods
Justin Forbes and his promontory
Was it Grazia or someone else who knocked me off
my bike?
Lady Preston: did she know about Matt's activities?
And were her pictures – if they existed – relevant to
the situation?
And were Matt's activities illegal in the first place?
And where is Will?

Not that I added that to the list, of course. But I had sent him an awful lot of information and had had of late remarkably little feedback. Or did I mean contact? I hung my head, figuratively at least. I'd told myself all my dealings with him had to be professional. Hadn't I? And any moment I'd be teenage-weepy because his dealings with me were being professional.

I added one more note – mental, not literal:

When can I go home? If not home, if not to Diane's,
then to Jo and Lloyd's?

Another five minutes of urgent conversation ensued. The hands on the big office clock confirmed it.

'Elaine, I really do need that loo.'

She jumped, as if a chair had spoken. And why not? She was doing her job, just as I'd done my part when I provided the material. More Gaviscon tablets.

I repeated what I'd said. 'I have a feeling that even with

279

this ID I'm not just supposed to wander round till I find one,' I added dryly. I had a feeling that even if she took time to escort me there'd be no Cagney and Lacey moments.

She pointed vaguely. 'OK. It's third on the right when you go out of here.'

I found not only the loo, but a coffee machine. I had enough change for a hot chocolate. Just the one.

It was probably only my warning cough that told them I was back in the room. That and the smell of the chocolate.

'Sorry – you wanted some coffee, didn't you?' Elaine said. 'You know what it's like, Jane – you get engrossed . . . Now, we've done all we can with the people on these images. Do you want one last scan? Or can Steve here go home?'

I hoped it looked as if I was giving it due consideration.

Whatever I was going to say, Steve gathered his stuff and slid off.

'What I would like is some information you may or may not be able to give me. This is a people-trafficking operation – right? And you must have evidence other than mine that these men were involved with it.' A wary look was coming into her eyes. 'Did you find the little boats I mentioned, at Churcham and at St Luke's Bay? And what about that little shelter I told Will about – the one he warned me not to approach?'

Elaine came across to me. 'Jane, I know it's frustrating for you, but this is our case and we can't risk compromising it to make you feel more involved.'

'I can see that – but the truth is I am involved. I got involved the day I was knocked off my bike and was rescued by two kindly people who have subsequently disappeared and had their place torched. All the times I've asked local builders to work on my new property only to have them make the feeblest excuses to run away. When I helped you deal with Zunaid. If I knew what you wanted,' I added, 'I might even have more information for you. If it's not appropriate for you to question me more tonight, I might as well push off home. Oh, I can't, can I, because someone torched the house next door.'

Elaine's head jerked up. 'To the best of our knowledge, as we told the media, it was a vagrant who started it accidentally.'

I spoke in my driest, most cynical headmistress voice: 'So there were no traces of accelerant anywhere?' I was only guessing but I'd bet my pension that I'd touched a nerve. 'You see, I'd say that there was a pattern emerging.' Speaking of patterns, I could see one in Lady Preston's behaviour now: her interest, genuine or spurious, in the kids' exercise. Her desire to come into school and see who was doing running practice – could she be checking up? Looking for someone? Someone concealed within the all-too solid and well-guarded walls of her estate?

She was looking at me apprehensively. Was I going to make a scene? Actually, I wasn't. Rule of combat number one: never engage when you're tired and/or emotional. 'There are a couple more people I'd say have been behaving oddly towards me, in particular. One is Justin Forbes—'

'The big-shot lawyer?'

I knew he was a solicitor, but had no idea he was so important. I parried. 'The same. He has the most wonderful home in Churcham, not so far from that bivouac, and a lookout post with a powerful telescope in his garden. He calls it his promontory,' I added irrelevantly, but failing

281

to suppress a silly giggle. 'He's another umpire, who tried to date me. Goodness knows why. Nothing in common, cricket apart.'

'He might simply have the hots for you? Like some others I could mention?' Elaine asked.

I would deal with the emotions caused by her second question in my own good time. 'Emphatically Lady Preston does not have the hots, at least not for me. Lady Preston, Matt Storm's employer. I believe she may officially have accused me of stealing certain works of art,' I added with an ironic smile, trying to lighten the atmosphere – or was it to appease her? 'The more I think about Lady Preston, the more I think she . . . needs to be questioned, at the very least.'

'Come on, Jane – get real. She's the lady of the manor. Old money. Influence. Hell, she and her family own most of the area.'

'And does that mean she can do no wrong? We're not living in a feudal society any more.'

'No? Haven't you seen your fellow villagers touch their forelocks?'

'Are we still living in an age when an aristo could phone the chief constable and stop work on a case? Hell, we've got crime commissioners to make sure that policing is done well. At least that's what they're supposed to do, and at great expense, of course. Come on, Elaine: just listen to me for a moment. From day one, the woman's been shoving her unofficial nose into the school. She gains unauthorised entry. She tries to see who's in my playground the day there's news of Zunaid's turning up: I think it was to check on him and any others.'

'You're getting paranoid, Jane.'

'Hear me out. On one occasion when I was talking to her in the grounds of her pad—'

'Stop right there. You were there by invitation? Well, then.'

'Well nothing. I heard children's voices. They stopped, very abruptly. And again when I was having a meeting with Matt Storm. Yes, that Matt Storm. The Matt Storm we suspect is a people smuggler. The Matt Storm with the vicious dogs. When I was with him discussing a school project I heard children's voices. As before they were quickly silenced. Then we have the small matter of Zunaid being attacked by dogs – never identified,' I added. Did I sound accusing? Perhaps I did. What if the local media were silenced by Lady Preston's diktat? Or even if she had influence over the police press officer . . .

'You're making very serious allegations.'

'You've cheerfully listened to allegations about other people – welcomed my photos. Please give what I've said some credence.'

'Have you told Will your suspicions?'

That silenced me. 'Why should you be asking that?'

'As Will's DI, I need to know exactly how much you know about what he's doing. And also what your relationship is with him.'

'Like you,' I said with something of an ironic bow, 'he's discretion personified. And as for a relationship, we all know that it would be a total breach of his professional ethics to be anything other than friendly with me. We're not lovers.' I couldn't stop a grin emerging at a memory. 'He did snog me once – but only so that a possible criminal thought we were what my mother used to insist on calling a courting couple, not a police officer with someone who was showing him a possible crime scene. And then Will gave chase, telling his colleagues what he was up to. Right? As for what he's doing now, I haven't a clue. I sent you both the photos at the same time. You responded; he didn't. The last I heard from him was when he told me not to approach that encampment down in Churcham.'

'Really. Nothing since? You're sure?'

'Of course I'm sure.'

She looked very serious.

'Elaine, is Will OK? We might not be lovers, but he's a decent guy and I like him.'

'We hope he's a decent guy. The thing is, and this is for your ears only, he's gone off piste. AWOL. Off air. Whatever.' Another Gaviscon. Two. By now she was actually looking ill.

'Seriously? My God.' I sat down hard. My brain made such unacceptable leaps I didn't dare voice them. I already suspected Lady Preston's influence. What if Will was her mole?

'We're looking for him. Exhaustively.'

'His phone?'

'Not traceable just now. Which makes you wonder . . . Of course, we'll be questioning further all those we've picked up. But if you've got any ideas? No? OK. Now, it's too late to start on that statement now. The person due to take it will have gone home long since. To be honest you look a bit washed out. So we'll adjourn till the morning. Nine. Here.'

'I'm on duty at school at seven tomorrow morning, you know.'

'The way things are going, school may have to manage without you,' she said sharply. She didn't look angry, however, just miserable.

'Are you OK, Elaine?'

'Of course I am. Just a touch of indigestion. And my back . . . It's been a long day. And I really do not want to have to argue about things I can't control.'

'I'm sorry. Let me just say this. You have a team to rally round if one person is absent,' I said. 'In schools as small as mine there's just no one to take up the slack. You can't leave the children alone to study – they're kids, not students!'

She managed a smile. 'It always irritates me too when the media call them that. Students at five years old. I get aerated when they have people on British cop programmes called Detective Carberry. Or Detective Bowman, I suppose. We all loathe it. So, OK: children. Kids.'

I smiled back, if grimly. 'So unless you arrest me, I can't see me staying away.'

'We'll give you time to put all your arrangements in place and send a car for you. We need the statement, Jane, however much your kids need you. It shouldn't take all that long. We know that in the past you've been a victim many times over, and I for one recognise that you're still trying to be a decent public-minded citizen, helping equally overworked public employees to do their job. And now,' Elaine yawned, giving a huge stretch, 'let's call it a day. I'll see if I can find you a lift.'

CHAPTER TWENTY-SEVEN

Next morning, halfway to school in a taxi, I got a text from the police – one of Elaine's team saying they could release my car. I could collect it from Ashford during the day.

Thanks. But since the news didn't come from Elaine herself I didn't ask any of the questions I wanted answers to.

But here, mercifully, I was at Wray Episcopi School with more than enough in my in tray to take my mind off anything that wasn't strictly work.

What was on today's schedule? Allergy recognition training, and an action plan in case of anaphylactic shock. Right across our lunch break. Three-line whip, nonetheless – and that would include me. A staff meeting back at Wrayford after school – I'd spent so little time there recently they'd hardly recognise me when I turned up. And some time I was supposed to be giving the police a statement. Apart from that? News of Zunaid? I must contact Pam. The surveillance at the pub? I checked my watch: yes, Diane would be up and about, itching, no doubt, to share any gossip.

'Nothing at all. Zilch. Zero. *Rien*. Nowt. I was really disappointed. Maybe the officer occupying your room was too. At least she's getting a free breakfast. Now, how's it going with Will – did you get to spend the night together?'

I must be circumspect. 'Actually I was with Elaine looking at the photos we took at Churcham. I took the opportunity – you know how keen the police are on professional standards – to stress he'd always behaved like a perfect gentleman. Or a perfect police officer, and I know the two aren't necessarily synonymous. So that's the way it is and that's the way it has to stay.'

'It was clear he really liked you. And the way you ignored all the other guys chasing after you, I thought you fancied him.'

'Hmmm. Maybe I do fancy him. But fancying someone doesn't justify destroying his career. Remember what I said about Pat: if they thought he'd exploited someone vulnerable he could end up in jail.'

'Which is where that bastard Pat should be! Wife and children indeed!'

'Goodness me,' I said as lightly as possible. 'You have got a bad case of Monday-morning-itis, Diane. Let poor Pat be. He worked his socks off. He was always there when I needed him, and, job done, went away when I didn't. End of. Same with Will. A good hard-working cop.' I hoped.

'You can't tell me you didn't love him. Pat, I mean.'

'I can't tell you anything at all because the first staff are arriving, and goodness knows I've neglected them. See you tonight, all being well. But please, please say nothing about me and either Pat or Will.'

It wasn't just any staff arriving. It was Pam. And she arrived with a beaming Zunaid who ran up to me to be swung in my arms. 'Pam stay with me,' he declared.

She kissed the top of his head and told him to go and wash his hands so he could help lay out breakfast. 'No, I'm not staying with him, nor him with me, more's the pity. But his foster mum's sister runs a B&B and needs some help, so I can live virtually next door to him and give him his breakfast and put him to bed – well, that's more than some real grannies get. The only trouble will be where he goes to school, Jane: don't you have to go where you live?'

I mimed rolling up my sleeves: 'You leave the authorities to me. After all, his only real friend is here, isn't he? Georgy? Pam, I'm so pleased for you – and I'll be so pleased if you can both stay. Because you'd try and get a job wherever he fetches up, wouldn't you?'

'Here for now, anyway. Now where's that imp gone?' she asked loudly – it was obviously part of a regular game.

'Imp here!' I heard, and turned to the next task. Without any enthusiasm.

Then a Range Rover drew up outside. By the grim expression on the young woman's face, she wasn't there to help the kids across the road. Since it was too early for Donna, I opened the door for her myself.

'Ms Cowan? I'm Detective Price. I'm part of the team working on the fire next to your cottage. I'm afraid I have some bad news for you. You may want to sit down.'

Gesturing her inside and seating her in Donna's office, I found my face too stiff to smile or say anything sensible.

We sat. I waited.

'The body . . . Bodies. Not identified yet, may never be, actually, but we know it's not a simple vagrant lighting a fire to keep warm. The fire brigade have found traces of accelerant. The thing is – the victims were children. Two children. Quite young. And that's not the worst part,' she said.

'Killing two children isn't bad enough?'

'Of course it is. But for you it's just the start. They think you may know the children from school and they'd like you to identify them. Now. I've come to take you to the morgue.'

In the midst of the physical agony gripping my stomach, I had to think. Fast and hard. Because anyone introducing herself with the term that Elaine loathed so much, anyone presenting herself without showing her ID, anyone so obviously on her own – no, it was reason as well as instinct that told me she wasn't a police officer. 'I'll have to make some calls first, Ms Price. A school doesn't run itself.'

'We don't have time.'

Were the bodies going somewhere in a hurry? I hated the grim joke my head had framed all by itself. Certainly I wasn't going to say it aloud. 'I have to tell my secretary and my deputy where I will be,' I said. 'I'm legally in charge of a hundred kids. I can't just walk away. Sit down and make yourself at home while I make the calls.' I even passed her the magazines Donna kept beside her desk.

'I told you we have to go.'

Shrugging, I sat down anyway at Donna's desk. The first call was to Elaine herself. Hell, voicemail. I left a message anyway. 'Jane Cowan here, Tom,' I said clearly. 'Now, listen, Tom, if you want to be deputy head, you're going to have to keep better time than this. Look,' I continued, 'I've got the police here saying I need to ID two bodies. I have to leave now, but you have to be here to let the students in.' She'd pick up on the term I'd told her I disliked, wouldn't she? 'Oh, get a helicopter if you need one. No more excuses! OK?' I ended the call. I must try not to panic. 'Sorry,' I said, my visitor getting to her feet, 'there's another person I need to talk to. My secretary.'

'Can't you do it from the car?'

'I've got her number here,' I said, hand on the landline phone.

'The car, Ms Cowan.'

'Not till I've used the loo.' Which is where I retired, using it as disgustingly loudly as I could while I texted Pam. Then I pretended the loo wouldn't flush.

Yes, Price was waiting for me right outside the door.

Like a lamb I accompanied her to the car. She flung open the passenger door, to release a strong smell of horse.

So my suspicions were right.

What if Elaine hadn't picked up the subtext to my message? Or even the message?

I could cut and run, but where? Back into school? What if that put Pam and Zunaid at risk?

Put your brain in gear, Jane – now!

While Simon was still on the loose trying to kill me, the police showed me how to make secret 999 calls. You dial as usual, but make no reply when asked what service you need. The call-handler will ask a series of questions; if you can reply to them you must. If you can't, you just press 55. That triggers an amazing response: it saved my life once. I had an idea it might just have to again. Holding the phone as far out of her sight as I could, I tapped – I knew to a millimetre where the 9 was.

'What are you up to?'

'You said I could text my secretary. I have a job, Officer Price, remember.'

'No need to take that tone with me.'

'OK, OK.' I shoved the still live phone into my trousers pocket. And prayed. Then I had another idea. 'Look, if you give me a lift,' I said in my most reasonable voice, 'you'll have to get someone to bring me back. Why don't I follow in my car?'

She gave herself away again. 'And there I thought it was stuck by your cottage. Get in. Now.'

My kidnapper was either very stupid and underprepared or absolutely sure I wouldn't be escaping alive, or she'd have found a chance to blindfold me before we continued on our journey. She'd have confiscated my phone too. As it was, she drove blithely up to the gates I'd been through when I'd been to see Matt Storm about the school's nature research. The dogs were still there, but there was no sign of Matt himself. I prayed that he was still in custody.

We didn't stop in the yard but went straight through into the Great House's grounds. The house itself looked beautiful in the morning sun. Goodness, it had enough rooms to hide an army, let alone me. But it seemed I wasn't destined to have such grand accommodation. Built right up against the inside of the wall, where there might once have been cold frames or even kennels, was a row of windowless shacks, no better than the sort that used to sicken us in old footage of South African shanty towns. Worse. I'd seen better hen-coops.

I was thrust inside one. If you were as tall as me you couldn't stand upright. On the plus side, I told myself as I was thrust unceremoniously inside, the place looked pretty flimsy. Dare I risk another call? Hearing steps outside, I thrust the phone, still on, of course, right into my knickers. It was too big to slide into my vagina, in the time-honoured way of concealing such devices, and I might have to stand a tad awkwardly, but it might just escape an amateurish pat-down.

The footsteps passed the door. I heard voices, which I did not recognise. They certainly weren't the carrying tones of my hostess, and didn't sound like my kidnapper either.

I'd done enough calming breathing exercises in my time. I ought to try them now. But a pounding distracted me – I was almost surprised to realise it came from my ears. Goodness, I'd heard the same thing often enough when Simon was after me. I might not be about to faint, but sitting down and putting my head between my legs might help me use the phone again. At very least a listener would hear my laboured breathing.

Just as I could hear a lot going on outside. It was hard to get to my feet with anything like speed or elegance, but one thing I was not going to lose was that phone. I pressed my ear to a crack in the door, and listened. Mostly non-English speakers. I couldn't understand the words but I could recognise panic when I heard it. A large lorry, the diesel engine sounding like a drum. Some shouted commands.

The voices dimmed to a murmur. The lorry drove away. And then another? All went quiet. I was left with nothing but my own thoughts for company.

Not quite. Surely at long last those were Cassandra Preston's cultured vowels? And that was certainly a very familiar voice. Brian Dawes'. Whatever our relationship he'd not let anyone kill me out of hand, I was sure of that. I banged on the door, as hard as I could, screaming and yelling at the top of my voice. 'Brian. Over here. Please!'

'Is that you, Jane?' He was right outside.

'Please let me out, Brian. Please.'

'There's no key. Who's got the key? Cassandra? I demand you open that door. Now – what the hell? I'm going to try to kick the door down, Jane.'

'Hang on, Brian. Is that a helicopter?' It was a silly question because nothing else would make that noise. 'They'll have the right equipment.' I really did not want Brian – anyone – collapsing at my feet with a heart attack.

There was even more yelling. 'Armed police! Lie down! Down! Armed police!'

'Help me! In here, Jane Cowan's in here.'

'Bloody lie down. Face down.'

'There's a woman—'

'Do as they tell you, Brian, for God's sake!'

A brief silence. I kicked and screamed again.

'Stand away from that door, whoever you are!'

I didn't argue.

Suddenly there was splintered wood, a man pretending to be a ninja turtle, Brian Dawes face down on the ground with a gun to his head, and an incandescent Cassandra Preston, already being handcuffed. The sight of me gave her strength to shake one of her hands free: 'That's the bitch that's stolen my paintings! I'll fucking kill her!'

CHAPTER TWENTY-EIGHT

I might have felt a great deal happier if I hadn't been aware that I too was the focus of a number of armed officers. But it seemed that they didn't want me to prostrate myself beside Brian, just to stay exactly where I was until I had properly identified myself. Once I was established as a victim, then I was presumably going to be treated kindly and given a great deal of support. But that was more easily said than done. The armed men didn't want a genteel conversation. So I looked for Elaine, presumably the person responsible for this spectacular turnout. And for Will.

Presumably, if either were there they'd be tricked out like their colleagues in body armour. Or be kept well to the back. Or – I looked around and found not a single familiar face under those helmets and visors – not present at all.

What had felt like a miraculous rescue was beginning to feel like a protracted nightmare, although it was probably all happening in the space of a few seconds. Hands up, I persuaded my watery legs towards Brian, eventually managing to kneel beside him. Was it safe to put one hand down and on to his shoulder? I risked it.

'This is Brian Dawes,' I said to the nearest gun. 'He was trying to rescue me. Can't you treat him with some respect? Some dignity?'

Someone barked something at the officer aiming at his head. I couldn't hear what because this time the pounding in my ears was almost deafening. At least he lowered his weapon. Another officer grabbed Brian's other shoulder and heaved him, none too gently, to his feet. I kept my hand where it was – it was almost as if I was literally keeping in touch with reality.

We stood there motionless, unsure of what to do next. The best option seemed to be nothing.

At least we could see something of what was going on. The so-called Officer Price was being shoved unceremoniously into the caged back of a truck, next to a bulkier figure – probably Cassandra Preston. In the distance two horseboxes were surrounded by armed officers, keeping a hostile eye on the trickle of people, almost all young men, being disgorged. It wasn't much of a welcome if you'd given your life savings to be trafficked across an unfriendly set of borders.

'I thought she was a friend,' Brian said, his quavering voice lacking all its usual self-confidence. 'Not a close one. Drinks and nibbles. Dinner occasionally. Bridge. That's the only reason I'm here – to deliver this.' As his hand moved towards his inner pocket the nearest officer twitched his gun. 'A thank you card,' Brian continued dryly. 'And now here I am – here you are too! – and we're being treated as criminals.'

'You tried to save my life, Brian. Thank you. And when they get round to taking my statement, I shall make sure I say so.' I turned to the nearest gun. 'Officer, I am going to make a move that you may find worrying: I am going, very slowly, to put my hand in my trousers to remove a mobile phone. Just look away, Brian.' I did as I'd said, producing it and holding it with my fingertips. As if to celebrate, it started to ring. 'May I?' I asked the gun.

'Let it go to voicemail.'

'Very well. But it's time someone had the goodness to let us go. Elaine Carberry, for instance. Is she here? Very well,' I said, letting my voice carry as if across a playground, 'it's time I spoke to the officer in charge.'

As if by a miracle a figure approached me, still in standard body armour but carrying his headgear. Somewhere in his late thirties, perhaps, he was holding out his hand as if we'd just been introduced at some social event, and his smile was immensely reassuring. 'Ms Cowan? Acting Superintendent Tom Arkwright. I'm in charge of this operation. Some of my colleagues really could do with a word or two – when you've had a cup of tea and a slice of cake.' In answer to my unasked question, he said quietly, 'I'm afraid Mr Dawes won't be able to join us just yet, but if he can he will later.' Such calm efficiency, such lovely northern vowels, reduced my blood pressure to less stratospheric levels. 'I think you may know a friend of mine, Caffy Tyler,' he continued, managing to escort me without my being aware that I was being separated from Brian.

'I do. Before I go anywhere else, Mr Arkwright, no matter how tempting the cake, I need to go back to my school.'

'Of course. You'll need to set things in motion for the rest of the day. My mum was a teacher. Wonderful with wall pictures. Not as good on cake as my auntie, though.'

'It's not just the school day. I've got one of the refugee kids on the school roll and when I twigged that the so-called Officer Price wasn't on the side of the angels I texted the dinner lady to get him into hiding. I can't believe they're both still locked in a kitchen, but I just want . . .' I wasn't sure what I wanted.

'Let's go find out. Hey, Ms Cowan – or may I call you Jane? I know Caffy does – where did you learn all that clever stuff with your mobile? I'm not saying you shouldn't, mind. In fact, I wish everyone knew.'

I was in the car, beside him. He warranted a driver, to whom I gave directions. Wasn't he a bit young to be a superintendent? Not to mention a bit gentle? Dear me, wasn't I into stereotypes this morning. I responded to his question with one of my own. 'How much do you know about this case, Mr Arkwright?'

'The answer is zilch, to be honest. Anyway, any friend of Caffy would call me Tom.'

'I've already got a Tom in my life. He's deputy head at one of my schools. Wrayford. Not the one we're heading for, Wrayford Episcopi. Sorry: I feel pretty confused myself.'

He nodded. He had the sort of face it was easy to talk to. And ask questions of. 'If you're nothing to do with the case, why are you involved?'

'Because I'm in charge of the sixth cavalry: the men and women who ride to the rescue no matter what. Ah, is that your place?'

'It is. But could you park round the corner and let me

300

walk in? It'll keep the atmosphere something like normal.'

He was happy to wait, already poring over his smartphone.

So much had happened to me I was shocked to see that the school day still hadn't started. Cars were arriving, kids being decanted. What about the breakfast arrangements for those signed up? There wasn't a queue of kids banging empty plates and wailing with hunger, so everything must be all right.

Donna greeted me phlegmatically enough, as I apologised for being late. 'Some problem at Wrayford, is there?'

'I'll tell you all about it later. Meanwhile, is Pam here?'

'Yes, and that Zunaid, the little imp. He's only managed to lock them both into the kitchen, hasn't he?'

'I'll go and sort things out,' I said, 'before we have a food riot.' And then I'd ask the friendly northerner to organise a police presence at the school, just in case. Even with Cassandra Preston in custody, I still felt uneasy.

But despite my qualms, I persuaded them to open the door.

'There was a bad woman here,' I told them both. 'But she's gone now and isn't coming back. I hope you've not eaten everyone's breakfast, Zunaid.'

'Not quite,' Pam answered, ruffling his hair. Her face clouded. 'He's been drawing me some pictures, Jane. I think you ought to see them. And maybe one or two of your police friends too.'

'And his support workers,' I agreed, taking in the subject matter and swallowing hard. It was possible the pictures could be used as evidence. 'I'll photocopy them.'

I reckoned without Zunaid. He shook his head violently and thrust the papers behind him. 'Pam. Present for Pam.'

'Of course. Can you go and put them somewhere safe,

301

Pam – like the photocopier?' I added under my breath. 'I'll collect the copies if you leave them with Donna. And then you'd better make sure your friends get some food, Zunaid.' I found myself bending to hug him. He wriggled away, and went off in pursuit of Pam.

Sometimes spending time in a police station is like waiting for a hospital appointment. So I gathered up a pile of work, my bag, and even – almost as an afterthought – the little overnight case I'd brought back from Jo and Lloyd's. My mobile charger. And all the photocopies of Zunaid's pictures.

Tom Arkwright was easy charm itself as I rejoined him in the car. 'But the trouble is, Jane, since I work for a discrete unit, I don't know all the details of what my colleagues are up to. This morning's shout, for instance: we came in response to a bright call-handler knowing what you were doing, not to a summons from Inspector This or Sergeant That. I can see someone ought to see those pictures – clever little bugger for his age, isn't he? – but I don't even know who's handling the case. Not officially. I know Caffy was talking about a guy called Will Bowman – didn't she say he'd got the hots for you?' he added impishly.

'Will's not answering my calls, and I didn't see Elaine Carberry this morning. May I say the unsayable, Tom?'

'In my office, you can say anything,' he said, 'and show me anything.' But there was something quite steely in the way he closed down that topic, turning it quickly to the weather, and how lucky we were to have had so much fine weather before the rain, scheduled for later in the day, came in, bringing autumn with it.

* * *

302

The cake was as good as Tom Arkwright had promised, but he asked me to defer any questions I had until I could meet a senior colleague. Senior to a superintendent, even if it was only an acting superintendent? I was prepared to be bemused. I felt as if I'd dropped down a rabbit hole back in Wray Episcopi and come up in a uniformed Wonderland. But I was soon back on earth with a bump. Would I mind handing over my clothes? There might be traces of fibres or chemicals that would help the prosecution. I turned down the offer of a paper suit, suggesting I'd feel better in the clothes from my case. It was a small victory, but one that made me feel better, especially as I had a chance to apply some make-up too.

The first person to speak to me was a woman in her late sixties, surely way beyond the age for police retirement. On the other hand she had a pleasant manner, a notepad and an empty room. She introduced herself as Mrs Cox.

Now I could ask my questions.

'Officers' whereabouts? Nothing to do with me. I'm just a statement-taker. A volunteer. I used to teach. You sit and tell me what happened and I write it all down – I'll prompt you if you get stuck. So don't worry. We'll get through it all together.'

I didn't doubt it. We got through it quite quickly, since I'd had plenty of time to marshal all the relevant information into a consistent narrative. The first time we hit a problem was when I tried to talk about this morning's activities: it seemed that they weren't part of her brief.

'I'd say they were germane to the matter in hand, Mrs Cox.' She preferred the title – I wanted to keep her onside. 'And being kidnapped's pretty serious, you know. Why don't I read through that statement while you go and see what to do next?'

The spelling and sentence structure were perfectly acceptable, but she hadn't used exactly my words, though I'd been under the impression that I was dictating to her. I changed the words back to my own, initialling each alteration. Another tiny gesture, but another step on my way back to being a fully functioning human being. More important, perhaps, to being recognised as one.

Mrs Cox was clearly displeased by my editing, reminding me pointedly that she was a trained teacher. Should I go for a cheap point by pointing out that my headship might trump hers? I felt acrid enough. Instead, with a smile, I asked about her career.

But now it seemed wasn't the time to make a formal statement about this morning. I needed to be debriefed first. So I fetched up in what Mrs Cox said was a waiting room. As far as I was concerned it had all the hallmarks of a soft interview room, right down to appropriate cuddly toys. Now would I get a chance to ask about Will? And Elaine, of course, if she wasn't the one coming to interview me.

The last person I expected to see was Caffy Tyler bouncing into the room. I'd tell Will I saw her as a Tigger next time I saw him. She'd popped in to see her Tom, she said, and learning I was here thought I might be cheered by the sight of what they had in mind for my house – version two.

'Or you might just want me to hold your hand, literally or figuratively, that is,' she said. 'Tom says you've had a hell of a morning. And everyone's busy dashing round like headless chickens because of liaising with the Border Force and social services and the dear old NHS. And there's not much in the way of reading matter, is there?

You could do with *War and Peace*. Something pretty long. *Clarissa*, perhaps.'

'I always turn to *Middlemarch* if I get the flu . . .'

Sometime later, our discussion of the merits of the various Brontes was interrupted by a lugubrious-looking man who said he was Bob Thatcher, the chief superintendent in charge of the case. With a swift hug, Caffy took herself off.

'I very much hope,' I said, wishing Caffy could have stayed, 'that you've come with information, not just questions.'

He looked decidedly taken aback. 'About what?'

'More accurately, about whom. Two of your officers I've come to regard as friends, not just chance acquaintances. Elaine Carberry and I were chatting happily away only last night. It's less than twenty-four hours since I was sending Will Bowman what I considered important photos and accompanying information. I'd have expected one, if not both, to have dropped by to say hello. So where are they, Mr Thatcher?'

His face shifted from lugubrious to nail-hard. 'I can tell you where Elaine Carberry is. She's in A&E in William Harvey with suspected gallstones – a very painful condition, I gather.'

'Gallstones! I'm so sorry – I thought she was off colour last night, but she's such a pro she insisted she was fine.'

'She called me a few minutes ago: she only just picked up your voicemail, and needed action. Only you'd sorted it yourself,' he said with a grim smile. 'As for DS Bowman, you tell me, Ms Cowan.'

'The last thing I heard from Will was a warning not to

return to what I was convinced was a crime scene down in Churcham. I sent him map references and photos. I got a text telling me not to go back.' I showed him my phone. 'You know what,' I added, in the face of his silence, 'it occurs to me that information I've passed to one or both of these officers might conceivably have got into the wrong hands.'

He frowned. 'Whose, for instance?'

'How should I know? You know the internal politics of your department and presumably the contacts your colleagues have to work with.'

'Where was this possible crime scene?'

'It'd be easier to show you than tell you. Much quicker.'

'Give me the references anyway. And then – I don't need to tell you that this is way outside the box! – we'll go.'

We drove in silence. We ran up the path in silence. We didn't exchange a word when we came across the body. He was calling for the air ambulance. I was checking for a pulse. Even when we thought it was pointless, I was doing mouth-to-mouth.

We drove back in silence.

CHAPTER TWENTY-NINE

'They told me to talk to you, Will. Any rubbish. Anything. And to read to you. So I've brought *Winnie-the-Pooh*.'

'Is that the best you can do?' Elaine asked, making me jump out of my skin.

I got to my feet so we could exchange a hug.

'How are you?' I asked.

'Fine. Or is that the wrong thing to say in Intensive Care, or whatever they call it these days? Actually, not bad. As you can see, they've let me out. I'm on this zero animal fat diet. Hey, I'm losing weight already, so it can't be all bad. Then eventually they'll fish the gall-bladder out – keyhole surgery, probably day surgery, and then I'll be as fit as a flea. More to the point, how's he?' She jerked her head in Will's direction.

'They say he's improving. Yes, I think he is. At least now all the swelling's gone down you can tell he's a human being.'

307

She squeezed my hand. 'I saw the pictures of when you found him. A lot of people wouldn't have fancied doing mouth-to-mouth – case of finding the mouth to work on. Sorry.'

We stared down at the tubes, the wires, the machinery.

'They say his brain should heal as the rest of his body does. The physios are at work on that; I'm just doing my bit with his brain in the evenings. Last night I told him all about the new house Brian's found for me until PACT can finish work on my own.' I hadn't told him that now Ed van Boolen was clearly not going to be dating anyone for a long time, Brian clearly thought he was the heir-apparent for my affections. I'd tried to make it clear he wasn't, but hated to be brutal. The incident – to use police understatement – at the Great House had shaken him to his roots, ageing him overnight.

I edged her away from the bedside. 'I'm just wondering, Elaine, if we should be talking to him, rather than about him. The does-he-take-sugar syndrome. Will can't reply, but that doesn't mean he can't hear.'

'Fuck, fuck, fuck! It's my fault, all this, Jane. This is for your ears only, mind. I got his text as he headed to Churcham, and passed it on, asking for backup. But then I started to throw up. Big time. And I didn't chase up what was going on. I took my eye off the ball.'

'Once you'd said you needed help, surely it should have been despatched?'

'It should. Only we—no, I mustn't say anything. Please don't look at me like that. It's an ongoing situation, Jane, that's what we call it. So while you can speculate all you like, don't speculate to me. OK?'

I gestured back to Will. 'Why don't you tell us what you can? So we can both hear?'

She shrugged, but followed me to the bedside, and even took Will's hand. 'Lady Preston's been denied bail again,' she said, slowly and very clearly, as if the injuries had affected his ears, too. They might well have done. I mustn't sneer. 'And the girl Price who pretended to be one of us – no, you wouldn't know about that, but I daresay that if you lie there long enough Jane'll tell you all about it – anyway, this girl's been denied bail too. But she says she was just a stable hand and was only obeying orders, which is an excuse we've all heard before somewhere, haven't we? Her ladyship is still chuntering about her pictures and I bet they'll come up in court.' She turned to me: 'We've looked; you've looked. They're not there. Probably never were there. So don't give them another thought. The old cow's off her head. But not too crazy to stand trial, I hope. She's up on a nice long list of charges, including murder. The bodies in the cottage next to Jane's,' she added belatedly.

I touched Will's hand. 'I know you tried to tell me that the fire had been started by a vagrant, and I think you were just trying to soften the blow. This Price woman that Elaine mentioned – she said that they'd found two children. It turned out it was about the only bit of truth that she was telling.' Despite myself, my voice cracked. Today wasn't the day to tell him the rest of their tiny story. Or perhaps it was. 'The villagers rallied round wonderfully. You may recall that we don't have a vicar at the moment, so do you know what Carol, the lovely churchwarden, did? She only contacted the Archbishop of Canterbury direct and said that since they'd probably never be identified properly the kids ought to be buried in a village where they – their graves, anyway – would be cared for. Wrayford, in other words. And would he come and do the service. And by the way, could he bring an imam with him, since there was every chance the kids might be Muslim. He said yes. And yes to an imam. It's happening tomorrow. He's going to gear the service towards children, because Wrayford and Wrayford Episcopi schools will be there. Zunaid will plant a shrub. Everyone's been asked to bring a toy, not to leave on the graves, but to give to some of the other children Lady P had trafficked. She and her estate manager.'

Elaine said, her voice veering between gruff and whispy, 'Zunaid gave Pam some pictures he'd drawn. He's quite a little artist, that kid. Do you remember how he was taken to hospital with dog bites? Him and little Georgy, a Romanian kid who stayed with him? Two kids? He drew some pictures with four kids and a dog to show Pam what happened. Two dogs with blood on their enormous teeth; one child up a tree; one following the first up the tree; two lying on the ground. Him and Georgy, those two. So someone was left with two bodies. We think that the fire was probably a way of disposing of evidence, though we can't be sure. Matt Storm is a taciturn guy. He may yet turn Queen's evidence of course . . . As for that bastard, Gerry Paine, managing to sink his racist notions so long as he was making money from the people-smugglers: how does he look his kids in the eye? Are you OK with them staying at your school, by the way?'

'They've done nothing wrong. They need stability.'

'Don't we all?' She dabbed furiously at her eyes and took a couple of deep breaths. 'This low-fat diet is making me all emotional. God knows why. Anyway, we've nailed one mystery. Who ran Jane off the road.'

I touched Will's hand. 'Did I tell you about a crazy woman trying to bottle me at the pub barbecue? It was while you were talking to the fire service about my – Brian's – cottage? Well, Elaine saved not just my life but also my skin. Grazia Baker, wife of Marcus Baker and mother of a not terribly loveable couple of kids. It turns out she was so jealous of me because I'd fainted in Marcus's arms, the only way to deal with me was a prickly hedge. So apparently my fake faint at the cricket match convinced her that to maintain her husband's fidelity she must . . . er . . . bottle me. Nice lady. As for her husband, though – did he mean to kill me when he threw a ball from close range during that match or was it just a lousy throw? Somehow I don't see the case going to court. But he has been suspended from the team.' Elaine looked at her watch. 'I've got to push off, Will, but Robin will pop in to see you tomorrow. Look after yourself.' She covered her mouth at her gaffe. But Will gave no sign of resenting it.

We had finished *The House at Pooh Corner* for the fifth time. It was hard to keep positive, despite what the medics had said, especially as the next item I had to read to him was my analysis of the costs involved in admitting a child with severe behavioural difficulties into Wrayford School. I had got only two sentences into the introduction when Elaine came in, visibly slimmer but clearly in a bad mood.

'They keep postponing my appointment to see the consultant,' she exploded. 'Have you any idea how hard it is to avoid animal fat altogether? I fell off the wagon over the weekend – ended up in A&E again. Hey-ho. And how's Will?'

'I'm sure you'd like to hear how things are going, wouldn't you, Will?'

'Oh. Yes. Of course. Well, young man, you missed a trip to France for starters. Just when we needed someone who spoke French. You'd have been first choice. We're liaising with the French authorities because we're still trying to nail Justin Forbes for his part in the trafficking case.'

'That's the umpiring solicitor who lives in Churcham,' I said. 'The guy with the promontory.'

'I suppose that's one word for it,' Elaine observed. 'I've heard others. How big is it, Jane?' By now her giggles were audible enough to have attracted the attention of a nurse. 'Sorry. Anyway, we think we've got enough evidence from his phone and his vehicle movements to nail him. And Robin may have found him on his radar too: circulating images of what we're sure are Middle-Eastern kids being horribly sexually abused. Good job you didn't date him, Jane. Creepy bastard. How's Brian Dawes, by the way?'

'That's a fine example of a non sequitur,' I said. 'Brian's very subdued.' As much to deflect her as anything, I added, 'By the way, have you got any news on Harry and Doreen yet? It's been ages! They can't just have disappeared off the face of the earth.'

'One of my lads digs through the records of unidentified bodies every morning. And we've trawled through all the local scrap dealers for that Fiesta. Now what have I said?'

'Nothing.' But she had. The first verb she'd used. 'It's just that Ed had access to quite large diggers and such. Elaine, what if the car – what if Doreen and Harry are buried in someone's beautifully landscaped garden?'

'I'm on to it.' She was on her way already.

I sat, reading my dry paperwork aloud. In my head were some of the archbishop's words from the funeral service: that sometimes, in response to prayer, God said yes, sometimes he said no, and sometimes he said not yet. The trouble was, I had no idea what he was saying about Will.

A couple of days later in the middle of running practice I got a text from Elaine.

Guess what? We've found a cuckoo in our nest. You may even know her. Your 'friend' Ed's sister. That's the reason there was no backup for Will when he was being beaten up – the English guys claim it was some of their 'clients' that did that, by the way – and why despite all the information we should have got, we never made any progress. It hurts when it's one of our own. E xxx

PACT were making steady, if undramatic, progress with my new house. Despite Mrs Penkridge and the terrible state of the garden, with no Ed to deal with it, I felt more optimistic. Perhaps I could make it a home.

Out of the blue a phone call came from Caffy one night after I'd got back from the hospital: could I do lunch the coming Saturday? Her place? Come about eleven. And I wasn't to use the front door, but go round the back.

Who could resist such an afterthought?

She lived in one of the loveliest houses I've ever seen. Georgian, with all that that implies in terms of restraint and elegance. It glowed in the soft autumn sun.

'Yes. Paula and her team did all the work on this: I was just a junior then. Then, for various reasons I won't bother you with now, the owners more or less adopted me. Now they're getting older I can keep an eye on them. Not that I'd ever admit it. They're in the West Indies at the moment – they'd be happy for me to show you round.'

It was like having a personal tour of a National Trust property, without a whiff of overt heritage. Every room declared it was someone's much-loved home, without having to resort to silver-framed family photos coyly placed on a grand piano.

She let me look my fill, as if it gave her pleasure to see me so happy. At last she said, 'Let's go and sit on the terrace: it's sheltered enough. And you're to drink whatever you want. If you go over the limit, my lovely Tom will come and collect you and we can sort out your car as and when.' She poured champagne. 'You need a break, Jane – soon. Not working, I can tell you that now, like you did over half-term, and not sitting beside Will all the hours God sends.'

'I don't just sit. I work. I talk to him. I hope and pray.'

'Of course you do. Tom knows several of the consultants there. They say you're next in line for a halo. But it may not work, Jane – have you thought of that? Go on, swear and shout and pace up and down. And even if your loving kindness raises him from the dead, what then? Will his brain ever function properly? Will his personality be the same? Will you fall in love? Or find it was all a chimera? No, I'm not telling you to give up on him. Never in a million years. But you've lost enough of your own life, one way and another.'

314

I was furious. 'What have the consultants told Tom?'

'Nothing except what he can see for himself. What you can see for yourself.'

'What would you do?' I heard myself ask.

'No, I don't give advice.'

'You're not my therapist!' I shot back.

'I wouldn't dare be! Once upon a time, Jane, in circumstances quite unlike yours, this man got a crush on me. When I couldn't requite his passion, he killed himself. It took me a while to get over that. I didn't love him. I didn't even like him all that much. But it was all too easy to blame myself. In the end I realised that if he could choose what to do with his life, I could choose what to do with mine.'

'Will didn't choose this!'

'Of course he didn't. But I'm talking to you. About your life and your choices.' She took my hand. 'Despite the police urging you to keep a low profile, you chose to be not just a teacher, but a head teacher, with all those young lives in your hands. Can you tell me – no, tell yourself – that you're not neglecting them? You're certainly ignoring your own needs. Yes? Now, that's the end of my lecture. Before you drink any more and you're not safe to swim, how about a dip in Todd's pool? Plenty of cossies in the changing rooms . . .'

I was just setting off for church next morning when the phone rang. 'I've got great news – well, interesting news.' Elaine dropped her bellow to an ordinary conversational level. I could hold the phone nearer my ear. 'That Fiesta. We've found it. Another step to nailing the bastard, since it arrived in Sir Something Whatsit's garden at the time lovely Ed was working on it. Or that's what the experts say.'

'Harry and Doreen?'

'Not such good news. They were in it. The car, not the plot. Almost certainly dead when they were buried, though.'

'Why? They were decent people!'

'Decent people renting out accommodation to people some very unpleasant folk had trafficked. No doubt they were afraid the poor old pair would give the game away if they carried on being nice to strangers.'

'So the first aid on my knees signed their death warrant. My God.'

'Yup. Bastards.' Her tone changed. 'Hey, when I yelled about good news, you didn't think – I mean, hell, Jane – you didn't think I meant about Will?'

Of course I had. 'Of course not. Even though I'm not next-of-kin I think someone from the William Harvey would have let me know as soon as there was what they will insist on calling a material change. Any news of your gall bladder operation?'

'Tomorrow. Home at teatime. Come and have a cuppa as soon as you can.'

'Parents' night. But I could do the next evening?'

She'd never know how much effort it took to say that. Or to say I'd go on a weekend course designed to help heads like me integrate refugee children into the classroom. Or to promise to coach the new women's cricket team one night a week.

Any time I was passing, of course, I always popped in to see Will. Always. I had read all the Pooh stories scores of times now.

What if he woke and found I wasn't there? Would I ever forgive myself? But what if he didn't know me anyway?

Caffy and my therapist had to put up with a lot from me for a few days. In the end, though, the advice came silently from Lavender and Nosey. I must leave a substitute in place.

They'd moved Will out of the ITU to a room where I suspected all he was getting was palliative care. A room with windows. At least if he opened his eyes – if he ever opened his eyes – he'd see sky and distant trees.

'Will,' I said, taking his hand as always, 'I'm going to be really busy for a bit. But you know I shall be thinking of you, and will come to see you whenever I can. I promise. But while I'm not here, there'll be someone here on the bedside chair, always watching over you. Yes, I've brought Winnie the Pooh.' I tucked the bear's paw into Will's poor rigid claw. 'And you know that Pooh's always ready for an expotition.'